# HIDDEN CHANCE

# HIDDEN CHANCE

## Secrets of the Hermit's Hideaway

*by Ron Gamer*

Adventure Publications, Inc.
CAMBRIDGE, MINNESOTA

# dedication

To my terrific grandkids: Avary, Davis, Nate, Grace and Henry. May each and every day be a new adventure—continually capped with a happy ending!

Cover and book design by Jonathan Norberg

10 9 8 7 6 5 4 3 2 1
Copyright 2007 by Ron Gamer
Published by Adventure Publications, Inc.
820 Cleveland Street South
Cambridge, MN 55008
1-800-678-7006
www.adventurepublications.net
Printed in the U.S.A.
ISBN-13: 978-1-59193-209-3
ISBN-10: 1-59193-209-2

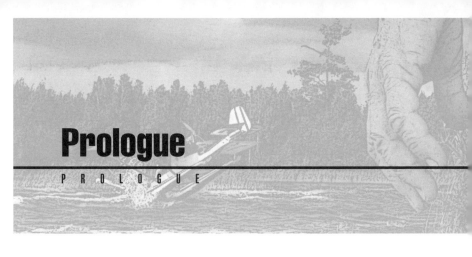

# Prologue

P R O L O G U E

*He'd timed it perfectly. The boat slid ashore without a sound.*

*The man sat alone in the dark, listening. His ears caught the splash of a fish snatching a midnight meal. Minutes later an owl hooted; as if telling rodents beware—feeding hours are still open.*

*To Max Grogan, these nature noises were pleasing as a familiar melody. Like the night before, there were no people sounds—no noisy TVs—no thumping stereos—not even a friendly card game between neighbors.*

*That meant the fools were in the city—catching forty winks before charging off in early traffic—counting the hours until quitting time come Friday. After leaving work, they'd pile into pickups and SUVs—head up the highway—hoping to be the first to arrive at "their lake."*

*"Their lake!" Ha!*

*Well, they could think it was "their lake." Too much time had passed to convince anyone otherwise. If the courts hadn't robbed him, these summer homes wouldn't exist.*

*In the meantime he'd pull a Goldilocks. Under the cover of night he'd tour a few cabins—try each on for size—and before leaving, claim a souvenir.*

*But always careful not to take anything too fancy, nothing* expensive—nothing that would be immediately missed. That'd bring on the law—the same system that stole the land to begin with.

The man stepped out of the dinghy; satisfied the cottages stood vacant. He fished a small light from a vest pocket and began hobbling toward the nearest dwelling.

A crooked leer cracked his disfigured face. Sitting in dark shadows, the boxy retreats reminded the little fellow of cartons of Crackerjacks. They were easy to open, often contained good things to munch, and each would yield a small prize.

# Chapter One

C H A P T E R     O N E

The trim, dark-haired teen coaxed the tractor through the huge hangar door. She closed the throttle and switched off the key. Like a pup in training, the engine barked and shook before playing dead.

Savoring the silence, she wiped a hand across a sweaty brow. From behind the tractor a new sound suddenly arose. She jerked around to look over her shoulder. Dime-sized drops were splattering on the concrete apron.

Good. She'd pulled in without a minute to spare.

The girl returned her gaze to the rear of the gigantic airplane garage. Her unlined face formed a pleasing smile. A silver-haired man in his seventies had shuffled into view.

"There you are Jazzi!" he exclaimed. "Finished mowing so soon?"

"Just about, Uncle Bob. I cut most of it, but it started raining. I didn't think you'd want to plug the mower with wet grass."

"Good choice, as always. But I'm glad you called it quits," the man said, tottering closer. "There's someone here I'd like you to meet."

He turned toward the workshop and second story loft

built into a corner of the immense room. "Buddy, would you come here a minute? It's time you meet my Jazzi."

Jess flushed at the use of her nickname. "Please Uncle Bob. Call me Jess or Jessie. Jazzi's just between you and me. Okay?"

Robert "Bob" Ritzer's lips twitched into an uneven grin. With a nod of his head, he agreed. "Sorry Jess. You're right. It won't happen again. Promise."

A coverall-clad youth came trudging across the vast space. Stopping alongside the elder, he extended his hand.

"Hi. You must be Jessica. Bob's told me lots about you. I'm Wilbert McLean. My folks call me Will, but friends call me Buddy."

Jess wiped a moist palm on the side of her cutoffs before thrusting out her hand. She clasped the offering and gave a quick, shy shake. "Okay, Buddy it is. Most people call me Jess."

Shoving the hand into a pocket, Jessica took stock of the newcomer. A husky five-ten, somewhere between fifteen and eighteen, reddish hair, pale skinned—unlike her own weak coffee with lots of cream coloring—with a friendly smile on a broad, freckle-dotted face.

"Buddy's gonna help tear down the Cessna," Bob said, focusing beyond the wide door opening.

Jessie followed her uncle's gaze. Perched atop a giant flatbed trailer were the fuselage, pontoons and wings of a seaplane. She thought it amazing that a salvage company had been able to pluck the overturned aircraft from a remote wilderness lake.

Even harder to believe, after a flurry of faxed paperwork, it had only taken seven days to truck the injured mechanical bird back to its nest.

A week prior, the prized red-and-white Cessna had been bobbing upside down on a remote Canadian flowage. Amazingly, here it was already, perched on a flatbed in north-central Minnesota.

Not that it would be flying anytime soon. The airplane needed a complete teardown and rebuild. Such an undertaking might take months, maybe a year or more.

The good news, if it could be termed that, was by then Uncle Bob might be fully recovered. With luck, even have flying privileges restored.

"So what d'ya think Jess? You up to giving Buddy a hand now and then?"

Jess turned to read her uncle's face. Was he serious?

"Jeez, Uncle Bob. "What I know about tools could be written on the back of a stamp. I'd just be in the way. Besides, aren't you supposed to use a trained mechanic? You know . . . someone with a license to do that kind of stuff?"

Before the old man could speak, Wilbert "Buddy" McLean rushed in. "Yep, usually. Especially if the plane's gonna be flown in a club or used as a rental.

"But that there," he noted, nodding at the fuselage, floats and wings strapped tight to the trailer. "That there is your uncle's personal property. He's allowed to take it apart. It's the puttin' back together that'll leave an ink trail."

The young man hesitated, staring through the drizzle at the stack of aircraft parts. "But you're right. When we get to doing that, we'll need licensed mechanics. They'll need to sign off on a blizzard of paperwork."

It annoyed Jess that this newcomer thought it necessary to give a half-dollar answer to a ten cent question. She'd directed the query at her uncle, not some know-it-all neighbor kid.

Her dark eyes flashing, she said, "Oh . . . is that right? And what makes you such an expert?"

"Whoa, Jess," Bob intervened. "Don't get your dander up. Buddy knows quite a bit about rules and regulations. He plans on flying the big boys someday. As a matter of fact, he passed his flight test just last week, one day after his seventeenth birthday. Not only that, he's built and flown his very own fat ultra-light."

Chastised, Jess stammered, "Fat ultra-light? What the heck is a fat ultra-light?"

Bob gave a weary sigh. "Go ahead and explain it, Buddy. Too much yakking tends to drain my tank."

The teen was more than willing to take over.

His green eyes zeroed in on Jess. "Okay. Think of an ultra-light as an airplane in training. The main difference being, they weigh a lot less. Ultra-lights have wings and a tail, an engine and a prop, just about everything you'd find on the Cessna. The exception is that there's a weight limit. That means all the parts have to be feather-light . . . even the engine."

Jessie's forehead scrunched in confusion. "Are you talking about a model airplane? You know. The kind kids take to a park and fly with a remote control?"

"No, no, no," Buddy sputtered. "Ultra-lights are real airplanes . . . well sort of. It's just that because of their size and weight, they have their own rules."

Without looking up, Jess muttered, "What kind of rules?"

"Well, for one thing—depending on the pilot's experi-ence—some single-seaters are only allowed to fly so far off the ground. Another rule is how fast they can go, 'bout the speed of a car on a freeway."

"And you actually built and fly one of these tinker-toys?" Jess asked while wondering, whether this kid was truly brave, or had merely been missing the day the common sense wagon passed by his house.

"They're not toys, Jess," Bob said. "Last summer I helped

Buddy assemble a two-seater. Unlike entry level kits, Buddy's has a wrap-around windshield and partially enclosed cabin."

The man paused for a breath. "Technically, under some rather confusing rules, it's termed a sport plane. It's one that can be used for training other pilots or carrying a passenger. My guess, once you see Buddy take off and land a few times, you'll want go up yourself."

Jessie's brown eyes bulged. "Ha! That'll be the day," she said. "After that bumpy ride and close call in Canada, I'll pass on going up in a flying go-cart."

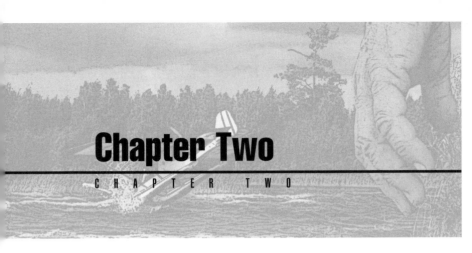

# Chapter Two

C H A P T E R   T W O

Morning broke with a flourish as orange streaks flared over the edge of the earth. Not wanting to go unnoticed, glassy lake water reflected a second edition.

Finished writing, Jess set down the pen and stared out the window. Wow, she marveled, too awesome to even try capturing with a camera. A four-by-six print would never cut it.

And to think; a month ago she couldn't have imagined being up and at 'em so early on a mid-summer's day. But that was just one of a whole list of things she wouldn't have thought possible.

The girl would never have guessed one's life could make such an abrupt turnabout.

It was hard to visualize the change had started with a life-threatening event; a touch-and-go episode that just thinking about caused a shudder.

Yet, she realized she was better person for the experience. And on the plus side, she'd made several new friends. She'd just penned a thank you to the tall, quiet one.

Or was it more than that?

The angry whine of a small engine intruded on her

thoughts. She looked off into the distance. As promised, another new ally was coming to call. Buddy's ultra-light was winging over the water like a giant dragonfly clad in over-sized shoes.

Her pulse quickened.

Was she really going up in a rickety-looking aircraft built out of tubing, strands of wire and swatches of fabric—a flying machine wannabe?

She was having some serious second thoughts.

\* \* \*

Jessica eased the screen door shut. The seniors might still be sleeping. No, that wasn't likely. Not after Buddy's eardrum-piercing low pass.

Jess couldn't believe what she was about to do—ride second seat in Buddy's homebuilt.

For the past two weeks the young aviator had been a daily fixture at her uncle's little airstrip; a flat, grassy swath cut between stands of birch, pine and poplar.

Her uncle had mentioned that the one-hundred-sixty acres had once been part of a dairy farm. But like so many others this far north, the soil was too rocky, the climate too cold, to eke out much of a living. Following a fire that destroyed the farmhouse, the property had been abandoned.

Somewhere along the line, the land had been reclaimed by the county. The fields had lain fallow for decades. So long, that when her uncle purchased it, a bulldozer had been used to clear away trees and brush.

With a half-mile of shoreline on a semi-private little lake, the property was perfect for Bob's purpose; establishing an airstrip. The man loved to fly—had been doing it most of his adult life.

A few years before retirement, Bob constructed a comfortable cottage near the lake's edge. With the adjoining acreage, he and her aunt Betty had the best of both worlds. They had a seaplane base from which to come and go during warm weather. Then after swapping pontoons for wheels, a landing site, complete with a large hangar for winter storage and repair.

It had been in that building that Jess had come to know Wilbert "Buddy" McLean. The youth had been there every day, taking things apart.

Each morning, while the wind was still sleeping and the lake was soft, Buddy would come buzzing over the tree tops. And because the ultra-light was amphibious, he had the choice of water or grass on which to land.

Jess assumed that since Buddy had only used the grass strip once, he preferred setting down on water.

Though the airplane itself was small, engine noise made up for what it lacked in size. The contraption reminded Jessie of a miniature poodle—scads of high-pitched bark but very little bite.

Just after first light, Buddy would circle overhead. Then, with a last burst of engine clatter, he'd set down and taxi in to Bob's pier—the same dock on which Jess now stood, nervously awaiting his arrival.

Before stepping out she had slipped into a pair of her uncle's coveralls. Uneasy, she fiddled with the long front zipper, pulling it up and down, up and down.

Her temples wrinkled with worry, Jess studied the amphibian as it drew near. When the plane was within a few yards of the dock, the engine went silent.

A sudden hush enveloped the lake.

The quiet was short-lived. Often the comic, Buddy belted out one of his "made up on the spot" rhymes. "All right, girl, you're standing tall! You didn't wimp out and sneak off to the mall!"

Getting only a scowl for his poetic effort, he underhanded a rope. In a serious tenor, he growled, "Hey, wake up and catch this cord. Just hold tight. I'll do the tugging."

Jessie's hackles rose to the rhyme's reference to wimping out. "And here's a cheery good morning to you, Mr. Poet-Pilot. Why'd ya think I'd wimp out? What? Won't any of your girlfriends fly with you? Or were they all busy that day?"

Clad in a one-piece flight suit, Buddy busied himself aligning blue-trimmed floats parallel to the pier. Satisfied, he swiveled on the seat, placed a size twelve shoe on the pontoon's step-pad, and pushed up to the wharf.

"Girlfriends, shmirl friends—who's got time for that? As a matter of fact, Miss Jessica, you're about to be my first passenger."

Jess rose to her full five feet, four inches and challenged Buddy's gaze. "You've gotta be kidding! I don't know if I should be flattered or frightened. How is it that I'm to be numero-uno? Was everyone else you asked too smart to say yes?"

Cracking a smile, Buddy said, "Nah. I never invited anyone before. It wasn't legal until I got my license. Besides, as little as you must weigh, I won't even know you're along."

Ten minutes later they were off. The youthful aviator used five of those minutes tutoring Jess on what to touch and not to touch. He went over the use of rudder pedals, throttle control and steering stick.

Jess listened with only one ear. She'd heard a similar lecture before departing on the Canadian venture. Now that the little pontoon plane was up close and personal, she was busy making a visual check.

She saw that the engine and propeller were mounted up and behind the narrow, nearly door-less cockpit. A pusher, she recalled being told, not a puller like the Cessna. A second difference was the seating arrangement. Unlike sitting side-by-side as in most modern aircraft, two thinly padded seats were placed one in front of the other.

But what caught her eye most was the absence of twin steering yokes. There were no wheels to turn, push or pull. Instead, poking up in front of each seat were joysticks similar to those used for computer games.

"You got all that?" Buddy asked, drawing Jess back to the moment.

"Ah, yeah. I think so," she sputtered, wondering how much of his speech she'd tuned out.

"Okay, then. Let's get strapped in."

Pontoons were soon pushing water and after a couple long breaths, the ultra-light was airborne, its small engine squawking full-speed ahead.

During liftoff Jess was too tense to do anything but clutch her hands and squeeze.

Buddy had figured as much. Only when the aircraft leveled off did he talk into his headset.

"This is your captain speaking. We're currently cruising at four hundred feet. If you'd look down to your left, you'll see the western shore of Birch Lake. Birch is one of the smaller bodies of water located in the central lakes region. Note the lack of dwellings or docks. Surrounded as it is by larger lakes, Birch has managed to escape development."

In spite of her nervous state, Jessie's lips formed a feeble smile. He sounded kind of lame, but at least he knew what he was doing. Looking down as directed, she saw he was right.

From this height, Birch appeared to be more of a pond than a real lake. And its tree-lined shore was dock and cabin free.

She hadn't taken notice of that detail the day they'd left for Canada. Once off the water, the Cessna had climbed straight out. Plus, she'd been sitting in the right front seat. Much of the scenery right below had been blocked by a silver pontoon.

It had been her first flight in her great-uncle's seaplane and she'd been overwhelmed by the view. Like precious gems nestled in a forest of wavering green velvet, countless lakes glistened under brilliant sunshine. Some lakes were big, some were small, and countless others were in-between.

She discovered that this ultra-light made a perfect viewing platform. Without full doors, there was no Plexiglas to peer through. With exception of the engine whine and some wind curling around the windshield, Jess thought it similar to a Ferris wheel. The customer had a bird's eye view every direction but the tail.

Using his normal voice, Buddy resumed chattering. "Here's my plan. Our family's cottage is located one lake over. Pike Lake is bigger than Birch. I haven't flown with a passenger since my flight test. I'd like to do a couple water landings before heading back."

Jess jerked straight up in her seat. "What? You need to practice before you can land at Uncle Bob's? Thanks for not telling me before we took off."

Buddy grinned as he eased the plane into a bank. "Relax. I don't really have to practice. I just thought you'd like to see where I spend summer vacation."

Relaxing was the last thing on Jessie's agenda. She was still finding it hard to accept that she was here in the first place. Somehow Uncle Bob's assurances that it was safe, and Buddy's teasing that she was a "fraidy-cat" had eroded her "no way" into a "maybe" and eventually an "okay."

Buddy pitched the nose down before Jess had time to reply. They were pointed toward an arm of an L-shaped lake. Unlike Birch with all open water, this waterway was sprinkled with islands.

The first island reminded Jess of a middle-aged man's scalp. It was shaped like an oval. A thick forest circled the outside; a tiny, bald bump filled its center.

A quarter mile of open water separated the first island from the second. Viewed from on high, island number two resembled an hourglass. But unlike the first, the figure-eight form had a full head of hair. A tangle of green sprouted from one end to the other.

While she'd been staring ahead the amphibian had bled altitude. Tree tops flashed below the floats. Jessie's hands got to know each other again. Suddenly the airplane sailed over water; a shimmering, wrinkled, silver-blue field.

Adding a touch of throttle, the pilot kept the craft air-borne. He flew just above the surface, directly toward the first island.

Jess thought Buddy was pulling a stunt. That he was going to fly near the wooded shoreline and then haul the stick back into a steep climb.

She was about to scream a protest when the engine relaxed. Then, while Buddy pulled aft on the control, keeping the snout above center, its floats touched.

The ultra-light began bumping and bouncing as if mimicking a carnival ride. That sensation soon ceased as its pontoons stabilized—the engine working just hard enough to keep the floats from settling in.

# Chapter Three

C H A P T E R   T H R E E

Max couldn't believe it.

If he didn't have bad luck, he wouldn't have any luck at all.

Clad in camouflage clothing and hunkered in the woods, he touched his forehead. Good. The Halloween mask he'd perched cap-like on top his scarred skull was still there. He cursed under his breath. Damn—his first daylight crossing and what happens? The McLean kid chooses to soar up and down in the mini-plane. Did the kid take off and fly away as he had every-day for the past two weeks, not to return until late afternoon?

The one morning he chanced sneaking over after sunup?

Oh, no—that'd have been too much to ask.

Now Max was stuck. He didn't dare leave. Not until the clueless teen either parked at his own pier or flew back over to Birch. What a crock of sour cheese this turned out to be!

He didn't even dare venture into the clearing to spend time with his trinkets. For if the contraption were to fly over the island, his gig would be finished—kaput. Two years of midnight forays gone in a puff of noisy exhaust.

And worse, if the teen were to yap, what might result? Maybe a toss in the slammer—fitted for a set of oversized orange clothes—courtesy of the county?

*No thanks. For now it was best just to lay low . . . stay put . . . let the fool kid tire of soaring around in the water beetle.*

*Max didn't want to wait until after sunset, but if that's what it would take to keep his secret safe, he'd do just that.*

* * *

Buddy did two more liftoffs and landings. After the first takeoff he'd pointed out the pier and path leading to his parent's cottage. The cabin was isolated from its neighbors. Actually, most of the shoreline looked unspoiled. Fewer than a dozen dock fingers poked out from a thickly treed beachfront.

On the second go-round, the ultra-light soared high enough to view Pike and Birch at the same time.

Jess was surprised to see how close the distant end of the airstrip was to the McLean cabin. Not more than a short trek through a forest of young pines and leafy trees.

"So what do ya do when it's windy or wet? Walk over?" Jess inquired once the amphibian leveled off.

"Naw, don't have to. Used to though, before Dad bought an ATV. Our property runs right up to Bob's. With all the trees you can't see it from the air, but last summer I hacked out a trail. I use the four-wheeler if it's gonna be windy. And if it's raining, I use Dad's old pickup . . . drive around on the gravel road."

Buddy shoved the stick forward, pushing the nose down. Not wanting to distract him, Jess kept her lips locked, watching the water rise. Neither said a word until fat pontoons and small waves brushed.

"Whaddaya think? Is that fun or what?" Buddy asked.

Jess had to confess, that once over her initial fear, it'd been a rush. And she'd been impressed with Buddy's piloting skills.

Except for the brief time when the floats were uncertain whether they should fly or be wave runners—the ride had been silk. But it wasn't Jessie's style to hand out quick praise. She saw no reason to serve up a steak-and-potato platter to the new pilot. The young man's ego already seemed well fed.

Instead, she chose to dish out a burger and fries. "It was okay. It wasn't as scary as I first thought. You do a pretty good job of bringing it down, though. But I have a couple questions. How can someone your age afford to build an airplane? It must have cost a fortune."

Buddy cleared his throat, and then in a tone Jess hadn't heard before, said, "My grandpa helped me out. He knew how much I wanted to fly"

"Cool, he must be a great guy. Do you take him up in the plane?"

"He *was* great," Buddy said slowly. "Ah, he died of cancer, so…"

"I'm sorry," she said.

"It's okay, Buddy replied. With a reassuring smile, he added, "And yeah, he flies with me all the time."

As his words trailed off, Jess felt a stab of sympathy.

She stared through the windscreen, choosing her next words with care. After a lull she asked, "So . . . have you named this motorized kite? You know, like some people tag boats. And more importantly; why in the world are we so close to this island?"

Buddy had taxied to within a few yards of a sandy cove. He didn't immediately reply. Instead, he shut down the engine, unhitched his harness, and then leapt out of the rear seat. Splashing knee deep in water, he began pushing a pontoon.

Only when the fronts of the floats were nestled on land, did he speak. "Yep, I do."

"You do what?" Jess asked, unhitching the safety belt before slipping off her shoes.

"You asked if I've named this little bird. I have."

"So, what is it? Or is it a top military secret?" She asked, gingerly lifting off the front seat and stepping on the float's footpad.

"It's no secret. Just don't laugh. I've named it *Jonathan* . . . *Johnny* for short."

Clutching her shoes in one hand, Jess grabbed the open window frame with the other, and then jumped into shallow water. The early morning air held a chill. She was glad she'd kept her shoes dry. Dropping to her bottom on a patch of damp grass, Jess began undoing a knot.

After a lull, she caught up to her thoughts. "You got to be kidding! *Johnny?* What kind of name is that for an airplane?"

Satisfied pontoons would stay put, Buddy plopped down alongside. "Have you ever read *Jonathan Livingston Seagull?*"

"Read it? I never even heard of it. What is it?"

"It's a make-believe story about a unique bird—a gull that's more fascinated with flying than feeding. I figure my amphibian is a lot like that seagull. It can soar on high, land on water . . . or with wheels extended, set down on terra-firma. And to top it off, it doesn't need to be fed very often."

"Speaking of the ground, my butt's getting wet," Jess complained, springing to her feet.

Peering down, she asked. "So why'd you park here? Or aren't you real anxious to start playing with tools today?"

Buddy wrestled himself upright and then swatted the sand and weeds from his backside.

"Not really. We're ready to start taking off the engine. But Bob said that he and Betty were meeting someone in Aitkin first thing today. I don't want to try any technical stuff without him looking over my shoulder."

Jess slipped on her shoes and then bent to tie the laces. Finished, she stood erect and said, "Well, if you're not in a big rush, I'm gonna sneak into the woods. All I had for breakfast was a glass of O.J. You can guess what that means."

"Oh, is that right?" Buddy chuckled. "Are you sure it was the juice and not a case of nerves?"

Jess gave an honest answer. "Well . . . maybe a little of both. "Either way stay put. Unlike you, I don't need anyone looking over my rear. I can do this on my own, thank you very much."

A month earlier, having been raised in the city, Jess wouldn't have dreamt of setting foot in a forest. That wasn't totally true anymore. After a week of being marooned in the middle of nowhere, she'd outgrown that panic attack.

She had been the one female in a four-person play. Needing private time and space every now and then, it hadn't taken long to learn how to steal in and out of camp.

She also realized, this being an island, she couldn't get lost. No matter which direction she hiked, she'd reach water. Following shore would bring her back to the starting point.

Buddy let out a yell just as she was about to slip into the woods. ·

"Look around if you like. Take all the time you want. I'm gonna work on *Johnny*. But first listen up. You do know what poison ivy looks like, right? See leaves of three, let 'em be—or you're itchin' for some misery."

Jess spun on her heel, and with a glower, yelled, "There's poison ivy? Here? Thanks a lot, pal! I don't have a clue what to look for."

The sudden outburst caused Buddy to backpedal to the water's edge. He was beginning to realize what Jess lacked in size, she more than made up for in tenacity.

"Ahh . . . ," he stammered, "I'm not certain that there's any here, but there could be. Not to worry though. Just don't touch any low plants with shiny leaves."

Crossing her arms, Jess shook her head and scowled. "Yeah, that's easy for you say." Then she turned to examine the ground where she was about to step. Seeing only ferns and tree seedlings carpeting the forest floor, she stomped off.

* * *

Buddy had said "no hurry." So with mission accomplished, Jess decided to do a little exploring. She had yet to see any three-leafed plants. The big joker was probably spoofing; maybe get her anxious before take off.

Nah, she didn't think so. Buddy liked to clown around, but not about flying. That was one subject where he was all business. But on other issues he was a regular comedian; often spouting a backwoods rap that could bring tears to her eyes.

Deep in this musing, Jess became careless. She'd neglected to watch where she was walking. While tramping up a small rise, a root reached out to snag a toe. The next instant Jess found herself sprawled flat on the ground. The impact whooshed away her breath, leaving her gasping for air.

When she could breathe without wheezing, she rolled over and sat up. Then she saw that tripping had been a good thing. For filling an opening not five feet from where she sat, were dozens of sinister looking plants— each displaying trios of glossy leaves.

Getting to her feet, Jess brushed off the leaf litter, scolding herself for being careless. Then she stood quiet, studying the route, determining if a detour was needed. Easy enough—just skirt left and then go right again.

She took a stride and stopped. Had she heard some-thing, like a twig being stepped on? Peering down she saw that both her feet were planted on soft damp leaves. It wasn't her.

Standing motionless as a gravestone, nerves tingling, Jess strained her ears.

Nothing but normal forest sounds—crickets fiddling, birds chirping, a breeze sighing softly through the tree-tops.

Maybe Buddy had been right. Maybe she was a combo of "fraidy-cat" and "wuss" put together in a "two-for-one" special. But thinking deeper, she recalled Travis's counseling words while in Canada. He said forest animals were far more frightened of you than you are of them.

Right!

A squirrel began to chatter, scolding Jess for invading its territory. It took a couple of nerve- wracking squawks before she recognized the source of the complaint. And when she did, she relaxed.

Get a grip, girl, get a grip, she chastised herself. Because Travis had it right—she had nothing to be afraid of but her own stupid panic.

Moments later Jess came to the edge of the clearing seen from the air. After propping against the smooth bark of a young aspen, her eyes explored the opening. Finding a meadow surrounded by forest wasn't all that unusual. They'd flown over similar glades in Canada.

Leaning against the tree, Jess experienced a tingly sensation. It surged up her spine and quivered the hairs on her neck. It was almost like a sixth sense was reporting for duty. And the message it conveyed was menacing— she wasn't the only one in the woods.

Jess had to force down the lump in her throat. She stood up straight and peered every which way. There was nothing out of the ordinary—only trees, shrubs and woody plants.

She held her breath and listened, but the only sound was the soft whimper of wind and a few birds sharing the morning gossip.

Jess exhaled, shook her head and tramped into the clearing. Afterward when describing what she'd stumbled upon, she'd emphasize two words—"really weird."

But right then she needed to rush back to the beach. Buddy seemed to have an answer for everything. She looked forward to hearing the explanation.

* * *

Buddy was hard at work removing bug splats from the plane's windshield when Jess bolted from the underbrush.

"You're not gonna believe it! I found something you just gotta see!"

Bent over and wheezing, Jess had a brain flash. "Or maybe you already know! Maybe that's why you told me to look around . . . to take all the time I wanted."

Stuffing the rag into a back pocket, Buddy made a face. "Girl, what are you babbling about? What'd ya do? Run into Big Jim?"

Jess stood large and returned the stare. "Big Jim? Who the heck is Big Jim?"

"You did, didn't you? You bumped into Big Jim? That's what we call the bear that likes to raid our garbage can. We nicknamed it Big Jim because no matter how we fasten the lid, Big Jim can always find a way to jimmy it off."

"Bear! You mean there are bears out here, too? Why didn't you tell me that before I started traipsing around?"

There was a pause as Buddy decoded the question. "Oh. So you didn't run across Big Jim? I thought it'd be strange for a bear to swim out here when there are such easy pickins' on the mainland. Well, if it wasn't Big Jim, what was it?"

Jess chose to play coy. "I'm not gonna to tell ya. You'll just have to see for yourself. Come on. Follow me."

With that, Jess spun on her heel and walked briskly into the woods. Puzzled, Buddy stood motionless. Then, realizing Jess was traipsing off without waiting, he came alive. "Hey, girl, wait up."

\* \* \*

Pilot and passenger were rooted in the middle of the meadow. Spread flat before them lay a large, earth-toned tarp.

Buddy hoisted one corner of the thick tarp, expecting to see sun-starved vegetation. There were scores of dead plants, but that wasn't what triggered the next response.

On a second layer of clear plastic, arranged in rows like cars in a parking lot, were scores of everyday items. Some of the gadgets looked to be recent additions. Others were old and moldy. Many looked to be some-where in between.

Large spoons and small spoons, forks and knives, cups and saucers, even a broken mixer shared space with an array of worn-out watches, muff-less ear phones, book ends and outdated tools.

"Oh . . . for crying out loud! I don't believe it! See that pocket knife?" Buddy exclaimed, pointing a finger halfway down the second row.

"That's mine! I got that for my fifteenth birthday. I kept it on a shelf in my bedroom. It disappeared last sum-mer. I searched everywhere. I even blamed my little brother for throwing it off the end of the dock."

Surprise waning, Jess said, "But apparently you didn't."

Buddy turned, cheeks flushed with annoyance. "Stop with the word games. Apparently I didn't what?"

"Hey! Put a lid on it! I mean that you didn't look every-where. If you had, you would have found it."

Rebuked, Buddy released frustration on a grass clump. With the tip of a shoe, he kicked the plant, scattering a spray of plant litter.

"Jeez . . . take it easy. You still gotta fly us out of here."

She said it so unruffled, so calm, that Buddy had to agree. He took in a big gulp of air, peered up at the blue sky and grimaced. "You're right, you're right . . . I need to cool down, sit tight, think about this until tonight."

Jess reached out to brush a mosquito off his cheek. "Try to remember what I'm about to say; you're a pilot, not a poet. And I think we should put the tarp back just the way we found it. Then, before we need to call nine-one-one for a transfusion, let's get back to the plane and get the heck out of here."

Jess swatted her cheek, smudging several fingers with bright-red blood. She studied the stained digits, made a face, then wiped the hand on the side of the coveralls.

"Let's go. We can talk about this in the hangar. I'm tired of feeding your little flying buddies."

"Yeah, maybe you're right. But just to prove we're not seeing things, I'm gonna take back my knife."

\* \* \*

Thirty minutes later *Johnny* was tethered to Bob's pier. The short hop to Birch had been uneventful. Like every good pilot, once at the controls, Buddy had cleared his head of all other thoughts.

The rising sun had encouraged a fresh breeze. Buddy needed total focus to plant pontoons safely on top of a light chop. He wanted to make certain the floats didn't skip. The last thing needed was to flub the landing, have to do a go-round.

The front passenger would never approve.

Neither said word one during the five-minute flight.

Buddy was all business working stick and rudder. Jessie was lost in thought, trying to unravel reasons for the weird find.

As soon as Jess stepped out, she'd sprinted to the house. She couldn't wait to inform Bob and Betty about the stash. But when barging inside, Jess was greeted by silence. The house was empty.

Then she remembered. Bob and Betty were going to town. Jess glanced at the kitchen clock; nine-thirty.

No doubt they'd be gone for a while yet. Snatching a couple of bananas from the fruit bowl, Jess went out through the side entrance. It provided a shorter route to the shop door.

Buddy came plodding into the workshop as Jess was stuffing the last bite of banana into her mouth.

"Don't suppose ya brought one for the pilot?" He sighed, plopping down on an empty stool.

Jess answered around a mouthful. "Not to worry." She nodded toward the banana on the workbench.

Smiling, Buddy picked it up. "I get up too early to eat at home. The cabin's not very big. Don't want to wake my mom or little brother. Besides, Bob usually sets out a plate of rolls and a carton of juice. Guess he forgot this morning."

Jess watched, captivated, as Buddy stuck one end of the banana into his mouth, chomped and then, using his teeth, peeled back the skin.

Noticing her ogle, Buddy mumbled, "What? You've never seen a banana peeled that way?"

"No, that's really weird. Everyone I know is civilized. They use their fingers."

Buddy took a bite, chewed and swallowed. "There's nothing weird about it at all. That's the way monkeys do it. Saw it on the Learning Channel."

Jess swiveled her head side-to-side. "Monkeys, huh? Oh man, you make it, way too easy."

Keeping one eye on Jess, Buddy chomped a second bite. Gulping, he said, "I'll tell you what's crazy—the stuff under that tarp. What'd ya think we should do about it?"

Jess reached over the workbench and plucked a pair of pliers from a wall peg. Then she swiveled back and forth on the stool, snapping the tool open and closed. After a time she said, "Well, I suppose the right thing would be to call the cops, tell 'em what we found. Don't you think?"

Rotating back and forth, Buddy studied a crack in the concrete. Looking up, he said, "Hmm, I'm not certain we should do that. Not just yet, anyways. First off, there aren't cops—as you call 'em—out here in the country. We'd have to contact the Sheriff's Office."

"Yeah . . . whatever. That's what deputies do, isn't it? Investigate break-ins and burglaries?"

Buddy took a moment to play "spin-the-stool." He did a three-sixty and then planted a shoe. Slamming to a squeaky stop, he said, "Let's think about it. Individually, none of those items are worth much. Most look well used. I doubt that the sheriff would make the case a priority, if he took it at all. For all we know, some of those things could have been dug out of people's trash."

Jess squeezed the pliers shut with a snap. "Your knife wasn't taken from the garbage, was it? You said you thought your little brother took it. But obviously he didn't. That is, unless he sneaks out of the house at night when rest of you are in La-La-Land."

Buddy spun another full circle. "Naw, that's impossible. He's only nine. He's not even allowed to take the rowboat out unless someone's on the dock to watch."

"So where are we then? Maybe tell Uncle Bob. See what he thinks?"

Buddy bit at the corner of his lip. After a time he said, "No, for now let's keep this under our hats. Maybe go back there in a couple of days. We'll see if anything's been disturbed. On Saturday, when neighbors are at cabins for the weekend, I can ask around and see if they're missing anything."

Jess frowned. "You better be real careful how you phrase the question. You could wind up being the number one suspect. I can see the headline now: 'Teen uses pilot's license to pile up secret stash of trash.'"

Buddy's eyes widened. "I hadn't thought of that. You're right. Let's go back to my first thought . . . I'll keep it under my hat, like a cat, until we figure out how to sniff out the rat."

Jess snickered, "Cats, rats. You're a real piece of work, Mr. Wilbert McLean . . . a regular poetry pervert."

Buddy grimaced while checking his watch. "Speaking of work, Bob should be back anytime now. I better get a move on. We'd like to get the engine pulled by the weekend."

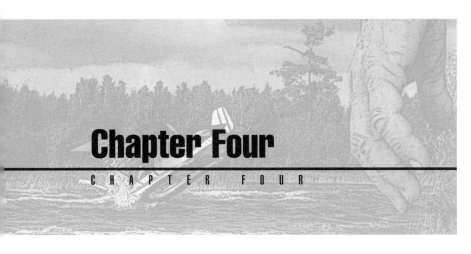

# Chapter Four

C H A P T E R   F O U R

Jess retraced her steps to the house. A lonely banana didn't cut it. Once inside, she went straight to the kitchen. After pouring a bowl of frosted flakes and buttering a slice of toast, she sat at the table, reflecting on recent events.

This was not how she had expected to spend the summer. The last few months had been a nightmare and her recent past an emotional roller-coaster.

The first jolt was when her dad announced he was getting married. The news shocked Jess like a bolt from the blue. Her mother hadn't been dead that long, barely a year.

To add insult to injury, the next week she was told they were moving. Almost overnight they'd vacated the comfy old inter-city two-story. Before she had a chance to say, "I won't go," she was living in the suburbs.

From that point forward things headed downhill like a truck without brakes.

Jess blended in at her old school. Many classmates had attended the same elementary. Most could be called friends. More importantly, the student body was diverse. There were students of every nationality: black, white and shades in between.

That Jess was of Eurasian heritage—her mother had been Vietnamese, her father was white—hadn't been an issue.

Not so at her new building. With coal-black hair and sand-tinted skin, Jess thought she stuck out like a dark sock on a white carpet.

Or at least that's the way she'd imagined it.

But looking back, Jess realized most wounds were self-inflicted. She'd been angry and upset. When she'd enrolled, she was carrying a redwood-sized chip on her shoulder. In reflection, given half a chance, most of the new classmates couldn't have cared less about her heritage.

She simply hadn't given any one a chance to get to know her.

Disheartened and lonely, Jess made some dreadful choices. The worst decision being the day she joined a clique of burnouts. One girl had an older boyfriend. He owned a car. Everyone piled in for a trip to the mall.

Acting cool to be accepted only compounded the error. When offered a cigarette, Jess took it.

She soon had a habit.

The crash came in April. Formally a B-plus student, her grades quickly dropped so low that her dad and step-mom were called in for a conference. Sitting in a closed room, encircled by people with power, Jess broke down. She sobbed until the reservoir was empty.

And then she came clean.

She confessed to skipping school, picking poor role models, and even owned up to smoking cigarettes. Sniveling back tears, she unloaded a heart full of hurt. Sadness caused not only by her mother's passing, but by recent events.

Her tale of woe caused other moist eyes. Even the counselor found cause for a tissue. After a period of silence, her dad began a stuttering apology. He should have known such far-reaching changes would come with a cost.

He clasped Jess's hands in his own and said he was sorry. Tears over, the counselor insisted they initiate a plan. Guidelines were needed for a fresh start.

First on the agenda was taking care of her schoolwork. The number two priority—reduced contact with the new crowd.

As luck would have it, her father's aunt and uncle pulled in just as the family arrived home. The older couple had driven to the city to attend an anniversary party.

After hearing the problem, Uncle Bob made a proposal. He had a close contact in Canada. The friend managed a swanky fly-in fishing camp and was always in need of seasonal help.

Rather than attending summer school, Jess could spend her vacation working at the resort. Bob said he'd be happy to provide transportation. He was planning a flight that direction anyway—a "fly and camp" gift for two special young men.

At first thought, Jess had misgivings. She couldn't imagine spending three months stuck in the boonies, trapped in the middle of nowhere. But she changed her mind after her dad reviewed the alternatives.

There were only two, Canada or summer school.

Clear as high-definition TV, Jess pictured weeks of sitting in a stuffy classroom. When that mental video rolled, washing dishes and making beds didn't seem so bad.

As it happened, she never made it to the lodge. Winging over the Canadian wilds, a squall dictated an emergency landing. Setting the Cessna on an unfamiliar lake, the foursome thought the worst was behind.

But their troubles had only begun. A pint-sized tornado

dipped from the storm clouds, flipping the floatplane.

Then to add to the teenagers' woes, the stress was over-whelming for their elderly aviator. Uncle Bob suffered a mild stroke. They were stranded for more than a week before reaching help.

Upon their return to the states, it was determined Jess would spend the rest of the summer at Birch Lake. Her uncle hadn't fully recovered and here were chores galore. Jess would have plenty on her "to-do" list.

From outside came the sound of car doors clunking, jolt-ing Jess from her reverie. Jumping up, she placed the bowl in the sink and hurried to the door.

She gawked through the screen. Clad in worn Levis and a faded Vikings sweat shirt, his lanky frame lounging against Bob's Buick—was Travis Larsen. Travis was the one teen who'd kept a clear head throughout the Canadian ordeal.

She knew the Larsens and Ritzers were good friends. It was the reason Travis and his pal, Seth, were taking a fly-in trip in the first place. The outing had been a unique birthday present for both boys.

But what was Travis doing here? The Larsens lived four hours away, far up in northeastern Minnesota, long miles up a dead-end road.

Bob was about to open the trunk when he spied Jess lurking behind the screen. "There you are, Jess! Come on out. Betty and I brought home a surprise."

Jess suddenly felt self-conscious. Clad in the baggy cover-alls, she had to look like something the cat dragged in. Her hair had to be a bird's nest. It hadn't felt a comb since she took off her headset. And with all the tramping in the woods, her cheeks had to be one large dirt smudge.

"So why does it matter? "she thought, unlatching the door. It wasn't like Travis hadn't seen her looking worse. She stepped out and raised a hand. "Hi. I sure didn't expect to see you today."

Startled, Travis turned, ran fingers through a mop of sandy-brown hair, and grinned. "Well . . . what can I say? I guess that goes ditto for me!"

He peered through the car's open window. Betty was sitting behind the wheel, waiting for the trunk to be emptied.

"So I take it this is the big secret you were whispering about at the cafe? Did Dad know she was here before we drove down this morning?"

Betty nodded, smiling eyes lighting up her grand-motherly face.

"He wasn't sure you'd want to come if you knew we had company. But don't worry, if you're not comfortable sleeping in the house, you can bunk in the hangar loft. It's cozy and private. You can have it all to yourself."

# Chapter Five

C H A P T E R     F I V E

"Honest, Jess," Travis pleaded. "I had no idea you were staying here. No one said a word about it to me. I thought you'd be home in the cities."

Jess focused on the far shore to where a tall pine stood guard along the water's edge. Evening light was playing tag with rippled water, staining a golden cast on century old boughs.

Supper over, dishes done, the two teens were sitting on the dock. Travis was watching a loon diving for dinner. Jess slid forward so her bare feet could tread water.

After a quiet pause, she said, "At first, I thought so too. But if I did go home, it'd been a real bummer. Dad's out of town working on a big project. I'd be alone with my new step-mom. And I'd have to finish summer school. Mark that down as a double *ugh*."

Jess leaned sideways and gave Travis an elbow nudge. "Anyways, I'm starting to like country living, waking up with the birds."

Displaying a playful grin, Travis returned the arm smack. "Hey girl, anymore abusive behavior like that and you'll be taking a bath."

Then turning somber, he said, "I'd have thought you'd be bored to death hanging out here with nuthin' to do."

Jess stiffened, turned and stared at Travis, her mouth an open cave. "What are you talking about—nothing to do? There's plenty of things need doing around this place. Just mowing the airstrip is a full-time job."

Travis toyed with a splinter on a dock board. Breaking it free, he snapped it in two, then flicked the bits toward a lily pad. One piece plopped dead-center on the green, platter-sized leaf.

"All right! Three-pointer!"

"Give me a break," Jess groaned. "Like you're into ball games . . . not! But tell me the truth. What are you doin' here? Did you get your fill of camping out with your buddy?"

Travis tipped back, measuring Jess with his eyes. She never did say how old she was, and neither had Bob. But from the way she carried herself, and her lightening quick retorts, he thought closer to seventeen than his recently turned fifteen.

"You mean Seth? Naw, you got it wrong. I had this day penciled on the calendar for months. My folks are taking a trip, just the two of them. They're driving across Canada and then up the Al-Can Highway. They'll be gone for a couple weeks."

"What about your little sister? Where's she staying?"

"Beth's at a language camp near Bemidji. She wants to learn French. Go figure."

On impulse, Jess swished her feet, splashing water. From behind came a squawk and a flapping of wings. Startled, both teens turned in unison.

A dull-colored mallard had been leading a flotilla of fuzz-balls. Hearing the sudden splatter, the mother bird had done an immediate about-face.

"Sorry, little ducks," Jess said, "I didn't hear you sneak up on us."

"Yeah, you better apologize. Mamma duck almost had a quack-up because of your foot washing."

Jess hit Travis with a second elbow shot, harder than the first. "Ha-ha. Funny, you're not. But really, Trav, why'd ya come down? You could have stayed with Seth, couldn't you?"

Travis gave Jess a pretend glare while rubbing his upper arm. "I suppose. But we had it planned long before all the storm stuff, that I'd stay here and take flying lessons. Get a few hours at the controls before I start ground school."

Jess pulled up her feet, and then tucked them underneath her body like a bird. "What'd ya mean ground school? What's flying got to do with the ground, other than you don't want to ever hit it too hard?"

Travis tugged off his cap, brushed the hair from his forehead, then pulled the hat back on. "Good question. I'm not really sure. But I think it means all the other things you gotta know about before flying solo. Reading maps, how to use the radio, stuff like that."

"I guess that makes sense. So, what are you gonna do now. I mean, with my uncle unable to fly and the float-plane in pieces?"

"Well . . . we weren't gonna use the seaplane in the first place. Bob's got a friend with a little two-seater—an old Cessna 150. I'm told most pilots start out in one of those before moving up to a bigger rig."

He paused, frowning. "I hate to say it, but you're right. Bob won't be able to fly, not until next year, if even that. But I was supposed to stay with the Ritzer's, so like it or not, here I am.

"Anyway, from the way you were whining about things to do, it sounds like you're getting tired of mowing. You'll have to give me a lesson on runnin' the big tractor. That little one I used today just doesn't cut it."

A fish jumped, putting a halt to conversation. Both watched the splash ring expand and then marry with other ripples.

Jess turned to face Travis. "So . . . what do think of Buddy? Did you check out his little bug-on-floats this morning? Maybe he'll teach you some of the basics. He's really into it."

"Bug-on, floats? Cute. But I gotta admit; it's a good description. I can't believe you really went up with him. Weren't you scared out of your mind?"

Jess uncurled her legs, pushed up and then stood. "Yeah, a little bit. No, that's not true. More than a little bit. But you know what? He may be a lousy poet, but he seems to be a good pilot. Just don't tell him I said so."

"Hmm . . . I wonder why that is? But back to his airplane . . . no, I didn't get a chance to check it out. Remember, he didn't stick around after we were introduced. He muttered something about it getting windy. Next thing I knew he was through the door and gone."

Travis rose, flashed a teasing smirk, and said, "Bob told me Buddy flies over every day. My showing up here probably bothers him. Maybe he sees something else of interest in the hangar besides airplane parts."

Jess rolled her eyes, hoping Travis didn't notice the heat rising in her cheeks.

"Yeah, right . . . like he even knows I'm a girl! Hey kiddo, the mosquitoes think it's feeding time. Let's run up to the shop. There's something I want to tell you. Buddy and I have a secret, but not the kind you're referring to. It's more like a mystery. Now that you're here, maybe you can help us find some answers."

Travis knew better than to challenge Jess to a foot race. He'd made that mistake once before, coming in a distant second. Instead, he let her lead the way, content to hang back and admire the view. The girl loped with the grace of a wild cat, and he thought if pressed, could probably outrun one as well.

"About time," Jess joked, pulling open the workshop's small side door. "I see you haven't gotten any faster."

"Just saving my energy. Travis said, stepping inside and closing the door. Who knows? I might need a full charge if I'm gonna help solve this big mystery,"

"Make fun all you want. But I bet you won't be laughing after I tell you what we found. The more I think about, the creepier it becomes."

* * *

"Let's make sure I've got this straight. You were on an island. You went exploring and found a camouflage tarp. Under the tarp were dozens of odds and ends, some old, some new, and everything organized in rows."

"That's pretty much it. Oh, there's something I forgot to mention. There was a pocket knife lined up with the other stuff. You'll never guess who it belongs to—Buddy. He'd thought his little brother swiped it last summer."

"I gotta admit that your story makes me curious. But I'd like to see it for myself. Maybe tomorrow you and I can make a trip out to that island."

Jess wrinkled her nose. "How we gonna do that? Buddy's plane only carries one passenger. Besides, from the way he pulled a disappearing act, it might be a few days before you get an invitation, if ever."

Travis slid off the stool and sauntered to the interior door. Pushing it open, he stood in the doorway and pointed across the cavernous hangar. "Not to worry. Our ride is tied to the rafters. Didn't you notice the old canoe hanging from the ceiling?"

Jess sprung to her feet. "Are you serious? There're so

many airplane parts lining the walls I never took a close look."

She slipped by Travis, then felt for a wall switch. Finding it with her fingers, she flicked on a set of overhead lights. Sure enough, off in a corner, secured high on a set of rope pulleys, was a scarred and dented aluminum canoe.

"Okay, I see it. But we still have a minor problem. We're on Birch Lake. The island I'm talking about is on Pike. How are we going to get the canoe all the way over there?"

Travis lounged against the door jam and smiled. "How do ya think, Jess? We're gonna carry it."

"Jeez. . . sounds like a lot of work. You're going to need a good night's rest. I better get going so you can head up to the loft. See ya in morning."

And with that, she was gone.

# Chapter Six

C H A P T E R    S I X

A rattling vibration woke Travis from a pleasant dream. Startled, he jerked upright, and for a few seconds, was uncertain of his whereabouts. As he rubbed the sleep from his eyelids, his mind cleared and he recognized the source of the wake-up call.

The electric winch was starting to crank up the hangar's large overhead door. Through the loft window, Travis could see the huge panels were beginning to fold together like pages of a giant greeting card. As the door slowly inched up, light began to flood inside.

He must have overslept.

The last thing he wanted was to have this Buddy character catch him loafing in the sack. Slipping out of the sleeping bag, Travis stuffed his long legs into Levis and then pulled on a sweat shirt. Quickly donning socks and shoes, he ran fingers through unkempt hair, then tugged the ball cap tight to his head.

By the time Travis tip-toed down the steep flight of stairs, the door was nearly open. Sunlight poured through the huge gap, brightening the work area as if it were a movie set.

Travis spied someone leaning against the far wall, fingers

poised near the door's emergency stop button. Squinting against the glare, he saw it was Jessie's brawny new friend.

Cripes, Travis wondered, what time does this dude get up? It couldn't be all that late, could it? Looking at his watch, he saw it was only six-forty-five—still early. He had nothing to be embarrassed about.

After wheezing out a silent sigh, he chose to meet the day head on. He padded around the Cessna's fuselage, stopped, and called out, "Morning Buddy. You're an early riser."

The greeting caught Buddy off guard. He spun around as if yanked by a cord.

"Whoa! You startled me, man! I didn't know you were here."

Buddy noticed the pillow wrinkles crinkling Travis's cheeks. In bright light they were as clear as red lines on a roadmap.

"So what'd ya do? Sleep in the loft?"

"Yeah, I did. The house only has one bathroom. I thought it'd just be simpler if I used the one out here. Besides, have you ever heard Bob snore? The man could wake the dead."

Buddy's expression remained neutral. "Nope, can't say that I've ever had the pleasure. But anyways, I'm sorry if I disturbed your beauty rest."

Uncertain how to reply, Travis toyed with the floatplane's prop, running a palm up and down the outer edge.

There was an awkward silence before he spoke. "No problem. I was awake but I didn't want to go in the house too early," he fibbed. "I'm not sure what time Bob and Betty roll out."

The older teen gave the slightest of nods and then said, "I wouldn't worry about that. Chances are Bob's already been in the workshop. He may not be one-hundred percent, but he still gets up with the sun."

Then he placed a hand on his stomach and muttered, "Come on . . . let's go see if he brought us something to eat. I don't know 'bout you, I'm starving."

Travis received a second shock when he opened the shop door. Jessie was perched on a stool, nibbling a roll. And she had company—her uncle. Screwdriver clutched in one hand, a pair of pliers in the other, he was fussing with a two-way radio.

Bob glanced up as the boys shuffled in. Setting down the tools, he wobbled upright and said, "Good, I'm happy to see everybody made it through the night. But Buddy, I'm surprised to see you here. We didn't hear *Johnny* this morning. What'd you do, ride over on the four-wheeler?"

Staring at the plate resting on the workbench, Buddy said, "Yup. It's supposed to rain this afternoon, maybe even a thunderstorm. I pulled *Johnny* up on the beach and tied him tight to the trees. One soggy airplane is enough of a project, don't cha think?"

Bob noticed Buddy's eyes lingering on the napkin-covered platter. "Go ahead, boys. Help yourselves to a roll."

He gestured in the direction of a small refrigerator. "There's a carton of O.J. in the fridge. Buddy, once you feed the lions, we'll get started pulling the engine."

Bob turned toward Travis. "Guess you'll have to wait another day or two for your first flight lesson. My friend phoned last night. Said the 150 needs a new front tire. Besides, from what Buddy just reported, the weather doesn't sound promising."

Bob alternated his gaze between Travis and his niece. "Jess tells me that you two would like to take the canoe down and do a little paddling on Pike. What'd ya think, Buddy? Would it be all right if they used your dock?"

Clutching the carton of juice in one hand, a cup in the other, Buddy mumbled, "I suppose, if they want. They can load the Grumman on your old snowmobile trailer. I'll tow it over to our place behind the Honda."

Buddy considered Travis, making note of the younger teen's slender frame. Returning his gaze to the platter, he said, "It'd be a heck of a carry for this kid, toting it that far on those skinny shoulders. When he got there he'd probably be too pooped to paddle."

The room became silent as an empty church; the stinging remark lingering like the smell of stale sweat in a locker room. So still, the click-swish of the wall clock's second hand and hum of the refrigerator were the only sounds.

Bob broke the impasse. "I'm heading for the house. Betty should have breakfast ready. If any of you kids want more than juice and a roll, now's the time to tag along."

Two teens followed the senior through the side door. The third stayed behind, eyes fixed on the pastry plate.

* * *

"So what's really bugging you? Or did a bee sting your tongue?" Jess asked.

"Like you can't figure it out? Why don't you ask your bubble-butted friend?" Travis muttered. "It's time to switch. I'll paddle on the left for a while."

Jess shrugged changed her grip and began stroking with her right arm.

Earlier, following a pancake breakfast, Jess and Travis returned to the hangar. In minutes they had the canoe lowered to the concrete. Then they dumped the old Grumman on the trailer. As agreed, Buddy drove the ATV. Jess and Travis sat on the trailer's bed, making certain the canoe wouldn't topple.

When arriving at the cottage, Buddy had pulled close to the lake and parked with the engine idling. He sat staring straight ahead while Jess and Travis hefted the canoe. As soon as the Grumman touched water, he squeezed the throttle. Without so much as a good-bye wave, he took off.

A nugget Jess gleaned from the Canadian peril was that Travis was a people pleaser. He cared what others thought. And right now, she realized, Buddy was acting like a jerk. He'd transformed from poet-comedian to creep in the blink of an eye—a regular Jekyll and Hyde.

Why? She wondered. Because the big goof was clueless if he thought she'd be impressed.

"Where do you want to land?" Travis asked, prying Jess from private thoughts.

Jessie studied the wooded shore, hoping to spot the sandy cove.

"Ah . . . just around the corner, I think. There's a beach with a small grassy opening. That's where we stopped the other day."

Travis resumed paddling, thrusting hard, jetting the Grumman ahead in energetic spurts. He'd had ample opportunity to hone his canoeing skills weeks earlier. Bob had strapped a lightweight canoe to one of the seaplane's pontoons. In the wake of the flip-over saga the sturdy craft had been worth its weight in gold.

Jess also had opportunity for paddling practice. Using the canoe and an abandoned old boat, the four castaways rowed and paddled to a remote fishing lodge. The remainder of the rescue had been a simple event.

"Jess, look," Travis whispered. "Up ahead, there's a doe with a fawn."

Jess let the paddle drag, scouring the shoreline with her gaze. At first glance she only identified trees and brush. Then a flicker of white caught her eye. More of the frame filled in as she focused directly on the spot.

She realized that she was looking at the rump and tail of a mature deer. Standing alongside—its tiny head nuzzled under the doe's ivory-furred belly—was an adorable spotted fawn.

After a long moment, Jess swiveled so she could see Travis. "Cool," she mouthed. "Wish I had a camera."

Just then her paddle caught a wave, clanging the canoe. She swung around, only to see two white flags bounding into the forest. "Sorry, I didn't mean to do that. But that was awesome."

"Don't sweat it. Soon as we got close they would have taken off anyway. So where is this secret beach? Or maybe you made the whole story up so you could practice paddling."

"Dream on. It's right over there. Let's pull in."

* * *

Twenty minutes later they were standing in the middle of the meadow.

"I'm telling you this is where we found the tarp. Check it out. Look at the dead weeds."

Travis could see something large and rectangular had recently been removed. And by the appearance of flattened and lifeless vegetation, it'd been there for quite some time. He thought at least a year, maybe longer.

"I believe you," Travis said. "I can see you're not making it up. About the only thing that makes sense though, is that the person responsible knew you were here. Why else would someone take the trouble to haul everything away?"

Jess didn't have the answer. Instead, she edged along the perimeter of yellowed vegetation, searching for any kind of helpful hint.

Shuffling to Travis, she sighed and then said, "There was this one thing I didn't mention. That day, when I came to this clearing, I stopped—over there by that tree."

Jess hooked her thumb toward a medium-sized aspen and then went on. "I had a funny feeling, like I wasn't alone. It felt like someone was watching me. I listened and looked around but didn't hear or see anyone."

She paused, forehead furrowed in thought.

"Wait! There was something else . . . a hint of a smoke, like pipe tobacco. I didn't pay any attention to it. I thought it was a cabin owner burning leaves across the lake."

She gasped and then stood open-mouthed, staring at the sky. "Do you think someone was spying on me? Oh man, it freaks me out to think about it."

Folding his arms across his chest, Travis did a slow one-eighty. "I don't know, Jess. Let's check along the edge of the meadow. Maybe we'll come across something."

* * *

"Hey Jess, get over here!" Travis yelled moments later.

"What? What did you find?" Jess shouted, bounding across the open space.

Travis waited until they were standing side by side. He pointed to the ground. "There," he said, making a sweeping motion with a hand. "If you look real close, you can see where someone made two or three trips."

Jess fixed her stare to where Travis pointed. She didn't see anything unusual about the mat of leaves, small plants, dead sticks and broken branches.

"What am I looking for? I don't see anything."

"Try again. Only this time pretend you're looking for the easiest route to the far side of the island."

Placing her hands on her hips, Jess looked forward. Travis waited patiently. He wanted her to find the clues with her own eyes.

A light came on. "I get it. There," she said, "and farther on. Those ferns are bent or broken. They've been trampled. And you're right. It's like a natural path through the trees."

Travis took a step back before patting Jess's shoulder. "Way to go, Pocahontas. I'll make a tracker out of you yet. What say we follow the signs, see where they lead?"

Jess had grown up in Minneapolis. She knew about bus routes, traffic lights, bargain stores, shortcuts through back alleys and a thousand other city things. But she still had lots to learn about the outdoors.

"Can you really do that? Follow the tracks, I mean. Won't it take all day?"

Quite the opposite of Jess, Travis had been born and raised near the border of the Boundary Waters Canoe Area Wilderness. As he grew to be a teenager, the nearby lakes and surrounding countryside had become a big backyard for him and his buddy, Seth, to play in.

Rather than reply to Jess's query, the youth shook his head. He pointed deeper into the woods and then began stalking forward.

Travis had little difficulty following the faint imprints. By combining subtle clues with common sense, they were soon stationed on the far shore.

"There's no doubt that this is where he loaded the boat," Travis said, then added, "Assuming, of course, the mystery person is a he and not a she."

He dropped to a knee and then bent back a clump of grass. "Look, you can see the groove where the bow sat."

Jess didn't need any more proof. The eerie sensation had been real. Somebody had been spying. And then alarmed that his secret had been discovered, moved everything before word got around.

Hidden away as it was from curious spectators, this was

the perfect spot for a transfer. All the lake cabins were opposite where the canoe was beached. This side of the island faced a long stretch of vacant shoreline.

The only chance of being spotted would be by a passing fisherman. And if the move had been made after dark, no one would be the wiser.

So the obvious question would be—where would a thief take a boatload of odds and ends?

Possible answer—another island. Buddy had said the land belonged to the county, reclaimed years ago for back taxes. That meant anyone—anytime—could walk around, camp or even sneak over to hide treasures.

But today, if they chose to explore, she'd have a partner. She wouldn't be nervous about being spied upon.

The Boy Scout from the Boundary Waters would be at her side.

# Chapter Seven

CHAPTER SEVEN

"You know what, Buddy? I've learned a few things in seventy years of living. One of which is when work won't cooperate, you have to step back and take a timeout."

Things had been going badly for Bob's youthful companion. Buddy usually practiced a "slow and easy does it" approach. Not today. Instead, the teen was demonstrating the slam-bam method of mechanics—come apart or I'll tear you in two.

Breaking things had almost become a habit during the first hour of work. In a rush to get started, Buddy didn't notice that the wrench handle was under a gas line. Giving the tool a hearty thrust, the bolt wasn't the only object to budge. So did the tube, tearing free from a fuel strainer as easily as if it were a paper straw.

A similar snafu occurred minutes later. This time a spark plug wire fell victim to an errant twist of the wrist.

The elderly airman had seen enough. A recess was in order. Bob was no expert on teenage behavior. He was, however, wise enough to know Buddy had more than airplane parts buzzing about in his brain.

The senior wobbled over to the workshop. He paused at the door and gestured for the frustrated young man to follow. Inside, the elder retrieved rolls from the refrigerator. Indicating that Buddy should park on a stool, Bob put the platter on the bench, then lowered his bones into a well-worn recliner.

Settling in, he waited while Buddy took his time selecting his third pastry of the day.

"So tell me, Bud, why the long snout this morning? If I didn't know better, I'd guess you're turning into a mule or had just lost your best friend."

Buddy chose to chew rather than respond. But his feet betrayed him. His shoes tapped a nervous beat on the stool's support rung.

Bob cleared his throat with a "harrumph" before answering his own question. "I can only assume it has something to do with our new guest. Before Travis arrived you appeared to be in hog heaven . . . what with working on the Cessna . . . joking with Jessica . . . flying *Johnny* over every morning."

"I don't believe that I ever saw your cheek dimples so often and so deep. I was thinking the other day that if you were into eatin' rhubarb, they'd be a good place to store the sugar."

The odd comment piqued Buddy's interest. Between bites he mumbled, "What are you talkin' about—sugar in my cheeks? Why in the world would I want to do that?"

Displaying the stroke-affected grin, Bob laughed. "Fresh-picked rhubarb, my young friend, is one of Ma Nature's finest gifts. Trouble is, it's awfully tart. When I was a wee lad on the farm, I couldn't wait for the rhubarb to ripen.

"My brother and I would pour a cupful of sugar into a brown paper bag. Then, when Mom was busy elsewhere, we'd take our pocket knives into the garden and cut a few stalks."

Bob took a breather. He sat with his eyes closed, remembering—a smile lighting his leathery, weather-worn face.

Buddy tried to wait him out. When the man didn't speak, the youth grew impatient. "Okay. So you swiped some rhubarb. What's the sugar got to do with anything?"

The old man opened his eyes and gazed across the room. "Swiped is too harsh a word, son. After all, it was a family farm. We lived mostly off what we grew. But think. I've already told you that unripe rhubarb tastes tart. It needs a little sweetening. So we'd trot over to the woodlot where we had a little fort."

Bob closed his lids again, dredging up the memory.

"It was really only a crude collection of corn stalks, sticks and cast-off lumber. But to get to the point, whoever had the sugar sack would pull it out of their back pocket. We'd twist the top so a rhubarb stalk would just slip inside. Then we'd give the bag a shake or two. Sugar grains would stick to the sappy wound, sweetening the first couple of inches. Ah yes, it was better than a treat from the general store."

"So tell me, Bud. Smart as you are, you know darn well this isn't just an old man's rambling about rhubarb. What's the lesson to be learned here?"

Buddy found it difficult to make eye contact. Instead he studied the floor.

"Well?" Bob asked gently.

The teen lifted his head until he stared at a place over Bob's shoulder. "That I'm acting like sour-puss. That maybe, like your rhubarb, I could use some sweetening?"

"Close enough. I'm not saying you have to be young Mr. Larsen's best pal. But cut the boy some slack. He's a good kid. And bear in mind, you're nearly a full-grown man."

Bob coughed and went on. "If you want to stay in good standing with a certain young woman, I suggest you file away my sugary tale. And try to remember the words of this old saying. They always ring true. 'You're bound to catch more with honey than you will with vinegar.' Try it. You won't be sorry."

* * *

Travis tugged the canoe up on the beach. He wrapped the bow line around a tree, tied a knot and said, "It'd be quicker if you go that way while I go this way. We'll meet halfway around. Okay?"

After climbing into the Grumman, the paddlers had agreed not to dawdle. Ominous gray-topped clouds were gathering, promising rain.

Once on the water, the teens placed all their energy into pulling short oars. In five minutes of steady stroking they'd circled the island, then pointed the bow toward island number two.

Now, standing at the edge of dense forest bordering the lakefront, Jess was feeling ill at ease.

"Why can't we stay together? It wouldn't take any longer, would it? Besides, you're more apt to notice something strange than I am."

"What? Are you still afraid of the woods? I thought you got over that."

Jess turned and kicked at a rotten stump. Boys and their need to act macho, she bristled, giving the decomposed wood a second taste of a toe.

Whirling to glare at Travis she said angrily, "Okay, fine. You go that way. I'll go this way. If I see anything strange, I'll holler. But don't hold your breath. You probably won't hear me. Buddy and I flew over this island. It's a lot bigger than it looks from here."

Without giving Travis a chance to compromise, Jess turned and trotted away. Quickly swallowed by leafy foliage, she vanished from view.

Travis was left standing alone, shaking his head. He wasn't surprised by anything the girl did. While marooned in the wilds, Jess had often acted in a similar fashion.

Seth and he had begun referring to Jess by another name. They tagged her "Somethun' Else." To the boys, it seemed that every time they thought they had her figured out, she'd go and do just that—something else.

And the strange thing, Travis reflected, was that he found it alluring. Unlike some other girls he knew, this one had a mind of her own. He checked the bow line and then, still smiling, began hiking in the opposite direction.

* * *

Jess didn't slow until well out of earshot.

Then she stopped, leaned against a tree and laughed. She really expected to see Travis chasing after, trying to catch up.

Giving it more thought—nah—he probably wouldn't. The boy from the Boundary Waters was so darn gullible.

Though sincere and honest to a fault, she knew Travis wasn't skilled at reading between the lines. But then again, who could blame him? Living as he did, a gazillion miles from civilization. She'd have to be more direct with her words. Just tell the tall hunk she enjoyed his company.

Jess had just pushed away from the tree when movement caught her eye. All senses went on alert. She'd only caught a glimmer—but it was something dark, bounding her way through the heavy cover.

Two words rushed front and center—Big Jim?

What to do? Stay put? Scream? Run?

In a heartbeat the creature came bumbling through the underbrush. Jess tried to scream but her vocal chords had iced-over. The best she could do was exhale a pitiful shriek.

Before she had time to flee, the beast was at her feet, slobbering, hoping to get a quick lick at exposed ankles. Like a Raggedy Ann doll, Jess went limp.

The beast wasn't the bear. It was a dog—a mangy black-and-brown mutt, a regular Heinz 57.

As rapidly as fear had squeezed her heart, made it race—its release did the opposite. She became light-headed and rubber-legged. If she hadn't been standing alongside a tree, she may well have tipped over.

Meanwhile, the stray continued to pant, tongue drooling and big, sad eyes staring up.

"Doggone it! You gave me a scare. What on earth are you doing here? Nobody lives on this island."

When the mutt dropped on its haunches, Jess noticed something odd. It was missing part of a front leg and had a collar circling its neck.

The dog seemed harmless, friendly enough that she lowered herself to one knee. She stretched out a hand to scratch behind its ears, one of which had a large gap of missing skin. The mongrel shut its eyes, closed its mouth and became totally tranquil.

Jess slowly worked her other hand toward the collar. She slipped two fingers under the leather and lifted it clear of shaggy hair. Sewn to the band with strands of wire was a small metal tag. Inscribed on its shiny surface was one word—*Lucky*.

Continuing to pet its head, Jess whispered, "So your name's Lucky is it? That's pretty weird. You sure don't look very lucky."

Hearing its name, the mutt opened his eyes and stared up. Jess thought the pooch actually smiled. No, impossible, dogs can't smile, she mused. But then again, she wasn't certain.

She'd never had a dog. For that matter, with the exception

of a pair of goldfish, she'd never owned a pet, period. Her father claimed he was allergic to animal hair. Flashing back, Jess wondered if that was the real reason. There could certainly be other possibilities.

Jess slowly rose, and then stood, considering what to do. She didn't want to abandon the animal. Wearing a collar with a name tag, it obviously had an owner.

After discarding several notions, she decided the best approach would be to continue the trek. Maybe the dog would follow. When she rejoined Travis, they could make the decision together.

Jess said to the dog, "Since you seemed so eager to meet and greet me, I'm gonna let you tag along. Not that I could convince you otherwise, I suppose. But no doubt you're like most dogs—when you catch a whiff of something interesting, you'll run off to do your own thing."

Lucky not only tagged along, he led the way. Jess was amazed that, despite missing part of a leg, the dog had little difficulty traveling over or around forest debris.

They were minutes into the hike when Lucky stopped. Like a well-trained hunting dog on point, he froze. Only his ears twitched, as if straining to hear.

After a time the mutt swung his head toward Jess. He gawked at the girl, as if making a difficult decision. Then abruptly, with only a wag of his tail, he bounded into the brush.

Before Jess had time to react, her new friend disappeared.

* * *

Still sporting a grin, Travis walked along the lakefront. In order to avoid windfalls, he'd sometimes venture inland a few yards. But being woods-wise, the diversions presented little challenge. Mostly, he trudged along the shore, eyes down, searching for any signs of activity.

His thoughts switched to Buddy, and how rude he'd been

first thing in the morning. What was the guy's problem? Yet Bob seemed to think he was an okay fellow. If he didn't, there was no way Bob would let him hang out in the hangar—much less tear apart the seaplane.

And, according to what Jess had confided yesterday, she too thought he was a regular guy.

No, there had to be some kind of burr under Buddy's blanket. And no doubt, Travis concluded, he was the cause of the irritation. Travis's arrival fit with the "two's company—three's a crowd" saying.

His remark why Buddy wanted to hang around the hangar was on target. Buddy had developed a school-boy crush on Jess, and he viewed Travis as a rival.

Travis grasped that he also had more than a passing interest in Ms. Jessica. He admired her fiery persona, her quick comebacks—the way she approached difficult situations.

And it didn't hurt that she was attractive. So if Buddy had trouble with that—tough. It wasn't enough to cause a lack of sleep.

Bringing thoughts back to the present, Travis realized that he'd come to a small cove. Partially obscured by reeds and stalks of wild rice, the little inlet was about the size of a high school gym. It would make an ideal location to come ashore unseen.

Travis backed into the underbrush. Then he began paralleling the water, one measured step at a time. The last thing he wanted was to be seen, especially after last winter's harrowing ordeal bumping into a pair of poachers.

He'd taken a dozen stealthy steps when a muted thud made him freeze. He knew the sound. It was the noise a person made stepping into a wooden boat. Without second thought, Travis fell to his knees and scurried farther into the forest on all fours.

When he was certain he was out of sight, he stopped to listen. There were a couple more boat-bottom thuds, followed by a man's gruff voice.

"Dang it, Luck. You were told you stay and guard the boat. I don't know why I even brought you along. You're worse at following orders than a spoiled kid."

Travis had heard enough. He didn't want to run into one crook, much less two. Rising, he made his exit, angling toward the lake. Although nervous as a mouse at a cat show, he was careful where he stepped. He didn't need a telltale twig giving up his getaway.

Upon reaching the lake, he slipped out of the brush and then shifted into high. He wanted to catch Jess. He could only hope that she'd slowed. For if she'd continued the pace she'd started with, it might be too late. She'd circle the island and wind up introducing herself to a couple of stash-storing strangers.

* * *

Jess more than dawdled, she stopped altogether. The girl was having somber second thoughts because of the way the dog tipped its head to listen.

She'd seen behavior like that before. A neighbor two doors down owned a black lab. Sometimes the man would walk the dog without a leash. Whenever the dog wandered too far ahead, the man would blow a whistle.

The strange thing was—Jess could never hear it. But obviously the dog did. It'd tip its head, drop in its tracks and sit. Sometimes the man would hit the whistle a second time. When that happened, the lab would scurry back to its master.

And this mutt acted nearly the same. Could it mean that someone had been blowing a silent whistle? But who and where would that person be? And did she really want to know?

Jess was still debating which way to travel when she

**61**

heard footsteps approaching fast and furious. Uncertain of their source, Jess sprang from the windfall and took a quick glance into the forest, hoping to see a place to conceal herself. Unless she was to run deep into the woods, a scraggly white pine a dozen yards distant would have to do.

But she'd have to hurry. The crash of breaking brush and splashing water were getting too close for comfort.

* * *

Running across an open field was one thing. But jumping over windfalls, dodging around rocks and occasionally even sloshing in the shallows took its toll. Travis was winded.

He'd jogged past the canoe minutes earlier. He had hoped Jess had failed to follow directions. That she'd returned to the boat and was waiting for him.

Not to be. The site was just as he'd left it—quiet and empty.

The pace had been too fast and furious. He needed a breather. Coming upon a fallen aspen, Travis stopped to catch his breath. After stepping over the plump tree trunk, he planted both feet and then plopped down butt first.

He rested with his head in his hands, breathing in short bursts, while his heart pounded like a jackhammer. Suddenly he was aware of a giggling chirp. Travis's radar came back on line. The peculiar sound seemed to have come from close by.

Travis jumped to his feet, ready to run. Then standing motionless, he looked around. Nothing seemed out of the ordinary. Ever so slowly, he turned to face the lake. Could the creepy noise have come from that direction? No, impossible, nothing but open water.

The sound repeated itself—louder and longer. Travis smiled. He was familiar with the giggle—Jessie.

Doing an about-face, he took a second scan of the woods. Again, nothing out of the ordinary.

"All right. You win. I can't see you but I know you're here. Red Rover, Red Rover, wherever you are, come on over. We gotta make tracks."

"What? Why?" asked a voice from above.

Travis looked toward the tree tops. A glimpse of Jessie's maroon sweatshirt caught his eye. He stepped farther into the forest. She was perched in a pine, resting on a ladder-like limb; mouth scrunched in a chipmunk grin.

"Real clever, squirrel face. But get down here. We gotta go."

Jessie's teasing smile twisted into a frown. "What's the rush? Afraid you're gonna be late for lunch?"

But by Travis's tone, she could tell he was serious. So without waiting for an answer, Jess climbed down.

Travis watched as she effortlessly lowered from one bough to another. In seconds Jessie's feet were resting on the bottom branch. And although almost a body length above the ground, she two-handed a nearby limb, swung out and dropped lightly to the ground.

Rubbing pine-pitched palms together she grumbled, "Yuk, remind me never to climb an evergreen without wearing gloves."

Resolved that the goop was impossible to remove, she asked, "Okay. So what's the big emergency?"

"We were right. I think they did move the stuff over here. I just about tripped over their boat. I'll tell you all about it later, when we're in the canoe."

# Chapter Eight

C H A P T E R      E I G H T

The transfer had taken more time than intended. It was already mid-morning. But he'd done it. All the souvenirs were squirreled away. Stuffed into garbage bags and cloaked with vegetation, they'd be impossible to find. Let 'em look!

Mission accomplished, it was time to head home. Not that many would view the old Airstream fit habitat for a human. But to Max it was more than shelter. It was the one place he could call his own.

The ancient pull-behind was parked deep in thick woods. Flat tires, peeling paint and plastic-covered windows screamed "hunting shack." And in fact, that's how it came to be in the forest in the first place.

Years earlier a distant relative had managed to snake the camper to the center of the property. He'd signed over the title after only a few hunting seasons. The city-slicker claimed he'd outgrown the need to kill Bambi. Said he was taking up woodcarving instead.

Max Grogan assumed a different reason. His distant cousin was a terrible marksman. The man had never hit a thing in a dozen years of trying. But Max wasn't about to argue. The gift had been one of the few highpoints in an otherwise dull and dismal life.

*Max waited for the dog to get settled in the boat. Then he took a slow scan in both directions. Pleased, he pulled down the mask, pushed the dinghy from shore and clamored aboard.*

* * *

"Did they see you? Did you get a good look at them? Were they young or old? Were they . . ."

"All right already! I surrender!" Travis begged. "One question at a time. No, they didn't see me and I didn't see them."

"If you didn't see 'em, how'd ya know there was more than one person?"

Travis was slow to respond. Switching the paddle to his other hand, he gave a hardy thrust, pitching the bow to the left. Sensing the change, Jess rotated her grip. She began stroking on the port side, helping to correct the canoe's course.

"Because I heard the first guy complaining to someone named Luck. I'm telling you, Jess, the dude was really ticked. He told this second fellow that he should have left him at home . . . that a spoiled kid could follow directions better than he did."

Jessie's shoulders began to shake with laughter. She laid the paddle across the gunnels and swiveled so she was facing Travis.

"What? What's so funny?"

"You know what? I think I met this Mr. Luck. 'Cept he didn't have much to say, hardly a woof."

"Say again . . . woof? You're not making sense."

"Yeah, I think I am. Your Mr. Luck is a dog named Lucky, a friendly mutt who almost gave me a heart attack."

Once they exchanged war stories, the paddlers made a decision. They'd circle the first island far enough to be out of sight. Then they'd beach the canoe and sneak along shore, hoping to catch a glimpse of the mystery man in the boat.

But by the time they'd hurried into position, they were too late. All they saw were waves and water. After thirty minutes of swatting mosquitoes and gnats, they conceded defeat.

Disappointed and bitten up, they trudged back to the canoe, ready to head home.

Travis studied the sky. Dreary clouds had closed ranks, darkening the day, coloring the choppy wavelets gun-metal gray. "We better move it or we'll be getting a free shower," he advised.

Jess stopped stroking long enough to check out the scowling sky.

"I think you're right. At least it's warm. I'm not made of sugar. I won't melt. But I'm little concerned about you."

Facing front, Jess had no idea the remark made Travis's lips curl. But he remained silent, not letting on that he was amused.

When he could talk without laughing, he said, "In the Wizard of Oz the Wicked Witch turned into a puddle when she got wet. You better pray you stay dry."

Jess laughed. "Say what? Are you calling me a witch? Watch your tongue, buster!"

Travis playfully skimmed his paddle along the surface. Jess was doused by a shower of droplets, causing her to giggle again.

But the next words that flew out of Travis's mouth put a halt to the playful exchange. "Yeah, or what? You gonna tell your boyfriend to beat me up?"

He regretted the words before the last syllable left his mouth.

\* \* \*

"Why didn't you go in the cabin? My mom would have driven you over." Buddy chided, shaking his head in disapproval.

The three teens had gathered in the shop. Two of them were waterlogged.

Ignoring Buddy's dig, Jess continued to rub her short locks with a fluffy towel. Travis was bent over in the chair, removing wet shoes and soggy socks.

Having finished drying her hair, Jess set the towel on the workbench. Then she spun about on the stool, challenging Buddy. "Oh really? From the way you disappeared this morning, we thought you were happy to get rid of us. Right, Trav?"

Travis sat up. These were the first words Jess had tossed his way since he'd spit out the boyfriend crack.

Upon paddling to the McLean dock, Jess had jumped from the canoe. She stomped up on land and stood with her back to the lake. She fumed silently until Travis had the Grumman beached. Then, without a word, she'd moved around the log-sided cottage to the entry of the ATV path. Only once did she glance back to make certain Travis was following.

The rain started as they came out of the woods. At first it was only a drizzle. But when they reached the airstrip's mid-point, the sky opened up. Jess turned on her afterburners, sprinting to the finish line.

Travis had started to bolt, but realized the folly of the effort. Regardless how fast he ran, he was going to get soaked. He slowed to a jog, and then to a brisk walk. By the time he entered the shop, Buddy had already scrounged Jess a drying cloth.

Jess flung Buddy a scowl. "Simple. It wasn't raining when we got to your dock. We thought we'd be back in time."

She glanced at Travis. "Besides, you never introduced us to your mom. Remember? What were we suppose to do? Knock on the door and say, 'Oh, hi. We're a couple of Buddy's buddies. Do you think you could drop whatever you're doing and drive us to the Ritzers?'"

Trying to avoid conflict, Travis faked working on a shoelace. Despite his sodden discomfort, he couldn't hold back a smile. When dissed, Jessie's comebacks could be as cutting as a butcher knife.

"Am I right Trav?" Jess repeated. "We didn't know we were gonna get wet, did we?"

"Huh? Ah, no. It didn't start raining until we were almost here."

Travis chose his next words with care. "But hey, it's warm out. So what's a little water? We agreed neither one of us is so sweet we'd melt. Ya think?"

Jess flashed Travis a quick grin, setting him at ease. "Nah. No chance of that happening. If anything, I'm worried that my paddling partner might rust."

Confusion furrowed Buddy's wide brow. "Rust? What'd ya talking about? Why would he rust?"

Jess winked at Travis before turning back to Buddy. "Because every once in a while Trav acts like the Tin Man. He opens his mouth before engaging a pea-sized brain."

She paused. "Do I hear any arguments, Mr. Larsen?"

Travis shook his head. Buddy might be baffled, but he caught the clue. Jess was telling him to think first, speak second. And if he didn't, the next time he might be traveling solo down the yellow brick road. But Jess had it wrong. Tin Man was in need of a heart, not a new brain.

Travis rose from the chair, about to pad up to the loft for dry clothes. Shuffling barefoot toward the door, he said, "Jeez, Jess. We had this conversation in Canada. Hate to say, but you've still got the characters screwed up. The Tin Man was in search of a heart. Don't ya remember? It was the Scarecrow who wanted some wits."

He paused at the door opening, "But I hear ya loud and clear. Sorry about before."

Faster than an eye could follow, Jess snatched the towel, and then lobbed it across the room. Travis dropped the shoes and threw up his hands. Amazingly, he snagged the soggy mass mid-air. Quickly bundling the fabric into a ball, he returned the favor.

Realizing what Travis was about to do, Jess flopped from the stool. By narrowest of margins, the moist missile zipped over her head, smacking Buddy face-first.

Travis had been ready to run but the errant throw turned his feet to stone. Mortified, he stammered an apology, "Ahh, sorry . . . that wasn't meant for you."

Buddy put the bundle on the bench and then surprisingly, cracked a grin. "It's all right. I deserved it. Bob and I had a little chat. He politely pointed out that I've been acting like a jerk. So really, I'm the one who should be saying he's sorry."

The poet-pilot wannabe broke into another rhyme. "Like the Mad Hatter, I'm gonna do better. If you don't believe me, I'll send you a letter."

Jess and Travis locked eyes and then, as if on cue, groaned in unison.

* * *

Warm and dry, the trio regrouped after lunch. Bob was stealing an afternoon siesta. Having extra mouths at the table, Betty had taken the Buick on a grocery run. Outside the day remained wet and dreary. A leaden sky teamed with a brisk breeze gave a fall-like chill.

"What we need is a plan," Travis offered. Clad in clean Levis and a green windbreaker, he toyed with an old headset lying on the work surface.

"Don't you guys think we should tell my uncle?" Jess asked. She'd changed into navy blue jogging pants and a gray sweatshirt. This one had a gold "U of M" logo scripted across the front, the words "University of Minnesota" emblazoned on the back.

Buddy laughed. "Tell him what? That we stumbled across some odds and ends? That there might . . . or might not be a sneak-thief roaming around Pike Lake? What could he do about it? Call the sheriff? And then what?"

The oldest teen had laid claim to the tattered chair. He shifted in the seat to first stare at Jess and then at Travis. "I agree with Trav. We need to figure out what's going on. Got any ideas?"

Travis slipped the headset around his neck and held on to the ear pads with both hands. "Yeah, I do. Those islands are public property, right?"

Buddy nodded. "Yeah, I'm almost certain."

"What's today, Friday? I suppose most of your neighbors come up for the weekend, go home sometime Sunday afternoon. That right?"

"Usually, 'specially now that Fourth of July has come and gone. What's that got to do with anything?"

Travis wiggled back and forth on the stool, considering. "Do you like to go camping? You know, sleep out in a tent?"

"What are you suggesting?" asked Buddy. "That we set up camp and spy, wait for this guy to come to us?"

Travis beamed. "Exactly . . . unless you can't handle being away from your own bed?"

He turned to Jess. "What d'ya say, kiddo? Would it bother you if Buddy and I stake it out? Say, starting Monday afternoon? That'd give Buddy time to finish pulling the engine. Meantime, you and I can get all the cutting and trimming done—plus any other odd jobs that need doing."

Jess measured the thought. "First off, aren't you forgetting about your flying lesson? I thought you wanted to get started as soon as possible?"

"It'll work out. I'm going up tomorrow, and again Sunday if the weather's okay. That'll be it for a few days. I won't be going again 'til the end of the week."

"And what d'ya mean . . . just you and Buddy? That seems pretty sexist. Are you gonna tack up a 'no girls allowed' sign?"

Travis snickered. "You care to join us? I thought you had enough of roughing it last month."

Jess leaned forward and slugged Travis on the shoulder. "I did. I'm just pulling your chain. You guys can have the island all to yourselves. Besides, even though I know you're both harmless, it wouldn't look right. Me being a girl, I mean. How'd I explain that to my folks?"

Travis turned to face Buddy. "What d'ya say? Want to spend a few days in the woods?"

Color climbed the older boy's neck then tinted his cheeks light red. "Don't think so," he stammered. "I really don't like camping. Besides, I really should be home at night. Sometimes my brother needs help."

"Why would he need help?" Jess asked innocently.

Buddy stared at the ceiling before letting out low, whistling sigh. "Joey arrived with a few strings attached. He's what some people call mentally challenged. Besides that, he has some physical problems . . . poor coordination . . . trouble balancing. Stuff like that. Mom doesn't mind me being gone during the day, but she likes me home in the evening—especially when Dad's not around. Joey doesn't always sleep straight through and we share a bedroom. He gets scared when he wakes up in the dark and I'm not there."

Travis and Jess remained quiet, studying the array of tools lining the workbench wall. Neither knew what to say, so they said nothing at all.

Aware of their uneasiness, Buddy continued. "You said everything was moved to the second island. I have an idea. I'll sleep at the cabin and then row the boat over first thing in the morning. I can pull in at the sandy cove and hike to where you're camped. Chances are the mystery man won't be able to spot me. I can even bring out breakfast. What d'ya think?"

"You can forget about bringing me breakfast. I can do that on my own. But we can wait 'til Monday morning to decide if it's go . . . make certain I don't get rained out."

The sound of the entry door opening halted further discussion, as Bob shuffled into the shop. Spying the teenagers, his face lit up. "Are you cubs all gettin' along?"

Seeing three heads nod, he declared, "Good! Then let's get to work. Buddy, maybe we can get the engine pulled before supper."

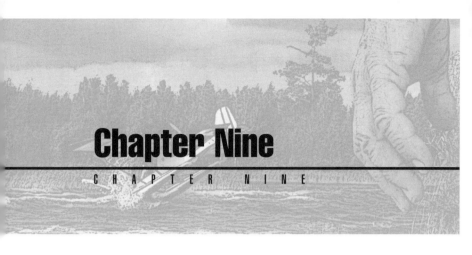

# Chapter Nine

C H A P T E R   N I N E

*Following his usual routine, the little man was up early Monday morning. He peered through the one grease-stained window not covered by plastic wrap. Streaks of sunlight angled into the opening. From the little he could see, it appeared to be a beautiful summer day.*

*Four checks had been marked on the calendar since secreting the cache. All weekend Max had kept an eye on the island from a concealed vantage point. Not a single visitor.*

*In fact, because of cool weather, there had been little activity on the lake. Three fishing boats and an elderly couple in a canoe were the only souls to venture out. Even the McLean kid's raucous seabird remained hunkered in its nest.*

*But that didn't mean the kid couldn't have approached from the blind side by boat. Max weighed the risk of a daylight crossing. Did he dare going over to make certain?*

*Why not? Most likely—with exception of the McLeans—the weekenders were in the city where they belonged. He shuffled the few steps to the trailer's tiny wardrobe. Opening its narrow door, he pulled a camouflage shirt from a hanger.*

*After stepping out of the Airstream, the man whistled for his dog. Moments later, the three-legged mutt and its master limped toward the lake.*

Travis dropped the backpack in the bow and then stood, thinking. What was missing?

He had borrowed Bob's tent, sleeping bag, cook set, cooler and even a full water jug—something he never needed near his home on the Gunflint Trail. Lakes in the wilderness canoe area were pristine. The liquid was pure. There was no call to carry drinking water.

Completing a mental checklist he decided that everything necessary for a two or three day outing was in the canoe.

Certain he had all the gear required, Travis pushed the Grumman off the beach. He tiptoed into shallow water, then gingerly climbed aboard. After settling into the stern, he waved to Buddy's brother. The youngster was seated on the front deck, watching Travis with the intensity of a hawk studying its next meal.

Travis had been introduced to the McLean family the previous day. Buddy had invited Jess and Travis over for a late-afternoon supper. Buddy explained that his dad always ate early on Sunday so he could begin the trip to the Twin Cities on a full stomach.

Travis worried that Buddy would spill the beans regarding the camp-out. But, thankfully, that hadn't been the case.

Buddy two-stepped around the real reason. He never mentioned the stash and mysterious odds and ends collector. Instead, he dwelled on Travis's zest for the out-doors. He even nudged Travis into sharing some of his earlier adventures, including the past year's close calls.

Joey was spellbound by the poacher story. The youngster hadn't so much as wiggled. Several times during the telling, Mrs. McLean gasped. She didn't want to believe men could be so cruel; leaving Travis in the wilderness at the mercy of the winter winds.

Her only observation was, "And after all that, your mother still lets you out of the house?"

Everyone laughed, including Jess. She was then asked to share the most recent adventure—the Canadian trip that had gone south the first day out.

After the tales were told, Mr. McLean—a larger and more wrinkled version of Buddy—put things in perspective. "From what I just heard, sleeping out on Loon Island is going to seem pretty tame for you. Better bring a good book to break the monotony."

As he began paddling, Travis pondered the remark. One thing he never experienced outdoors was boredom. Granted, this part of Minnesota wasn't as wild as where he lived—alongside the Boundary Waters Canoe Area Wilderness. Sightings of moose or wolves were rare around here.

But other critters thrived. Deer and bears, hawks and eagles, foxes and coyotes—all thought this was a splendid region to raise a family.

Travis had crammed one of his dad's old cameras into the pack. Except for several pictures Jess snapped after his first flight lesson, the film was blank. There would be plenty of opportunities to compose outdoor scenes. And if he was really lucky, maybe get a couple close-ups of the doe and fawn.

A wave slapped the bow, startling Travis. Lost in thought, he'd been paddling on remote control. Looking up he saw that the dome-shaped island was within rock throwing distance. Clad in shimmering shades of green and surrounded by sky-tinted water, the little land mass resembled a photo from a travel magazine.

The small clearing made an ideal campsite. Encircled by forest, the glade was well hidden from prying eyes. Within minutes of arriving, Travis had the tent pitched on the patch of yellowed grass. Then, after storing his gear inside, he uncased the camera. Although older than he was, the Pentax was professional quality and its zoom lens could bring far-off objects to within arm's reach.

He swung the strap around his neck, checked to make certain the tent fly was zipped, and started trekking across the meadow.

The plan was to stalk quietly inside the wooded shoreline opposite the hourglass-shaped island. Travis knew the odds weren't great, but maybe he'd get lucky. Perhaps the mystery man couldn't stay away. If the guy was so strange that he stole and hid items of little value, possibly he'd be crazy enough to make a Monday morning foray.

And if the man didn't show, that'd be okay, too. Travis was doing what he lived to do—exploring the outdoors. He'd get practice framing photos of plants and such. Hopefully, even a critter or two would stay put long enough to fill a frame.

* * *

Jess was sprawled in the workshop's one and only easy chair—bored to the bone. Unlike the boys, she had nothing of interest to keep her occupied. After delivering Travis to the cabin, Buddy had returned on the ATV. With a brief nod and a muttered good morning, he'd plunged into his work.

For a time she lounged with eyes closed, mulling over possible projects.

There was no need to start the tractor. The grass had been mowed on Saturday. And today, after finishing up with breakfast dishes, Aunt Betty had departed to her sewing room. The good-natured woman was stitching a quilt for a fundraiser. She'd asked if Jess would like to help, but the teenager had as much interest in needlepoint as she did working with wrenches—midpoint between zero and zilch.

Although the day was bright and sunny, the temperature remained too cool for tanning—not that she needed to brown her skin. It was dull activity, but something to do if the thermometer obliged.

Jess wracked her brain for a way to kill time. Lifting her gaze, she focused on the far wall. Hmm . . . she hadn't paid attention before, but next to the fridge, tacked to the pine paneling, was a colorful map. If she was seeing things correctly, Birch and Pike were featured dead-center.

Curious, the teen unfolded her legs, got up and crossed the room. Maps and charts were her area of expertise. She took pleasure in studying promising places to travel.

There were times she'd burn a whole library period making up fantasy trips. Not that she'd ever be able to actually go on one. Not at least 'til she was rich and famous, she mused with a faint smile.

Up close, Jess was amazed at the map's detail. Pike's islands were accurately illustrated. Even more incredible, there were small rectangles depicting where buildings stood.

Jess zeroed in on her uncle's property. Both the house and hangar were flagged by little black boxes. A three-quarter-inch purple streak marked the airstrip. Way too cool. She'd never seen a map with such in-depth features. Like a hungry fish to a scented lure, Jess was hooked.

Lost in study, time flew. When she checked the clock she couldn't believe that half an hour had passed. But she now knew how to spend the rest of the day.

She was going to take a hike—a very long hike. And if she had read the map correctly, she might learn more about a crook and his three-legged dog.

Dressed in jeans and the "U of M" sweatshirt, Jess slipped her fanny pack around her waist. She'd stuffed in several Granola bars, a plastic water bottle and a can of bug spray. And just in case, she even remembered to slip in her cell phone—with hopes it would work this far from a town.

She was ready.

From the map study, Jess had mentally filed a bird's-eye view of the area. There were several items of interest. First, she noted that the roads were scarcely more than graveled trails. She hadn't paid any attention to that fact during the ultra-light flight. She'd been too busy peering down at the water.

Second, the street abutting her uncle's acreage forked. According to the map, a "drive at your own risk" trail circled around the east side of Pike Lake. By hiking down Bob's drive, then turning as if heading toward the McLean's, she'd pass by that "Y".

For that matter, she recalled crossing the narrow, rutted road on the far end of the runway. She wouldn't even have to use the main road to reach it. The walk could be shortened by trekking along the airstrip toward Buddy's woods.

Except that she wasn't going to Buddy's. Her goal was the shoreline opposite the island where a mutt had nearly given her a heart attack.

Jess chose to keep her destination under wraps. She saw no need to play question-and-answer with any of the Bs—Bob, Betty or Buddy. So rather than seek approval, she penned a note. It simply read that she'd gone for a walk—a long walk. She'd be back in time to set the supper table. Placing the paper on the counter, Jess eased out the kitchen door.

An hour later, she slowed, then ground to a halt. Hiking the tree-lined lane had been a pleasant surprise. She'd had it all to herself. No traffic passed—nothing coming or going.

Instead of the drone of cars and trucks, she'd been serenaded by songbirds. She'd even spotted a porcupine clinging to a pine.

Thoughts about the, two boys had made time fly. What was she supposed to do about the jealousy thing? Ignore it? Play dumb? Choose to hang with one more than the other? Whatever, the green monster had certainly tainted Buddy's behavior a few days earlier. And it hadn't been for the better at that.

And then there was Travis—sweet, simple Travis. She could tell he liked her. But how much, she wasn't certain. Maybe she could think of a way to ask him. Hmm . . . one more thing to mull over.

There'd also been a couple of deer sightings. The first came when she'd spooked a small buck grazing inside the wood-line. Emitting a short snort, the animal bounded into the underbrush. Jess only knew it was male because she'd caught a glimpse of velvet-coated antlers. That was a lesson learned in Canada—that only male deer have horns.

The second sighting took place as she crested a rise. Fifty yards down-slope stood a fawn; spots beginning to merge into its tawny coat.

Sweat stinging her eyes, gnats buzzing about her head, she'd stood unmoving, captivated. The little deer paid no heed. Still as a statue, it stared into the woods. A wheezing, nasal bleat echoed from the forest. Without hesitation, as if it had spring-loaded legs, the fawn leapt off the road.

Jess waved a hand around her head. Motionless, far from the lake breeze, it was time to break out the bug spray. After a liberal dose of repellent and a swig of water, she took stock of her whereabouts.

A riot of greenery snuggled against the lane's shoulder. A casual sightseer wouldn't have a clue Pike Lake lay close by.

Jess knew the lake was through the woods to her left. She'd memorized this portion of the map. Access to land opposite the figure eight island would be along this lane. But she had no way of knowing the best route to the water.

She tramped beyond the deer crossing hollow and trudged up the opposite slope. Once past the crest the lane leveled. Stopping to scan ahead, she thought something seemed different. The right-of-way appeared a bit wider.

As she closed the gap, she saw the reason why. Stationed like sleepy sentries, skinny poles and sagging wires paralleled the lane. Marching in from the other direction, their ranks abruptly ended.

Interesting. Wait a minute . . . if the thief lived opposite the island, wouldn't he want electricity?

Pleased with the brainwave, Jess picked up the pace.

* * *

Travis held his breath. Fortune smiled. The breeze was in his face. That meant the doe and fawn shouldn't catch his scent. But despite the zoom lens, they were too distant for a decent photo.

He'd made that mistake before, using a whole roll of film snapping eagles. Feeling smug the photos would be of award-winning quality, he couldn't wait for the prints.

His hopes were dashed when the photos came back. The big birds were little more than white bumps on a skinny limb. Rather than life-sized raptors filling the frame, they looked more like sparrows perched on a branch.

Better to chance a stalk, risk spooking the whitetails— than snapping a picture from too far away.

On hands and knees, through ferns and forest duff, Travis inched forward. Not once did he look up. His father had said wild things sensed when they were being spied upon. He'd likened it to inborn radar—a natural awareness that kept them from being the meal of the moment.

Ignoring repellent, blood-seekers swarmed, looking for an opening. Several mosquitoes risked all and began drilling at his hairline.

Travis tried to ignore the pests. Finally their torment became too much to endure. He flopped flat and swiped at his neck.

Then he lay motionless, hoping the movement hadn't spooked the deer. Slowly rising to one knee, Travis peered around a tree. The doe stood fifty feet away, staring at Travis.

The gig was up. He was busted. Nevertheless, he raised the camera, aligning the viewer to his eye. All he saw was black. The lens cap was still on.

Moving a hand was all it took. The doe had seen enough. Bleating a whoosh of air, the whitetails swapped ends. With a good-bye flip of their tails, both the big deer and the little fawn bounded away.

Oh well, it'd been good practice. There'd be other opportunities. At least he hadn't wasted film.

Photo-op over, Travis meandered along the water's edge. What he needed was a comfy place from which to spy.

# Chapter Ten

C H A P T E R   T E N

*Max was satisfied. The collection was safe and sound. Hidden in a depression, covered with a layer of leafy branches, the bags blended with their background. Unless one knew where to look, they were darn near invisible.*

*Let 'em search.*

*Not that he thought anyone would. It had been an accident the girl had stumbled across his stash in the first place.*

*That had been a close call!*

*He'd been at the meadow that day, had just placed the latest trophy—a wooden cribbage board—on the plastic sheet. If he hadn't heard the grunt when she'd tripped, the girl would have seen him.*

*Wouldn't that have been a calamity! One look at his disfigured face and she would have run off screaming bloody murder. No doubt the McLean brute would have come rushing to her rescue. Or worse—called the cops!*

*Bad luck and good fortune—the incident had been a bit of both.*

*Bad luck that the store of souvenirs had been compromised. Good fortune that he hadn't been busted.*

\* \* \*

Jessie looked skyward. Wires sloped away from a weary looking power pole. Drooping like cables on an old-fashioned bridge, the cords sagged listlessly over the road.

Near the top of another tired upright, the lines met a pair of bottle-like connectors, then curved a half-loop before rabbit-holing into a tube. From there, the pipe tracked down alongside the pole.

Jess got it. If power was needed near the lake, the wires would have to be buried. In these woods, adult trees crowded together like commuters on a busy bus, and throngs of their stout branches merged in airborne arm-wrestling contests.

This had to be the place. Question: was she daring enough to investigate?

Ignore the "No Trespassing" posters?

Traipse about in strange woodlot? Possibly get lost?

Maybe even bump into the weirdo?

After blowing out a deep breath, she sauntered across the lane. Maybe she could go in a little ways, just far enough to where she could still glimpse the opening.

She slipped through the brushy road shoulder. This part of the forest hadn't been logged in decades, if ever. Trees were mature. The dense overhead foliage shut out sunlight. Plants on the forest floor couldn't capture enough energy to survive beyond infancy. A dank smell assailed her nostrils. The lack of light and musty odor reminded her of a cellar—damp and gloomy.

But the ceiling was a cathedral—high and arched. Standing in the understory, Jess could see farther than she would have imagined.

She leaned against the gnarly bark of an old oak and gazed at the ground. Travis had said to put your shoes in park, take a hard study ahead. Look for the easiest route, a natural path, the route you'd walk if going that direction.

Jess let her eyes roam. Nothing—not a bent leaf, not a twisted fern, nothing out of place.

What next?

Should she discard the idea—turn around and retrace her steps back to the airstrip?

No, she wasn't going to give up so easily. If this was the site, and she thought it was, the entry might be farther up the lane.

She didn't go far before finding footprints. Boot tracks—as well as several bike tire imprints, were cast in the road's soft shoulder.

Sometime between Friday's rain and today, someone had wheeled a bicycle in and out.

Coming and going?

Was this the place where the thief went about his business? Or were the prints left by a local out for a weekend jaunt—just someone exiting the roadway to answer the call of nature?

Noting a gap in the hedge-like foliage, Jess edged off the gravel. She stood, nervously nibbling her lip, studying the clue. Stems and branches had been clipper-snipped. Human hands had been at work.

Okay—question asked and answered. The tracks hadn't been left by a casual visitor.

A glance over her shoulder brought a sense of relief. Backlit by shafts of sunlight, the right-of-way was still easy to see.

Good. She could venture in a few more steps. If she kept to the trail, she wouldn't get lost.

After sneaking beyond the foliage, pinpointing the path had been a cinch. Years earlier someone had slashed a driveway. As proof, spaced along the path's edge were remnants of rotting stumps. But because the trail veered off at an angle, it was hidden from the road.

Jess saw that the trail had been recently used—sometime after Friday's downpour. Boot prints were etched in soft earth along the edge of a puddle

Nerves tingling, running muscles at the ready, she inched forward. Up ahead the ground began to fall away. The down-slope tree canopy became a leafy hedge, cutting off the view.

Jess swatted a mosquito, and then checked over her shoulder a second time. The opening had disappeared behind a wall of thick-hipped tree trunks.

Had she come too far? Maybe it was time to high-tail it and return another day with the boys.

And why was she here in the first place? She had no business tramping about in the woods. Raised in the city, wandering about in the forest was as foreign to her as a bear riding a bike.

The thought brought a smile. Hadn't she seen just that very thing on TV? A costumed bear pedaling around a circus ring?

So how far in did she dare go—enough to get a glimpse of Pike Lake?

Yeah. That's what she'd do—risk taking a few more steps, see what lay over the hill.

And see she did.

There was a clearing where the land leveled below the slope. And squatting in the center sat a tired-looking travel trailer. She'd seen others like it being towed down the highway. With their rounded corners and shiny skin, they'd always reminded her of comic book spaceships.

Once upon a time this trailer might have looked similar. Not now. Long ago someone had taken a paint brush to the exterior. Over the years the tan coating had either faded or flaked. The paintless areas were now dull gray, giving the trailer a spotted, chicken-pox appearance.

She'd heard the term "trailer trash," but had thought it referred to people, not the residence they lived in.

Another choice—should she sneak down—have a peek inside?

Or make a one-eighty, head for home—and report to the guys? But report what, that she'd stumbled across an abandoned shanty? No big deal. She needed something tangible, a clue she could touch to tell about later.

Jess eased behind a birch clump. Then she crouched like a baseball catcher. For a time she studied the camper. An olive-green box sat to one side. Half-buried from years of collecting leaf litter, it was the business end of the electrical service.

She'd seen one like it in a suburban yard. At the time she hadn't a clue to its purpose. Not until one morning when she'd arrived early at the bus stop. With time to spare, she'd strolled across the avenue. The plan was to use the boxy container as a bench. Drawing close she read the bright yellow words, "Caution—High Voltage."

Instantly she backed off. One could wait walking around as easily as crouching on a carton of current.

As she stared down at the cheerless dwelling, time seemed to stop. The surrounding woodlot was hushed—no squirrels scolding or birds twittering. That seemed strange. Had she scared all the critters away?

The only movement came when the breeze touched the canopy, causing leaves to flitter-flutter. On occasion, if the wind puffed with enough oomph, a few lower limbs wiggled. Whenever that took place, Jess caught the reflection coming off Pike. Its sky-painted water lay beyond the slope.

The wail of a loon jerked Travis awake. How long had he dozed? He checked his watch—nearly an hour.

The teen was hunkered between a pair of aspen. With a carpet of wildflowers and shaggy grass, it'd been a perfect place from which to spy. Out of the wind, and with warm sunbeams toasting his jeans, he'd nodded off.

Easing up on an elbow, Travis took note of nature's noisy alarm. The loon was busily grooming itself only a few yards from shore. Caught in full light, its sleek feathers reflected a bluish sheen; the white band circling its throat was as dazzling as a gold necklace.

What a perfect photo-op. Raising the Pentax, Travis removed the lens cap and focused. The timing couldn't have been better if the event had been penciled in a date book. Performing like the lead actor center-stage, the loon puffed out its chest. Then in a display of male conceit, it spread its wings—all the while prancing in place on rippled water.

Click—whirr, click—whirr, click—three full-framed shots. Travis was thrilled. The photos should turn out postcard perfect, with luck—magazine material.

But the clack of the camera brought down the curtain. The recital was over. With a flip of its beak as if to say, "that's all folks," the bird slipped beneath the surface.

Travis continued to cradle the camera. Sooner or later the bird would have to come up for air. Ten seconds, twenty seconds, more than a minute passed before the fish-eater popped to the surface. Regrettably the regal bird had put distance between itself and the photographer.

Travis focused but then chose to hold off. Long shots of swimming loons were common—familiar as clowns at a carnival.

He was lowering the telephoto when distant movement caught his eye. The nose of a boat was inching out from behind the island—from the inlet where he'd had the close encounter.

Travis's pulse quickened. Could it be—that on the very first day of the campout—he could be so lucky?

Talk about timing. First, waking up with a loon alongside the wildflower mattress—and now this—the possibility of seeing the mystery man.

He raised the camera. Why hadn't he brought along binoculars? But the zoom lens should work, with the bonus of being able to take a picture.

The craft continued edging out. Several long breaths passed before it was completely exposed. Travis adjusted the image, pulling the craft to within field goal range.

He pushed the shutter before realizing it was a wasted shot. The driver was slouched in the rear seat, facing the opposite way.

Propelled by a battery-powered trolling motor, the vessel began to gain speed. Travis needed to take immediate action before the boat was out of sight

He flopped flat to the grass. Then he cupped his hands and began screeching. Caw—caw—caw, sounding a dozen caustic crow squawks before chancing a peek.

It worked. Having turned, the figure was staring toward Loon Island. Travis pushed the shutter before dropping flat again. The glimpse through the viewfinder had been both brief and eerie. Travis had seen the likeness before. It was the face of a former president—the one with black hair—the guy who'd been an actor.

Impossible!

Besides being dead, the president had been a big man. The guy in the boat appeared slight—not much bigger than a sixth grader. This mystery was getting weirder by the moment.

Bewildered, Travis snuggled tight to the ground—fingers crossed that he hadn't been spotted.

* * *

Jess remained hidden for nearly a half hour. She saw and heard nothing—not a peep or a shimmy.

Once, from far off on the lake, she'd recognized the lamenting lyrics of a loon. A few minutes later, from the same direction, a crow had cawed. But with exception for those sounds, the forest had been quiet—country cemetery quiet—creepy quiet.

Only when her thighs and knees cried for relief did she rise. Then, after making one last scan, she scampered into the clearing.

Peering through windows had been a waste of nervous energy. Except for a small slider too high to see through, other openings were covered with plastic. At one time the sheeting had been transparent. Not now. Time and weather had taken its toll, tarnishing the film as if smeared with tallow.

Gritting her teeth, Jess reached up and knocked, pre-pared to bolt if the slightest creak came from within.

Silence. She knocked again, louder. No answer.

Now what? Should she see if the latch was locked?

Fingers trembling, she clutched the handle and gave the knob a gentle twist. She'd already promised herself, that if the door opened, she'd take one quick glance and then run for the road.

After taking a last look lakeside, Jess finished rotating the knob. The latch clicked. Emitting a squeak, the door cracked open.

Jess exhaled. Then, before the last of her courage flew south, she placed a foot on the cement block step.

Nibbling her lower lip, she pulled the door wide. The first

glimpse was that of the ceiling. Jess blinked in disbelief.

She assumed the inside would mirror the outside—messy and poorly kept up.

Not so. What she saw took her breath away. Puffy cumulus clouds, a distant V-shaped flight of geese, a pair of soaring coal-black ravens—so life-like Jess half-expected to hear their squawks—were artistically brushed on a background of blue. A color so vibrant, she could have sworn she was looking through a skylight.

Dropping her gaze, Jess realized every inch of wall space had been transformed. Highlighted above a tiny table—surrounded by trees and lifelike ferns—burbled a miniature brook. Whitewater splashed over rocks and boulders so realistic Jess half expected a flood to come surging toward the door.

The teenager stood statue-like, gawking at the wonder of it all. After a long moment and a shake of her head, she stepped up and went inside.

This wasn't some vacant, abandoned shanty, used once a year during hunting season. The camper was somebody's pride and passion, a work of art, a labor of love.

But why would he keep such a scruffy exterior? Jess thought she knew. It was a coverup—camouflage—a way to keep trespassers from becoming too curious.

Likewise the plastic over the windows, letting light in while keeping peeping eyes out.

Jess pictured the "Private Property—No Trespassing" signs tacked on trees along the right-of-away. The bold orange posters she'd chosen to ignore before leaving the lane. Whoever laid claim to this section of woods clearly didn't want company.

Illegal or not, now that she was here, it would be foolish not to take a mental snapshot. File away images of the entire interior. It wouldn't take long. The trailer wasn't large, really just one extended room.

She faced the rear. Defining the front from the back was what looked to be a closet and a bathroom. A narrow bed occupied the very back; a faded spread pulled tight as if done up by a maid.

An artist's easel, complete with a fresh canvas, was standing next to the bed. What appeared to be a mother loon with a baby on its back was sketched in pencil on white fabric.

More frames leaned against the wall. All but one had its backside facing out. The frame turned frontward was a masterpiece. With the clarity of a photograph, ducks were taking flight from a pond.

Were equally skillful settings brushed on the remaining canvases? Despite the guilty feeling, Jess stepped across. With great care she tipped back the second frame. Even from above and upside down, she was enthralled. It was a painting of a bald eagle soaring above lake, a fish clutched in its talons—glistening water drops obeying gravity.

The next canvas was of a doe with its newborn fawn. The baby's spots looked so genuine, Jess thought if she were to touch one, her finger would come away wet.

She quickly scanned two more canvases. Both were extraordinary. One displayed a bear with a cub; another featured a wolf ready to share a rabbit with its pups.

But the clock was ticking. It'd take too long to look at every one. Jess eased the frames in place and then did an about-face.

A kitchenette occupied the front sidewall. A two-burner stove took up part of a small countertop. Tiny twin cabinets bordered a doll-house-size sink. Above the basin a rectangular window let soft light filter inside.

Jess had never been in a camping trailer. But it made sense, that to save space, everything had to be economized. Even the recliner looked malnourished.

Aside from the unbelievable mural, Jess was impressed by how neat the place appeared. Not a speck of dust or wisps of cobwebs anywhere. The only exception was the stench of burnt tobacco.

A wood-framed photograph hung on the end of a kitchen cabinet. Jess edged closer. It took a moment to focus on the faded image. She'd seen the same view the day of the ultra-light flight.

Shot from an airplane, it was a black-and-white photo of Pike Lake and the adjoining property. The print had to be old. No docks or cabins lined Buddy's section of shore.

The only buildings were a house and a barn. Both sat near the edge of a large, open meadow. Jess knew the spot. The buildings had once occupied land that was now the end of the airstrip.

Examining the eight by ten as if there'd be test, Jess noted another curiosity. Drawn with the help of a ruler, a slim black line formed a rectangle enclosing Pike, Birch and much of the neighboring territory. In the lower right corner, hand-printed with black ink, were the words "Grogan Dairy Ranch-1956."

As if shocked by an electrical surge, Jess was suddenly jolted back to reality. A dog was barking, close by and growing louder.

She'd dawdled too long.

A wave of terror washed over her. She had to get out, quick. Spinning on her heel, Jess jumped for the door and then leapt to the ground. Then she bolted up the slope like a startled rabbit.

She didn't slow down until reaching the birch clump. Skirting behind the trees' protective cover, she dropped to one knee and peered at the trailer. The dog continued yipping, sounding closer with every yap. But the barking stopped when it broke into the clearing. The mutt closed its mouth and began snuffling around the door.

The door!

She hadn't closed the door! It was standing wide open!

Was there time to dash down, make things right? The dog's owner was probably still at the lake, securing the boat. But she couldn't count on that. Leaving her hiding spot was risky. The best plan was to run away while she could.

Half crouching, Jess backtracked on the trail. Only when she was certain she was out of sight did she rise. Then she began to jog, trying not to leave footprints in the soft earth where rainwater had pooled.

The dog started barking again. Jess chanced a fleeting look behind. Her heart sank. She was being followed. The scruffy canine was gaining ground with every bound. In spite of having met the mutt on friendly terms, Jess panicked. Throwing caution to the wind, she began running full out.

Trees rushed by in a blur. What had taken minutes to cover coming in took seconds going the other way.

The road opening loomed ahead. Only one more twist in the trail. Frantic, Jess paid no heed to where she stepped. The goal was the gravel lane. In her haste, she failed to focus on the big puddle—the place she'd found footprints.

Flying around the bend, arms pumping, Jess dashed straight into the goop. Only speed kept her from falling. Several slushy strides brought her back to firm ground.

But it was one step too many. As her left foot pulled free, so did its shoe—stuck in the muddy gumbo.

Sliding to a stop, Jess spun about. She needed the Nike. But the mutt had other plans. Ignoring the muddy slop, the dog raced in, snatched the tennis shoe in his teeth and reversed course.

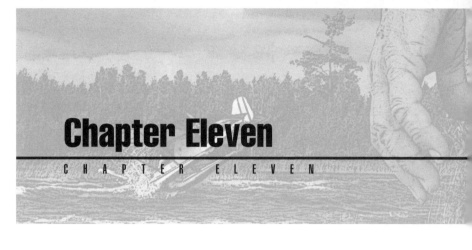

# Chapter Eleven

C H A P T E R   E L E V E N

*Max was anxious to get home. The one place he felt secure. He was upset—angry at himself. He needed to have his head examined, crossing over in such nice weather. What was he thinking?*

*Foolish—foolish—foolish!*

*He didn't waste time when the bow touched ground. He snatched the mask from his face and stuffed it in a pocket. Then with the aid of rollers, and help from a winch, he cranked the craft to its hiding place. The last job was to cover the boat with a tarp; a mate to the one he used to conceal his treasures.*

*He was also annoyed with the dog. As soon as the boat ran aground, the pooch had bailed. It pointed its nose in the air, sniffed, and then began to bark.*

*Max had no way of knowing Lucky had picked up a familiar scent. The scent of a friendly human he'd crossed paths with on another day.*

*The mutt stopped yapping long enough to stare at its master. Occupied with his chores, Max paid no attention. Lucky often yipped when they returned from an outing. The dog took pleasure warning squirrels and chipmunks to clear out.*

But unlike other times, Lucky didn't wait for Max to finish. Instead, yapping all the way, it bounded into the woods.

Max finished his camouflaging, then lifted the whistle to his lips. Dang it all! This was the third time in a week the dog had run off.

And what was with all the yipping? What'd the old mutt smell that he couldn't? Could it be the grumpy old garbage bear?

Nah—not likely.

Max kept smelly waste to a minimum. And the odd time or two there were leftovers—he buried them in a bag on the island. If the big bruin was that starved for a scrap or two, it could darn well swim over and dig it up.

No—Lucky was yelping for some other reason. Probably best not to call the dog in until Max knew the reason why.

The man let go of the whistle. He let the thin tube dangle from the cord looped around his neck. Then he pulled the mask from his pocket, and with practiced ease, slipped it over his head. No sense being careless. Despite all the "Private Property" posters, maybe he had uninvited visitors.

The smart thing to do was to forget going directly to the Airstream. The wise move was to sneak up to the road and check for tracks.

Max limped into the woods, all eyes and ears. There was no need for a map. This was the one remnant of property the county had yet to steal. Eighty acres of prime timber, and it was all his. He knew every inch like the back of his hand, was familiar with every tree and shrub.

Max knew where to look first. Traveling at an angle; he'd hit the road south of the old drive. He'd look for signs of recent travel. If there were footprints, and if they looked large, he'd stay out of sight.

But if he found proof that pesky youngsters had been poking around, he'd think of a way to scare 'em off.

Why couldn't they mind their own business? The young pests

*had already caused him too much grief. They had a good fright coming. He'd have to think of a way to get even—a scheme to teach 'em a lesson.*

*The thought brought a smirk to his scarred lips. He'd been on the receiving end of heckles and taunts his entire life.*

*Maybe it was his turn to do some dishing.*

\* \* \*

The mechanics were pleased.

It had proven to be a productive morning. Although it was only a few minutes past noon, the engine was out. The water-soaked power plant dangled from the end of a chain, ready to be lowered into the bed of a pickup.

Their work done, Bob and Buddy celebrated with sandwiches and frosty mugs of root beer.

They were camped in the kitchen, pulled tight to the table. Bob set his glass down, wiped his chin with a napkin, then grinned. "That hit the spot. It's hard to beat a ham sandwich and a cold soda on a summer day.

"Speaking of which, what are your plans for the afternoon? Going over to the island, see what Travis is up to? Or are you planning on sticking around until you-know-who comes home?"

Buddy's face flushed. Without lifting his eyes, he skirted the question by asking one of his own. "Are we through for the day? Isn't there something else needs doin'?"

"Nope, we've gone about as far as the rules allow. From here on in everything replaced will have to be signed off by a mechanic. Besides, it'll be a few days before I complete the parts list. Good thing I had full coverage. Without insurance money, we couldn't afford to rebuild the old bird."

Bob brought the mug to his mouth to sip a bit of ice melt. Setting the cup down, he said, "You didn't answer the question. What's up your sleeve for the rest of the day? Betty needs to run to town and I thought I'd bum a ride. There are a few things I want to pick up at the hardware store. You're welcome to ride along if you like."

Bob paused, the now-familiar crooked smile angled across his weathered cheeks. "Though I can't imagine why you'd want to tag along with us old folks. It seems to me you'd like to spend more time with kids your own age."

Buddy turned toward his mentor, frowning. "They're really not my age, you know. Neither one is old enough to drive."

The man chuckled. "Sorry, didn't mean to offend ya. But when you get to be as old as I am, everyone looks like a kid. Besides, when it comes to choosing friends there're more important things than a birth date. Take you and me for example. I consider you a good friend. And I'd hope you'd think likewise."

Buddy felt his face heat for a second time. "Well . . . yeah, of course I do. But that's different. We have something in common. We both have a passion for airplanes.

"Not that I don't think you're fun to be around. 'Cause you are. And I never think of you as old. Even after having a stroke you have more going on than a lot of kids my own age."

Bob nodded thanks, then said, "There you go, then. You've made my point. It's what's going on up in a person's noodle, not what year they were born or how fast they can run up and down a flight of stairs."

Buddy tipped his mug to slurp out an ice cube. He crunched it between his teeth, mulling over the remark. After a time he swallowed and said, "Flying. I think I'll take *Johnny* up for up for some exercise. He's been tied up too long."

* * *

Travis wasn't certain what he wanted to do—hang around the island, lounging by the tent or return to

base. Having accomplished the main goal—photo-
graphing the strange fellow—he saw little reason to
spend the night.

It wasn't that he wouldn't enjoy sleeping out. He always
did. The truth was—he was thinking about Jessie. His
stay at the Ritzers' was growing short. He'd soon be
heading home, hanging out with his pal Seth. More
than a month of summer vacation remained. He'd have
other opportunities to set up a tent, maybe do some
canoeing in the Boundary Waters.

Plus, with such nice weather, maybe he'd get a second
chance sitting left seat in the "150." The first lesson had
been a blast. Once in the air, Bob's flying buddy, Pete
Paulson, had turned over the controls. At first Travis
had over-steered, wobbling the trainer through the sky
like a wounded eagle.

But once he got the hang of it, he did fine. Well, most
of the time. There was that first landing.

Following Pete's instructions, Travis managed to align
the aircraft with the runway. Then things went south
in a rush. There were too many tasks in too short a
time—flaps, attitude, airspeed, elevation, alignment,
radio-speak. Like a computer asked to do three things
at once, his brain balked.

Pete just laughed. The soft-spoken instructor had simply pushed in the power, pulled back on the yoke and
said, "Not to worry. We'll go 'round and try it again."

And they had, nearly a dozen times. Each landing was a
little better, a little more under control. By the end of
the session Travis was getting the hang of it. But by
then it was time to call it quits. Lesson one was in the
book; a new leather-bound flight log Bob had presented
after dinner.

The teen's daydreams were brought up short. He heard
the drone of an engine—*Johnny*. Pushing himself
upright, Travis pulled on his shoes, then bounded for

the cove. He grabbed the camera bag, thinking it'd be neat to zoom in on the ultra-light. A flying photo would make a good peace offering.

Travis arrived at the inlet without a moment to spare. Buddy had already taxied the ultra-light away from the dock. He was about to push in the power. The flight path would bring him directly over the island.

Steadied against a tree, camera ready, Travis waited for liftoff. *Johnny's* engine revved, and its pontoons became water skis, spraying out a mist that reflected rainbows under the midday sun. In a much shorter distance than Travis imagined, the ultra-light became airborne.

The floatplane leveled only yards above the water, flying straight toward Loon. Between camera clicks, Travis was busy rotating the lens, keeping the subject focused. As the aircraft drew closer, its nose pointed up, and in seconds, it hummed overhead.

Travis had no idea how many frames he'd shot. Checking the counter window he saw there'd been five. More than enough, and all good, he thought. He'd been able to keep pace, keep the airplane centered.

Buddy should be thrilled.

Travis began trudging toward the tent and then stopped. There was a good way to spend the afternoon. The canoe—he'd paddle to the second island.

The weird guy was gone. He'd seen him leave, even snapped a photo of the man. Now would be the safest time to explore. He could beach on the back side and circle around on foot.

From there he could track the man's steps. He might even find the stash, get proof by taking pictures. It might mean staying over for the night, but that's what he was planning on in the first place.

Travis set the camera bag in the bow, pushed the Grumman into the water and hopped in. Back-tracking the mystery man should prove even more exciting than stalking whitetails.

* * *

The Grumman touched shore between a skeletal windfall and a fat boulder. On the paddle over, Travis had been entertained by the ultra-light. Buddy certainly seemed to be having a good time.

And why not? It was a terrific day for flying—a blue sky decorated with lacy white clouds. Even the wind was sweet. It was puffing from the south, folding the lake's face with sunlight- catching wavelets.

The one-lesson aviator felt a tinge of envy. Hopefully by this time next year he'd have his student pilot's license. Then he'd be the one soaring solo, dipping and diving, free as a bird.

It seemed odd, though, that Buddy kept flying over land, not water. What was that all about?

Travis had a sudden thought. Maybe Buddy would get lucky and spot the odd fellow making his getaway, see what kind of car the guy drove.

For a while, Travis stood on shore and stared at the sky. Then he remembered why he'd paddled over. He was on a treasure hunt of sorts. Putting his piloting dreams aside, he began to trek around the lakefront.

The teenager jogged and sloshed along the water's edge. Arriving at the weed-choked inlet, he stopped to look and listen. With exception of a few birds chirping, all was calm.

Even *Johnny's* mechanical cry had vanished. Travis reflected on that a moment—Buddy must have put the little bird to bed. He must have touched down, taxied to the dock and tethered his prize to a tree.

For a moment the teen stood fixed in place, listening and catching his wind. Breathing easier, he stalked along the cove's shoreline, searching for the pull-in place.

It was an easy mark and right where he suspected. At the very end of the inlet, he spotted evidence of a boat being beached—bent and broken shore grass. From the width of the bow print, the fellow had pulled in more than once.

Travis scanned the opposite shore. Nothing—only woods and water—no sign that a boat had been tied to a tree or pulled up on the beach. Confident he had the island all to himself, he began practicing woods-manship skills.

Travis loved tracking, the search for faint clues, figuring which way a deer or a moose meandered. This task should prove simple—the clues were man-made. Head down, eyes wide, he walked farther into the forest.

The strange little man had been cunning, never using the same route twice. It took three backtrack trips before Travis realized what the fellow had done—zigzagged helter-skelter through the underbrush. Starting over for the fourth time, Travis vowed to stay on one track, follow one set of clues.

Later he concluded that the creep had been tricky, but not sly enough. Much like the inlet where footprints gathered, each story had the same ending. It had taken more than an hour, but the route had been unraveled.

As he leaned up against a tree, Travis focused on several black garbage bags. The swollen sacks been tucked into a depression caused by an uprooted windfall.

The thief had covered the bags with a layer of ferns and broken branches. But he may as well have put up a poster. To an outdoors man like Travis, the wilting leaves and yellowing stalks shouted "look here."

And that's what he had done. Under the thin veil of vegetation, motionless as sleeping bears, lay four bulging bags.

For a time Travis stood quietly, pondering. The find reminded him of a recent experience, a life-threatening episode he'd just as soon forget.

The past winter, while searching for Travis, his buddy Seth had stumbled upon a poacher's stash hidden in a root hole similar to this one. Except that it had been an illegal wolf pelt and a rifle stuffed into a sack, not a mish-mash of household do-dads.

Travis couldn't help but wonder if this hoard of odds and ends offered up the same danger.

No, he thought. This was what people referred to as a horse of a different color.

The poacher who'd lashed him to a tree was an oppo-site image of the man he'd seen today. That scofflaw had been a tall, rangy fellow, overconfident and brash.

The man he'd captured with the camera seemed any-thing but secure. The guy was so bashful he hid behind a mask. And this stash, from what Jess had said, was mostly made up of worthless junk, nothing valuable enough to risk jail time.

Travis tried to pull up the word for people who couldn't stop stealing. He knew it ended in 'maniac.' Whatever— he didn't believe they were a threat—except maybe to themselves if they were caught in the act.

The question, now that he found the bags, was what should he do about them? He certainly wasn't about to tote 'em anywhere. No, that'd be foolish. He'd undo the twist-ties, snap a few pictures, then put everything back just the way he found it.

After checking the contents, Travis had to agree. Jess had nailed the description. Windup alarm clocks, din-ner plates, a jumble of silverware, an occasional tired appliance, a little of this, a little of that, were all stuffed in bags without rhyme or reason.

Travis opened each sack wide, snapped a photo, then

retied the tops. It took five minutes of shifting this way and that before the bags were settled back into their sleeping quarters. Once satisfied the bags looked untouched, Travis repositioned the drying vegetation. Then he stood back and took a final photo.

He checked his watch. Middle of the afternoon—lots of daylight remained.

What now? Paddle back to Loon—pack up—head for the McLean cabin?

Or—go back and hang out on the other island, cook dinner and sleep over?

Whatever, he'd neglected step one. First he had to trek back to the Grumman.

* * *

Buddy had more in mind than giving *Johnny* a workout. He'd seen Jessie's note on the counter. It said she was going on a long walk. His plan was to fly over the neighboring roads. Jess had to be hiking one of them. Where else would she go? Certainly she wouldn't have walked in the woods or trekked along the lake. No way—too many obstacles. Besides, from their together time on the island, he knew she'd avoid bugs and poison ivy.

But which road, he wasn't certain. It wasn't that big of a deal. *Johnny* wasn't as fast as a Cessna, but he could still cover the grid in a matter of minutes. And a whole lot safer, too. As long as he remained within gliding distance of water, he could always make a landing.

Buddy pulled on the stick. *Johnny* lifted up and over Loon. Busy working the controls, he didn't have time to be a sightseer. He never noticed Travis snapping pictures below.

Leveling off, he turned *Johnny* back toward Pike. The best sightline would be off to one side of the street. He paralleled the road bordering the airstrip first, assuming Jess would be trudging along the shoulder.

There was no sign of Jess, only a car and a pickup truck. The next target was the branch road. Few vehicles ever used the unimproved right-away. It would make an ideal footpath.

Buddy put the ultra-light into a lazy go 'round. Coming up on the cut, he realized there'd be a glitch. The right-of-way was narrow—skinny. Trees grew tight to the edge. From his seat in the sky, all he saw was green. A leafy canopy fanned over the road, forming a roof, preventing eyes from peeking below.

# Chapter Twelve

C H A P T E R     T W E L V E

Jess was pooped—spent—all done in. And there was mental agony, the fear of being seen . . . or worse. Walking with one bare foot was a torture test. No matter how hard she tried avoiding stones, sharp pebbles poked and prodded.

She was due for a timeout. A few minutes to catch her wind, figure out her next move. Jess scanned the shoulder, hoping to spot a good hiding place. Just ahead was the gap where she'd first entered the forest.

Not a perfect place but it would do.

Favoring the shoeless foot, she hobbled ahead. Reaching the opening she dropped to all fours and then crept into the foliage. She was about to crawl out the other side when she had a dark thought.

This was part of the property plastered with "No Trespassing" posters. No way did she want to set foot on that land again. She'd rather hide here in the bushes risking bug bites or poison ivy.

As she rested cross-legged, a more positive plan developed.

Her cell phone was stuffed in the fanny pack. She could call for help. Aunt Betty could pick her up. Or Uncle Bob could tell Buddy. He could make the run on the four-wheeler. It wouldn't take more than a few minutes for the Honda to cover what would take hours limping barefoot.

But first she needed a drink. The call could wait.

Although tepid as bath water, the liquid was as refreshing as a chilled soda. Saving a gulp for later, she tucked the bottle into the pack and then pulled out the repellent. Enclosed by weeds and brush, she'd become the meal of the moment. Mosquitoes, deer flies and gnats vied for first dibs.

Working quickly, Jess sprayed every inch of exposed skin—twice. She even bestowed a few foggy bursts to her jeans and sweatshirt.

After swapping the bug bomb for the cell phone, she pushed the on button. As she waited for the phone to power-up, a distant drone diverted her interest.

*Johnny!*

The ultra-light was coming her way. Jess pushed to her knees and scrambled into the open.

She hop-skipped to the center of the road and began flailing arms like a flightless bird.

Buzzing like a giant mosquito, the engine whine grew in volume and soon passed overhead. Jess gazed up and then realized she was under a leafy umbrella. Only smatterings of blue and white were visible. Unless Buddy possessed x-ray vision, he couldn't possibly see the road.

But as it turned out, it wouldn't have mattered anyway. The aircraft had begun banking back toward the lake.

The rush she'd felt moments earlier deflated like air from a leaky balloon. For a time she stood with shoulders slumped, staring at the ground.

Suddenly she jerked her head up. What in the world was she doing? Standing in the open, she was an easy mark!

She scurried into the foliage and refocused on the phone. The little screen displayed the phone's coverage—not a robust signal—but strong enough to make a call. Her uncle's number was already programmed. All she had to do was scroll, push the dial button, and wait for the call to go through.

It rang four times before connecting to Bob's ancient answering machine.

For a few seconds Jess was too rattled to speak. What was she supposed to say? "I've lost my shoe and won't be home for supper?"

Fortunately, before the recording session closed, she squeaked, "Hi. Not to worry. I'm on the branch road that circles Pike. I've got a problem. I lost a shoe. If I'm not back by the time you hear this, could you drive around and pick me up? Thanks . . . . ."

The twenty-second talk time had expired.

Jess snapped the cover closed. Then she sat unmoving. Who else might she call? Buddy's mom? No—not possible. She didn't know the number.

Should she punch in nine-eleven? Have the dispatcher send a deputy? Jeez, wouldn't that be embarrassing.

'Ahh . . . you see it's this way. I was taking this stroll, and then you know . . . like, I wandered onto some private property. There was this three-legged dog that scared the wits out of me. I panicked and ran so fast I lost my shoe. So . . . could you please send a policeman to take me home?"

No, she'd hold off making that call. Nine-one-one was for real emergencies. It wasn't designed for ditsy teenagers needing taxi service.

As she sat pondering, Jess became aware of a new sound—that of gravel being crunched.

Footsteps!

Cautious not to make any noise, she rocked to a kneeling position. Then she eased back a branch. Whoa! Up the road—silhouetted in deep shade—was a man. Not a big fellow, but from what she could make out, a most unusual one. From her vantage point she couldn't be certain, but it appeared the guy was wearing a mask.

Unbelievable! As if she wasn't already on pins and needles. Now this!

Frightened but fascinated, Jess continued to stare. She watched wide-eyed as the man limped slowly along the shoulder.

It had to be the trailer guy—the interior artist—the odds and ends souvenir collector! He appeared to be studying the ground.

What should she do? Wait? See what he's up to?

Definitely not a good idea! But what if he were to cross over past her hiding place?

No way—best to follow age old advice and get going while the going is good.

Jess gently let go of the limb, making certain it didn't snap into place. She slid the phone into the fanny pack, slipped the pack around her waist and eased the buckle closed. Then after throwing a last glance toward the gravel, she turned and headed out.

Staying on all fours, unmindful of prickly weeds and scratchy branches, Jess crawled toward the posted property. Without warning, and tugging like an unseen hand, a thorn snagged her sweatshirt. Startled, she had to fight off the urge to scream. But she found enough willpower to reach back and pull the spike free.

Crawling in slow motion she cleared the ditchline. Now in open woods, she began paralleling the lane. As the distance between her and trailer-man grew, so did her efforts. She stayed low, her hands and knees a blur.

Only when she was certain she couldn't be seen did she rise. Then, staying bent at the waist, she began trotting. Mercifully, unlike the dirt road full of piercing pebbles and pointy rocks, the forest floor was a carpet. So soft, the errant Nike wasn't even missed.

Jess didn't pause until she'd put a safe distance between herself and the odd fellow. After a moment of indecision, she turned into the forest. She'd head toward the lake. She shouldn't get lost. All she had to do was creep along the shore; all the way to Buddy's place if necessary.

After a time, Jess slowed, then stopped altogether. Was she heading the right way? She thought so. The sun was behind her, the backdrop looked familiar. Yes—up ahead was the hill, the ridge from which she'd first spied the trailer.

Moving at a more comfortable pace, she let her eyes scan forward. Suddenly there it was, the discolored trailer, squatting just over the hill.

Stalking closer, she eased behind a tree trunk. Down-slope, the mottled camper appeared as she'd left it. Except for the open door, the trailer appeared as forlorn as the first sighting.

No, something was different. What appeared to be a small dead critter lay next to the step-blocks. It hadn't been there before. She studied the clearing with her eyes, then returned the stare to the doorstep. Recognition. The object wasn't an animal! It was her mud-stained tennis shoe.

Did she dare dash in? Snatch the Nike, flick the door shut? Conceal that the camper had been violated? She'd run too far, too fast, for the limping man to pose a problem. He'd still be waddling along the roadway.

But the dog was a different issue. Was he already inside? Waiting for his master to return? And if he was, would he make a fuss? Yelp and yap, snitch on her?

As she knelt, scratching one of many bug bites, fortune smiled. Almost as if the dog had ESP, it barked. Distant and faint, the muffled yip filtered from the lane.

That meant the mystery man hadn't yet been home. He must have angled out toward the gravel to check for footprints.

Scenting a trespasser, the dog had probably taken a different route. And then after stealing her shoe, proud of his prize, the mutt had run back here.

Finding his master missing, the dog had gone off to search for him.

That had to be it. She had a chance to steal her shoe back. Jess scanned a full circle. She held her breath, listening.

Silence—the dog had stopped yapping.

Heart pounding, Jess studied the slope, searching for the easiest approach. After mapping the route in her mind, she dashed downhill. Seconds later she came into the clearing. Braking to a stop, Jess eased the door shut. Then snatching the shoe, she darted toward the lake.

Once there, she paused only long enough to slip into the footwear. Then she began scurrying along shore. Jess hadn't gone far when she came across the dinghy. The boat was pulled up on land and draped with an earth-toned tarp. The cover was a twin to the one she seen on Loon Island.

As she stood gawking, the dog barked. The yip sounded much too close for comfort. She needed to vanish—now! After throwing a glance the way she'd just come, Jess bolted along the beach.

* * *

Travis slipped the Pentax into a plastic sack, stuck it in the camera bag and tied the bag to a thwart in case the canoe capsized. That done, he stood tall, roaming the lakefront with his gaze. He hoped to spot a medium-size stone—

one big enough to act as ballast. Without a paddling partner, the bow tended to pitch above the surface.

That hadn't been the glitch earlier in the day. On the trip to Loon, camping gear kept the canoe stable. And on the paddle to this island, the breeze had been at his back. That wasn't the situation now.

On this crossing, the bow would be slanting into the wind. Without weight up front he'd have a difficult time keeping the canoe on course.

Travis perused the beach in the other direction. He spied the perfect counterweight. Some twenty yards down the shore, a head-sized rock's scalp poked above the surface.

Minutes later he had the pint-sized boulder tucked tight in the bow.

Travis pushed the Grumman offshore, then sloshed alongside until it floated free. He turned the bow toward open water. Only then did he clamber aboard, careful to keep his weight centered over the keel.

He was about to take the first paddle thrust when he had a thought. It wouldn't be much farther to circle the island the other direction. Having beached on the backside, he was already midpoint.

Although it'd take a little longer, it'd make for an easier float. The island would temper the breeze. And once past the stash-man's cove, the paddle to Loon would be straight into the wind.

Tossed in as a bonus prize, once he rounded the island, he'd be closer to the opposite bank. Maybe he'd catch a clue, see where the guy beached his boat.

Travis dipped the paddle and pulled. What a great day. He'd captured close-ups of a loon, a long shot of the mystery man, and had even discovered the loot.

It didn't take long before calm water was a thing of the past. On the first leg he'd kept the canoe out of the wind by hugging the beach. But after passing the cove, he chose to make a detour. Instead of paddling directly to Loon, he'd tour the opposite shoreline up close and personal. Maybe he'd get lucky one more time, go four-for-four and discover where the boat was hidden.

Having paddled away from island, dawdling wasn't an option. The breeze now had ample room to gather strength and exercise its muscle. It puffed with enough power to toss up ivory-tipped wrinkles. The small swells pushed with enough oomph that Travis had to consider every stroke.

The last thing he wanted was for the canoe to flip. He was a fish in the water and wasn't worried about drowning. But it'd be embarrassing to return with a water-logged camera bag.

There wouldn't be a problem as long as he paid attention. He'd grown up alongside a lake. He couldn't recall his first boat ride. He'd been told that as a toddler he'd been bundled along on portage trips. Too young to paddle, he was placed on a cushion on the floor.

After graduating kindergarten he was promoted to first mate—the front seat. Then sometime between third or fourth grade he'd been permitted—albeit with a life jacket strapped tight around his chest—to paddle to Seth's pier. At an age when most city kids were adapting two-wheelers to curbs and cars, Travis was becoming expert at handling watercraft.

Reading the furrowed surface, he pulled on the paddle, quartering the bow to the swells. The Grumman dipped and rolled. But then like the dutiful workhorse it was, the canoe resigned itself to the new course.

Because the breeze was blowing from right to left, Travis had to paddle on the port side. It didn't take long before that arm ached. He swapped hands, and using sweeping strokes, pulled from the right side. That proved tiring as well, and only made it more difficult to keep on course.

After a dozen heaves he traded hands again.

Five minutes of heavy paddling brought the Grumman close to shore. Buffered by the adjoining forest, wind pressure relaxed, waves reduced to ripples. He could ease off.

Travis laid the paddle across the gunnels and let his hands dangle. But he didn't rest long. The breeze caught the bow and like an unseen hand, began shoving it toward open water. Exhaling a perturbed grunt, Travis picked up the paddle and churned. Only when the canoe was within a few yards of shore did he slack off again.

Then he took a long look at the woods lining the lake. What was it that made this section of shoreline seem different from the rest?

It dawned on him. The trees! They were taller at the top, broader at the base—giants!

Gaping at the forest, he realized another difference—the understory. Unlike the island, or even the woods behind Buddy's, few shrubs grew beneath the leafy canopy.

Travis was suddenly snapped to red alert. Had someone called his name? Letting the paddle drag, he scanned the beachfront.

There . . . down the shore line! Were his eyes playing tricks on him?

Jessie?

# Chapter Thirteen

C H A P T E R     T H I R T E E N

Crouched behind a fat trunk, Jess chanced a peek at her back-trail. All clear. No strange little man, no three-legged dog—only fidgeting tree tops, trembling shadows. It seemed like a gift from Heaven when she swung her gaze lakeside. She had to rub her eyes in disbelief. Travis and the canoe were churning her way.

She waited a few moments before yelling. She wanted to be certain that when she did, Travis would hear.

But calling his name wasn't a reflex resolution. She debated whether to even show herself.

This was getting to be a habit. A habit she wasn't fond of. Once again, Travis would be coming to her rescue.

He'd done something similar in Canada. He'd tracked her footprints after she'd bolted from a bear. Then after calming her fears, he'd led her along a wild riverfront to safety.

Jess juggled the thought before caving in. Stuff the pride. It'd be easier to say "thank you" than hike all the way back to Buddy's.

She waited for the canoe to come close, curious as to why Travis was paddling along here in the first place.

According to what he'd said, the plan was to camp on

Loon. Snap wildlife photos and sneak peeks at the hourglass island. Something must have happened to make him change his mind.

Wait a minute—the boatman! Travis must have seen him crossing the lake.

All at once Jess felt eager to share. Jogging to the beach-front, she cupped her hands to her mouth and called out. "Trav! Trav! Over here!"

The teen's head swung around as if yanked by a string. Jess waved her arms. She laughed as Travis did a double take. After moment of staring, recognition set in. Travis thrust on the paddle, angling the canoe toward shore.

Just as the Grumman was about to bump, Jess shifted into hurry-up mode. She slogged into the shallows, grabbed the bow and in one smooth maneuver, hopped aboard.

Only when she'd settled in did she speak. Without facing Travis, she said, "I'll tell ya all about it later. But first get us away from here."

"Well, hello to you, too. What? I look like a taxi service?"

Then, with a quick series of correcting strokes, Travis directed the canoe toward open water.

Once he had the Grumman moving forward, he added, "Ya know, we're not gonna be making a speedy getaway from whatever ails ya. I only have the one paddle. Like it or not you're gonna have to just sit tight."

"That's fine. At least I'm away from that creep."

Busy keeping the canoe on course, Travis mumbled. "Are you talking about the man with the mask? The guy in the antique duck boat?"

They were far enough offshore that dread began to fade. Jess glanced down at the stone. "What's with the boulder? Planning on having a rock concert? Or is that your new paddling partner?"

Travis grinned; classic Jess. "You got it. His name's Billy Ballast, a rock star I picked up to hold the bow down. But now that you've got your butt aboard, he can take a dive. Go ahead, toss the old rocker out."

Jess picked the stone up in both hands and heaved it clear of the gunwale. Then she stiffened her spine, folded her arms and pondered the events of the past hour.

After a lull with only the splash of the paddle speaking, Travis said, "Say miss, you didn't tell me your destination. Are we headed for Buddy's or did you want to stop at my campsite? And maybe you'd like to clue me in to what you were doing over there. That's gotta be what . . . a three- or four-mile hike?"

Without turning around, Jess replied. "Why don't you pull in at the cove? You know, where we landed the first time. You can take a break while I tell you about it. If you thought the odds and ends stash was weird, I saw something that's really crazy."

\* \* \*

Travis held up his hand. "Stop! Time-out! Back up a minute."

Making eye contact, he let his palm drop. "You came across an old travel trailer parked smack-dab in the middle of the woods. And then you actually took it upon yourself to look inside?"

He rolled his eyes. "I don't know, Jess. That's pretty bold. Weren't you afraid of getting caught?"

The pair had arrived at Travis's tent minutes earlier. Few words had been shared. Each was waiting for the other to begin.

After snacking on breakfast bars, Travis started things off. Although bubbling with curiosity, he'd kept the first question simple. What was she doing wandering around so far from home?

That query may have been short, but Jessie's reply wasn't. Once she got rolling, the words flowed too fast for Travis to swallow. That's when he put his hand up to quell the gush. He needed time to digest it all.

In response to the question about "getting caught" Jessie's eyes grew large. She'd pulled her head back in an are you kidding gesture.

"I was petrified. That's why I hid in the woods, spying. And when I did knock on the door, I was ready to run at the slightest squeak. But there wasn't any. No one was home."

Jessie shifted to her other elbow. After tramping from the cove, the pair had sprawled on the matted weeds surrounding the tent. They lay on their stomachs, facing one another.

More comfortable, Jess shot Travis a defiant stare. "Anyways, if you'd quit buttin' in, I'll tell you what I saw. It was pretty weird."

She scrunched her brow. "No. Weird isn't the right word. Actually, awesome would be a better choice."

This time Travis listened without interrupting. When Jess was finished, he pushed to his feet, stretched, and then plopped down again. Only now he sat cross legged. Jess rolled over and did likewise.

"Wow! I thought I had something to report. What you just told me tops my tale. But I'll give it to you anyway."

Unlike Travis, Jess never interrupted. She remained mute until he came to the part about seeing her on shore.

"Well. We agree on one thing. The guy's more than a little left of the straight and narrow. And what's with the mask? He was too far away for me to get a good take, but it sounds like you got a picture. You said it looked like a president with dark hair. Are you talking about Ronald Reagan?"

Travis snapped his fingers. "Yeah, that's the one. I couldn't think of his name. But it seems so bizarre. Reagan was a big man, right? The guy in the boat looked to be about your size, maybe even a bit smaller."

"So what d'ya wanna do? Stay over, sleep in the tent? Or once you paddle to Buddy's, hike with me to Bob's?"

"There's no sense to staying overnight. I got what I came for. Give me a hand. We'll break camp right now."

* * *

Buddy finished tethering *Johnny* and headed up to the cabin. It was time to visit the cookie jar. Hungry young pilots need nourishment.

The phone jangled as he walked through the door—Bob. Would Buddy mind making a run with the four-wheeler? Pick up Jess somewhere along Wilderness Road? She'd lost a shoe and needed a lift.

Buddy jumped at the prospect. Here was the opportunity to redeem himself from his earlier behavior. "No problem, Bob. I'll leave right away. See ya in a bit."

Buddy's broad cheeks split into a wide grin. The Honda had only one long seat. Jess would have ride right behind, up close and personal.

Twenty minutes, later Buddy perched on the idling machine, perplexed. He'd traveled the length of the narrow lane—all the way to its junction with Pike Lake Road. Nothing—no signs of Jess—nary a car coming or going. Besides a power line, the only man-made item worth noting was an old mailbox. The rusty mail collector was nailed to a post at the junction of Pike Road.

So what now? Had she already hitched a ride? He didn't think so. There hadn't been any fresh tire tracks.

Buddy was about to twist the throttle when the engine coughed, sputtered and with one last gasp, died.

Great! Too many trips to the airport since fuel had been added. Now he was the one stranded. But unlike Jess, he didn't have a phone. That left only one option. He'd have to hoof it home.

At least he had comfortable walking shoes.

# Chapter Fourteen

C H A P T E R     F O U R T E E N

*Max was mad.*

*Forced to hide in the weeds like a timid mouse, he remained still as a stump. It had happened when he caught the sound of an approaching four-wheeler. Scrambling off the gravel, he'd managed to conceal himself just in time. The machine rumbled by only yards from where he hunkered in the roadside underbrush.*

*And then, just as he thought it was safe to get up and go, he had to skulk down a second time. The fool was returning from the opposite direction.*

*Even worse, as the four-wheeler passed, the knuckle-headed driver pulled over and parked. Max thought for certain he'd been discovered.*

*But he hadn't.*

*Instead, after removing a shiny black helmet, the teen lumbered across the road. Apparently he had bladder issues.*

*Max recognized the beefy kid—red hair and all. The water-beetle pilot—the Mclean offspring.*

*The boy finished his business and trudged back to the idling ATV. Once there he plopped his broad bottom on the padded seat, then he sat looking down the lane.*

Meanwhile the motor kept chugging, broadcasting a cloud of stinky blue exhaust—assaulting Max's senses.

Already lying flat like a worm, Max was thinking of wiggling away. All at once the engine coughed and quit. Max lifted his head, chancing a quick look. Through thick foliage he viewed the lad's backside. The teen was bent at the waist, peering into the fuel tank. Suddenly the youngster stood up and muttered something Max couldn't make out, all the while kicking a tire.

Max eased his head down, glad for his camouflage clothing.

Suddenly the silence was insulted by a string of curses. Then all went quiet again.

Max raised high enough to sneak another peek. The fat-wheeled machine sat along the shoulder. But the boy was gone, apparently hiking toward home.

Max exhaled softly. The kid got what he deserved. The sap had no business being here in the first place. There were plenty of other roads to ride.

Besides, a long walk wouldn't do the lad any harm. Judging from his size, the boy hadn't missed many meals.

There wasn't much Max dared do about the teenager. But the four-wheeler, that was a bird of a different feather. There was a gas can stashed under the trailer. Why not do the young fellow a favor? Park the machine closer to the McLean cabin?

Yup! That's what he'd do. He'd see that it got a lot closer . . . only it'd be much harder to find.

* * *

"I don't know, Jess. Your pilot pal shoulda' been back by now."

"Yeah . . . for sure. Do ya think I should call Uncle Bob again? Have Betty look for Buddy with the car?"

Travis glanced at his watch. It was closing in on supper time. "Naw . . . let's wait awhile. Give him a few more minutes. Maybe he had problems with the Honda."

Jess stared out at the lake, then smiled at an amusing mental image. She decided to share. "Hey! Wouldn't it be funny if he ran out of gas?"

Travis recoiled in mock shock. "Now why would you find that funny?"

Jess giggled. "Well, you know, him being a pilot and all. Don't they always read through a big list before take off? You know . . . it's funny because he acts like such an expert . . . that he, of all people, couldn't make such a stupid mistake."

Travis thumped Jess on a knee. "Girl, you are one sick puppy. If Buddy did run out of gas, I don't wanna be here when he gets back. Buddy's gonna be more than annoyed. And as I recall, he can get pretty excited over the smallest thing."

The teens were slouched on wide plank steps fronting the McLean's lakeside deck.

The sun had already slid behind a leafy umbrella. Sitting in full shade, the breeze felt chilly. Jess tugged the hood of the sweatshirt over her head. Her arms circled her middle, as if hugging herself.

Before leaving Loon Island, she'd powered up her cell phone. Bob said that Buddy had made a run with the ATV. His mission was to find her, bring her home. But now, because she and Travis canoed to the McLean cabin, they should stay put, wait for Buddy's return.

The better part of an hour had already passed since beaching the Grumman.

A knock on Buddy's back door had confirmed the cottage stood empty. A quick look in the backyard revealed that the McLean's' station wagon was in service elsewhere. Only a rusting pickup filled one of three parking slots.

With that discovery, the twosome had trudged around

to the deck. After dropping down on the steps, they began swapping thief theories.

Travis thought the strange fellow had more than one screw loose.

Jess held mixed emotions. She'd seen the trailer's interior. The man was more than talented. He was a marvel with a paintbrush.

So maybe the fellow was also a wordsmith. Could be he was gathering material for a book, exploring ideas for a new novel?

Travis thought that was a dumb idea, but didn't say so. Instead he argued that the guy had been dealt a deck far short of fifty-two cards. And the hand he was playing was stacked with jokers.

They did agree on one thing; the Reagan mask was more than creepy. Neither knew what to make of it.

After a time Travis stood to stretch. "My stomach's growling. What do ya say we head out? Maybe we'll bump into Buddy on the trail."

Jess popped up like a jack-in-the-box. "Okay . . . it's probably a good idea. 'Cause come to think of it, you're not the only who's starving. If I knew his number I could leave a message on Buddy's answering machine. Tell him what's what. But Uncle Bob has the number. We can call from the hangar."

Travis sauntered to the canoe. All the camping gear was stuffed in the canvas duffel bag. He hefted it from the bottom of the boat then decided it was too cumbersome to lug very far. The gear could spend the night on the deck. The only thing he'd carry would be the camera case.

* * *

Jess was first to spot the reluctant hiker. Emerging from the McLean woodlot, she'd paused in the narrow dirt lane.

"This is where I started. The map shows that this road—if you can call it that—winds all the way around the lake. If you go far enough, it reconnects with the one that goes past Buddy's driveway."

Travis examined the rocky right-away. "Jeez. I didn't even notice it before. I thought it was a firebreak."

Travis meandered back to the ATV trail. He pointed to the ground. "You know what? Buddy came this way a little while ago. Look. You can see fresh marks where the tires dug in."

Jess focused far in the distance. She caught a blur of movement where the road dropped out of sight. Her cheeks crinkled. "How much ya wanna bet we're about to have company?"

Travis followed her gaze. "What? You see somethun' I don't?"

Jess shrugged and looked away. But Travis recognized the cat's grin. He did a slow one-eighty.

"Okay. I give up."

Jess pointed her nose east. "Look that direction, near that hollow at the end of Birch Lake."

A red-haired head lifted into view—soon to be followed by a set of broad shoulders—Buddy.

When he was within earshot, Buddy barked, "How'd ya get here? Bob told me you lost a shoe, that you needed a ride."

Jess pushed back the hood. Sauntering toward the runway, she talked over her shoulder. "Well, it looks like I made the right choice. If I had waited for you, I still woulda' had to hike home."

Then she stopped and turned, grinning. "But let me guess. You ran out of gas, didn't cha? I thought that was the supreme no-no for pilots. Anyway, it looks like you need a break. Let's crash over there. I'll tell ya about my day."

Buddy reined in the urge to let off steam. He'd deflected Jess's ribbing by switching into poet mode.

"All right, all right! You made your point . . . and it's sharp as glass. I had to walk . . . 'cause I forgot to check for gas."

Travis stood off to the side, lips sealed. Buddy was soft on Jess. She could get away with teasing. But anything he added would be throwing fuel on a smoldering fire.

The three wandered over to a patch of grass dappled with yellow dandelions. They flopped down in a semicircle.

The sky had continued its western march, covered now and then by a sporadic parade of puffy white clouds. Long shadows were creeping from the woodline.

When they were settled, Jess began a condensed replay of her adventure. Travis chimed in twice. Once about getting a photo of the man, a second time to describe the new stash site.

Jess explained how she'd spotted Travis and how he'd given her a ride in the canoe. Then she changed directions. She sensed Buddy's jealousy was alive and well. From the way he'd jetted off on the Honda, he had clearly wanted to be the hero and make the rescue.

Giving the older teen her full attention, she asked, "So what are ya gonna do about the ATV? You don't want to leave it parked by the that guy's trailer overnight, do ya?"

Buddy pushed up to his feet and shook his head. "Gosh! Not now . . . 'specially after what you just said. If you two wait here, I'll run back to the cabin and then drive around with the pickup. You guys can ride along and help me load the Honda."

Travis hunched his shoulders and gave Jess a question-ing look. "What d'ya think? Do you wanna ride along? Or would you rather walk straight to your uncle's?

Either way, I think we've already missed supper."

Jess didn't reply. She unzipped the fanny pack and pulled out the phone. "I have lots of unused minutes. I'll give Aunt Betty a call and let her know we're okay."

Rested, it didn't take long for Buddy to jog home. After grabbing the keys, he threw a couple of wide planks into the truck bed. Soon the worn-out Ford was bouncing down the lane.

When it rolled to a stop, Travis and Jess jumped onto the tailgate. Once they'd crawled up close to the cab, Buddy punched the gas.

The old truck rattled over ridges, ruts and rocks, dispensing a murky haze to mark its passing. As if riding a bucking bronco, Jess and Travis clung tight to the sides. They didn't talk. The roar of a leaky muffler coupled with the complaint of clanking springs drowned out any thoughts of conversation.

The truck rocked and pitched. Travis had the feeling Buddy was purposely steering toward every hump and bump in the road.

But they made good time. A distance that demanded more than an hour of trudging was covered in minutes.

\* \* \*

"Gall-dang it! I parked it right here! How could someone steal it already?"

Jess and Travis sat on the rusted tailgate. Buddy paced back and forth, fuming.

Edging close to sunset, the right of way was retreating into deep shade. Jess was relieved she wasn't alone. With darkness fast approaching, the forest appeared sinister, as if the trees were creeping closer to the road.

A few moments earlier, Buddy had down-shifted, then suddenly slid to a stop. The rear passengers were pushed tight against the cab, engulfed by an atomic-sized dust cloud. Both were glad to have survived the ride. Continually bouncing on the metal bed had proved painful. They were happy to hop out and plant their feet on firm ground.

Without comment, Travis slid off the tailgate. He plodded along the shoulder, head down—eyes scanning the edge. He suddenly turned toward Buddy. "Yo! You can see the Honda's tire prints. Why don't you turn the truck around? I'll start following the tracks."

Sporting a scowl, Buddy plodded to the younger teen. "You can do that? Follow the tracks, I mean? I can see where they head toward the center of the road. But hey, they disappear on the hard stuff. How you gonna find them there?"

"I think it's possible." Travis said. "I think there are enough patches of loose sand here and there to leave a mark."

He looked at Jess. "So, do ya wanna tag along?"

In an attempt to chase away both a chill and the biting insects, she ducked her head under her sweatshirt hood. "Sure. But how do we know whoever took it didn't turn around and go the other way?"

"Good point. Let's check up ahead first. See if we find recent tire prints in that direction. If we don't, we'll assume the thief headed the way he came in."

Buddy put his hands on his hips and shook his head. "No way. He'd have to ride past the airstrip. The muffler's got a hole in it. You guys would have heard him. Plus, he would have passed by me."

"Yeah, you're right," Travis said, brow furrowed. "If we were even at your place when he drove by. But what if he just pushed the Honda into the brush?"

"Or since it's no doubt the trailer guy, maybe he saw you walking, scored some gas, then rode it down the road a ways and hid it the woods."

Travis hesitated. After a short break he stood tall, more than equaling the older boy's stature. "Just don't tell me you left the key in the ignition."

Buddy looked away, a crimson blotch staining his cheeks. "Ahh . . . " he stammered. "I had to. Sometimes it gets stuck . . . been that way for a long time. I didn't want to break it off. But then again I hadn't planned on being gone long. Soon as Mom came home I was gonna have her drive me back with the gas can."

Buddy gazed at the ground, then kicked a rock. "Besides, nobody ever uses this road . . . except maybe during hunting season."

He continued to scuff dirt with the sole of his shoe. Finally he looked up and added, "The turn-off from the main road isn't even marked. It just looks like an abandoned drive heading to the end of Bob's runway."

Jessie took a turn at speculating. "Hey guys, we're burning daylight. If we want to find the four-wheeler, we better get a move on."

Travis looked up. "You're right, Jess. Let's get after it."

All three shuffled to the front of the Ford. From there they fanned out. With eyes on the gravel, they crept forward. When they'd covered fifty feet, Travis lifted a hand—stop.

"No sense going any farther. I'm pretty positive that it didn't go this direction. All I see are your tracks from before. I'm gonna start checking the other way."

He pointed to the pickup. "Buddy, why don't cha turn that beast around? If it gets too dark, you can trail behind me with the headlights on."

Convinced he was right, Travis wasted little time distancing himself. He took long, rapid strides. Jess stalked behind, jogging now and then to keep close.

They'd gone nearly a city block when she hollered,

"How can you see anything? It's too dark."

Travis stopped and waited. "I can see okay. We know almost for certain the Honda went this way. And for your information, I am seeing tracks every now and then. But that's not what I'm really looking for."

Jess flicked a mosquito off her nose. "Huh? I don't get it? If you're not looking for tracks, what are ya looking for?"

Travis made a sweeping motion with his arm, indicating both sides of the lane. "Think about it. First off, if the dude was gonna ditch the four-wheeler, he wouldn't do it where it was parked. And when he did drive far enough, he'd need a place to pull off."

Travis pointed to the bumper crop of vegetation hugging the cut. "Check it out. Can you see any clues that he drove off the road? I don't. And we won't need full light to find where he did it. It'll be a natural opening."

Jess scrunched her forehead and blinked. Several seconds passed before her lips curled. "Hey, you know what? I think I know where that place might be."

Then she did what was becoming a familiar pattern. She slapped Travis on the arm. Before he had a chance to complain, she trotted off. She yelled over her shoulder. "Catch me if you can, Trav. I'm gonna find a lost ATV."

When Travis told her what to look for, Jess pictured the spot where she'd spotted the fawn. It'd make a perfect place to pull off. It was in a hollow; years of animal use had kept weeds and brush down, and there were openings on both sides of the road.

Jess ignored Travis's pleas to slow down. Instead, every time he drew near, she kicked it up a notch. By the time Travis caught up, Jess had found the first clue. She trudged to the middle of the road, awaiting the question.

For a moment Travis was too winded to do anything but gasp for air. When he could speak, he asked, "How do ya do it? How can you run so far so fast without being short of breath?"

That wasn't the query she'd expected. Before she could respond, and as if weighing in on the subject, an owl hooted. Not to be outdone, somewhere on Pike Lake a loon wailed. The primal cry gave Jess the shivers. She hugged her middle, while one foot tapped a nervous beat.

Letting her arms fall, she said, "Run? You don't call that running. What we just did is called jogging. And I suppose it's because when I was in grade school, I played soccer. Our team didn't have any substitutes. Everyone had to play the whole game. Tiring? For sure, but hey, it paid off."

Breathing easier, Travis put his hands on his hips while arching his back. "I thought it might be because all the boys chased after you on the playground. But whatever, why the rush? You know something I don't?"

"Maybe. When you told me what you were looking for, I remembered this place. On my walk this morning I saw a couple of deer cross the road. I noticed it was a game trail. You know, like the ones you showed me in Canada."

Travis nodded, then took a few steps to the shoulder. He dropped to one knee. Looking up, he said, "Jess, you're something else. Look here, tire tracks heading into the woods."

Headlights swept over the hill, accompanied by the roar of throaty exhaust. Seconds later the pickup clattered to a halt. Quiet reigned as the engine was keyed off. Buddy threw open the door and jumped out.

"What is it? What'd ya find?"

Travis gestured toward the woods. Blinded by headlights, the woodline appeared to be a black sheet.

"Tire tracks, going that way." He tipped his head toward

Jess. "It was her idea to look here. She remembered this spot from her morning stroll. It's an animal crossing."

Jess flashed Travis a quick smile and said, "So what are we waiting on? In a few minutes it's gonna be too dark to see the end of our noses."

Travis turned to Buddy. "Don't suppose you have a flashlight in that rust bucket?"

"Yeah, I think I do. But I don't know if the batteries are any good. Speaking of which, I better turn off the lights before that battery goes out, too. "

Buddy opened the driver's door and switched off the lights. While he was fumbling about in the cab, Travis stood with his eyes closed. Jess noticed and took a step closer, squinting at his face. "Hey, Beetle Bailey? Ya think it's time for a nap?"

Keeping his lids tight, Travis grinned. "I wanna give my eyes a head start."

The truck door slammed. Travis opened his eyes as Buddy came trudging up, clutching a silver tube. "It's not very bright, but it works."

Moments later the three teens stepped off the road. Holding the flashlight, but keeping it off, Travis took the lead. Buddy brought up the rear. Jess was content to be sandwiched in the middle. Between a shoe-stealing dog and hiding from the strange little man, she'd had enough surprises for one day.

Travis had no trouble moving forward. He knew that animals, like humans, tend to choose a path of least resistance. Now that his eyes had adapted to the traces of twilight, the trail was as obvious. And to make things even easier, the ATV's wheels had broadened the corridor.

Moments later the lead tracker made an abrupt stop. Not wanting to trip over roots or branches, Buddy had his eyes trained on the ground. Unaware of the leaders' braking, he crashed into Jess. She in turn slammed into Travis, nearly knocking him down.

Regaining her balance, Jess spun around and glared. "Jeez! Watch where you're walking! I don't like being the meat in the sandwich."

Embarrassed, Buddy was at a rare loss for words. After a few seconds of awkward silence he offered a meek apology. "Sorry. I was lookin' down. Didn't see ya stop."

The trio had arrived at a crest, the place where the ground made its first slope toward Pike. Travis flicked on the light. Holding it over his head, he played the sickly beam along the incline. On the second pass his eyes caught a flicker of red.

"Bingo!" He said, steadying the beam on target.

Buddy stepped up for a better view. Jess had already shuffled ahead. She'd spotted the red firefly on the first pass. But she'd kept mum. Let the boys find it for themselves.

It took a few seconds for Buddy to process the scene. Dressed in black tires and mud coated fenders, the rounded ATV blended with the dark surroundings like a fat turtle on a plump log. Even the taillight was decorated in earth tones. It's reflective qualities feature had been reduced to a cherry colored wink.

# Chapter Fifteen

C H A P T E R    F I F T E E N

*It had been another close call.*

*Moments earlier Max had shut off the noisy ATV. He sat resting in unspoiled solitude, relishing the quiet. The serenity was short lived. First to intrude was the bellowing roar of a leaky muffler. Within seconds, the cling-clanging of heavy metal added to the irritation.*

*The man cocked his best ear—recognition. The racket shouted "worn-out pickup".*

*It had to be the airplane kid—punishing the old Ford half-ton—the rusty truck that sat behind the McLean cabin.*

*From the sound of the engine's forced growl, the fool was driving like a maniac. He was no doubt chasing up the lane to fetch his motorized toy.*

*Ha!*

*Wasn't the big loaf of bread in for a surprise? Because for a little while, the four-wheeler was MIA—missing in action— stuffed away here in the woods. And it would soon be too dark to search.*

*Max threw his leg over the seat and wobbled upright. He began hobbling toward the road. Selecting a thick tree, he dropped down with his back against the bark.*

*With the arrival of sunset the breeze had retired for the day. The clamor coming from the truck cut through the evening air with the ease of a surgeon's scalpel.*

*Max's scarred face cracked a crooked grin. He was in for some free entertainment—a burst of verbal fireworks erupting from just over the rise.*

*A minute later the rattle-trap bounced across the man's sightline. As it passed, the driver down-shifted, then stomped on the gas pedal. From his hiding spot in the woods, Max caught only a brief glimpse. But it'd been enough to make an ID. He'd guessed right—it was the McLean pickup.*

*All the same, the man's pulse quickened. He'd spied something unforeseen. There were passengers in the truck bed.*

*Max sat up straight, a silent alarm ringing in his head. What had he been thinking? Hiding the Honda had been a foolish blunder.*

*Stupid!*

*When the red-haired kid discovered his loss, he'd rush home, call the cops. No doubt a deputy would stop by the McLean place yet tonight. Come morning a squad would venture the lane in search of clues.*

*And where would they look first? Without doubt a pair of doughnut-dunkers would pound the path to his Airstream, bang on his door—play a game of fifty questions.*

*Dumb! Dumb! Dumb!*

*What to do?*

*He didn't dare start the engine and back the Honda out to the road. It'd be too loud.*

*No, he'd have to push it part way, hope the kids looked long enough to spot the tracks, wander in a ways to have a look-see.*

*And that's what he attempted. But even in neutral, the four-wheeler was too much for one his size. He managed to push* the machine to the base of the hill. Once there he wrestled the key from the ignition, then froze.

There was talking—two young voices—out on the road. Then he heard the truck returning; its two headlights slicing through dusky shadows like twin sabers—the leaky exhaust belching fumes into the forest.

Max had no choice but to back away. Although twilight was clinging to life in open areas, the woodland was cloaked in gloom. The man scurried off the game path in the direction of his Airstream. When he'd figured he'd gone far enough not to be seen, he dropped behind a windfall.

Later, after the ordeal was over, Max figured Lady Luck had finally perched on his shoulder. Because once the truck parked, the teens wandered straight into the woods. The lead kid strolled as casually as if following a trail of bread crumbs.

Mere minutes after they'd entered; the trio stood yakking around the four-wheeler.

That's when Max realized his second stupid slip-up. The key he had pried from the ignition was parked in his pocket. And unless the oaf carried a spare, the teens would have to move the contraption with muscle power.

Max gawked as the trio tugged and pushed the Honda up the slope. And he listened as they shoved the contraption into the truck bed. Only then did he abandon his post.

Yet he began the trek to his trailer a more accepting human. The secret encounter had been a learning experience. His prediction was off base. There hadn't been any verbal fireworks. The teenagers had acted civilized—no yelling, blaming or name calling.

And from his hidey-hole, Max had collected every comment. The one that impressed most was the big boy's answer to the question, "Was he gonna call the cops?"

"Naw, no harm, no foul," was the reply. "It was my fault to begin with. I should have checked the gas before heading *out. Let's let it be. Whoever moved it was probably trying to protect their privacy. I can hardly blame them for that."*

*Wow!*

*These kids were nothing like the pups he'd put up with in his past. So civilized, they seemed an entirely different species.*

\* \* \*

Buddy threw back his head to drain the last drop of cola. Can empty, he clunked the container on the workbench. Then he thumped his chest with a fist and proceeded to burp.

Sliding off the stool, he stretched and yawned. "I better mosey home. Remember, I owe you guys. Thanks again for the help."

Jess sipped a bit of soda, then stuck out her lower lip in a playful frown. "Yeah, you do . . . big time."

She glanced across the room. Travis was slouched in the recliner, sipping a root beer. Locking eyes, she winked.

"What d'ya think, Trav? How much we gonna charge Buddy?"

Travis licked his lips and furrowed his forehead. After a moment he held up a closed fist. Slowly shaking his head, he flipped up a forefinger to indicate the number one. "Well . . ." he drawled, "First there was that death-defying ride in the back of the pickup. Person might well have lost a limb or worse."

Biting his lip, he added another finger. "Then there's the tracking fee. That's kind of a specialty. Talents like that don't come cheap."

Jess caught on. When Travis paused to come up with the next dig, she jumped in with both feet. Holding up three fingers, she said, "What about the woods walk? Rates double after dark, don't they?"

Nodding briskly, Travis displayed four digits. "Of course

they do. But the big bucks are gonna be for the uphill push, and then the giant shove into the truck. That job's gotta be worth a bundle."

Travis and Jess volleyed wisecracks so quickly, Buddy felt like a spectator at a tennis match, his head flipping back and forth.

Jess threw up all five fingers. "And finally, one last fee . . . the ride back to the cottage with three of us stuffed into the cab."

"Okay. Okay. I said I owe ya," Buddy said. "Maybe I can make it up by giving you guys a free flight in *Johnny*."

Travis thought that sounded just fine. He nodded and gave a thumb's up.

Jess wasn't as enthusiastic. She'd had her ride. And although it'd been a rush, one flight had been enough. She could wait until the real floatplane was up and flying. It had doors with windows that closed and locked tight.

"I don't know about you," she said, stifling a yawn. "But I've had enough excitement for one day. I'm going in the house before I fall asleep sitting up."

Buddy shuffled his shoes to the door. "You're right. It's been a long day. I'm gonna point my Ford toward home and go before you diss my poem."

\* \* \*

Travis awoke to drizzle drumming on the roof. Wiping away sleep-sand, he focused on his watch. Almost eight! He lay still, listening. Good! No sounds came from the dim hangar below. Maybe he wasn't the only one to sleep in.

What he needed right now was a hot shower, followed by a big breakfast.

From the sound of the rain, there was no need to rush. Other than Buddy's promise of a free flight, he had no plans. And with wet weather, riding second seat in the ultra-light wasn't likely.

Freshly scrubbed and dressed in clean jeans and a jersey, Travis knocked on the back door. He waited for a response before realizing he was getting wet. He opened the door and stepped inside. The entry was perfumed with the scent of sizzling bacon.

"Yo! Anyone up?"

"We're in here," Bob's slurred baritone boomed from the dining area. "Come on in. We've been waiting on ya."

Travis found a surprise when he entered the kitchen. Buddy, Jess and Bob were already at the table.

Betty was at the stove, pouring creamy batter onto a heavy griddle. Spying Travis, she smiled warmly. "I told them to be patient . . . that you'd be in any minute. Now that you're here, pull up a chair. Breakfast will be ready in a jiff."

Travis felt his cheeks tingle. He was embarrassed that the others had put their stomachs on hold while he caught a few extra winks.

The latecomer pulled out a chair and sat down. Bob nodded, then gave the teen an uneven grin. "Your friends were telling us about your adventure. Sounds like you all had an interesting day."

Between bites of crispy bacon and syrup-soaked flap-jacks, Travis shared a portion of the events. But like the others, he didn't mention the stash of odds and ends. Elbows on the table, chins resting on fists, the elders listened with interest.

When Travis finished, Bob said, "The man wears a mask? Strange. And you say you got a photo? I'd like to see it. Too bad you weren't using one of those new-fan-gled digital cameras. We could load it into the computer and pull it up on the screen."

He nodded at his wife. "I've got a doctor's appointment

this morning. Betty can drop off the film at the drug-
store while she's waiting. We can pick up the photos
next time we're in town."

* * *

"Uncle Bob didn't say we couldn't explore. He said we
should probably keep our distance."

Travis's jaw dropped. "Huh? You said before that you
didn't want to go back there. I guess you've changed
your mind now that you'll have company."

Breakfast over, the threesome had relocated to the
warmth of the workshop. Buddy was taking a turn in
the easy chair. Travis was perched on a stool, bent at
the waist, elbows propped on knees. Jess was slumped
against the opposite wall, peering at the map.

Buddy yawned, leaned back and kicked out his legs.
The relic of a recliner creaked a complaint. Placing his
hands behind his neck, the teen stared at the ceiling.
After a moment he said, "I've got an idea. We can use
*Johnny*. Before Jess arrived, I only flew twice a day. I'd
fly over here early in the morning. Then fly home in
late afternoon."

Yawning seemed contagious. As Travis began speak,
he interrupted himself with a yawning exhale. Shaking
his head to clear the cobwebs, he took a deep breath
and mumbled, "So? What's that got to do with the price
of rice?"

Buddy spoke to the light fixture. "Simple. We'll go up at
different times of day. Maybe catch the guy crossing
over. You could bring along the camera. If we spot him,
I'll make a low pass. You can snap some close-ups."

Jess pushed away from the wall. "How's that gonna tell
us anything? We still won't know who he is?"

"Or what he's up to," Travis added, glancing at Jess and
then at Buddy. "Anyway, it doesn't look like you'll be

**139**

flying today. No unless you wear a wetsuit."

Buddy pushed down on the foot pad. The chair groaned and creaked as it returned to the upright position. Sitting vertical, he said, "I checked the forecast. It's suppose'd to clear off by noon. Might be a bit breezy, but if you're game, we could make a short flight. Maybe circle Pike a couple of times, see if our friend is out and about. But in the meantime, I better get home. Mom wants to do some shopping . . . needs me to watch my little brother."

* * *

Rain tapered off midmorning then stopped completely. Patches of robin's egg blue began appearing between tatters of woolly gray. By noon most of the clouds had raced elsewhere.

But clearing skies were the product of an Arctic high— cool air plowing south from Canada. And although the sun's brilliant rays brightened the sky, its light offered little warmth. When Travis stepped outside, a chilly wind nipped and bit. Shivering, he reversed course, slamming the entry door behind him.

This was the middle of summer. The air should be hot and muggy—swimming suit time. But then again, this was also Minnesota, "Land of Ten Thousand Lakes," home to a zillion mosquitoes and zany weather patterns.

No way did he want a ride in the ultra-light. Not today. Much too breezy . . . too chilly, not at all what a July day should be like. What fun would it be? He was pondering the prospect when a tinny bell clanged.

The clatter paused, then began again. The second out-burst brought recognition . . . an industrial-sized bell for the phone extension.

Travis dashed toward the workshop. The ringing ceased before he touched the door knob. He pulled the door open anyway. He should have known—Jessie. She spun about on the stool and considered Travis. Before holding out the receiver, she mouthed, "Buddy. He wants to know if you want to collect on your ride."

Taking the handset, Travis covered the mouthpiece. "What about you? Maybe you want to go first?"

Jess held up both palms and shook her head, mumbling, "No way."

Travis nodded and brought the phone to his ear.

"Yeah, Buddy? It's me, Trav. Kinda breezy, ain't it? Not exactly a heat wave out, either."

He clammed up and listened.

After a long pause, he said, "You know what? Much as I'd like to take you up on the offer, I'm gonna pass. Maybe we can go tomorrow or the day after. I'll be around through the weekend."

He paused again, then asked, "Yeah? What time?"

After another break, he finished his side of the exchange. "Okay. About two o'clock? Jess and I'll keep an eye out. And Buddy, if you do go flying, take care. It's awful gusty."

Travis handed Jess the phone before plopping into the easy chair. Jess swiveled on the stool to face him. "Well? What'd he say? And what's with the 'be careful' advice? When did you become his mother?"

Travis reached down to snatch a paper plate shoved alongside the recliner. He crumpled it between his fists. With a flick of a wrist, he propelled the paper snowball at Jess, all the while beaming.

Jess never blinked. Just as the lightweight missile was about to strike, her hand shot out to slap it away. "Hey! Do you see a target on my forehead?"

Still grinning, Travis replied, "Nah. Quick as you are, I knew you'd hit a home run."

"I'm about to bat you, buster. No more surprises or else. So, is Buddy flying over or what?"

"Not really. He says he's gonna take the ultra-light up around two. That if we want, we could bike the trail over to the other side of Pike. If he sees the hermit out on the lake, he'll circle a couple of times and wag the wings."

Jessie's smile evaporated. She pulled her head back and arched her eyebrows. "Yeah? But I've got a couple of questions. One—where do we get bikes? And two, are you certain you want to? It's quite a ways from here."

Travis shrugged. "I thought you wanted to show me the hermit's trailer? You know, how it's all painted inside with wildlife scenes? Plus, maybe find out a little more about the guy. If Buddy circles, it means that the guy is either out on the lake or on the island playing with his stash. We could sneak in without being spotted."

Jess pondered the possibilities. "I guess. Like you said earlier, it won't be so scary if you're along. But I repeat . . . where are we gonna get the bikes?"

Travis nodded toward the door. "Same place we got the Grumman. There're a couple fat-wheeled antiques hanging on the wall. Don't look like they've been ridden in years. Tires are probably flat, but Bob has an air compressor. I can pump 'em up, squirt a little oil on the chains and we should be good to go."

\* \* \*

It took time to prep the outdated two-wheelers. Besides airing tires and oiling chains, Travis had to adjust the seats. He concluded that the last riders must have been pygmies. Both bike saddles had been left in the down position. Over time, the seats' shafts had rusted inside the adjustment tubes. After loosening the bracket bolts, it took a great deal of urging with a hammer to break each one loose.

While Travis labored, Jess returned to the house. She

was supposed to call home and check in at least twice a week. That was one of the conditions set forth being able to stay at Birch. She didn't mind phoning her father. His cell phone had caller ID. He always answered with a cheery greeting.

But she didn't look forward to talking to her stepmom. They had yet to meet on common ground. In the back of her brain, Jess recognized that it was as much her fault as anyone's. Still mourning the death of her real mother, it wouldn't have mattered if this new woman had been handpicked by angels.

Once the calls had been made, one long and upbeat, the other short and terse, Jess penned a note. It simply read that she and Trav had gone biking. They'd be back before supper.

Hmm . . . she mulled . . . weren't those the very same words she'd used yesterday?

Jess entered the hangar wearing the familiar hooded sweatshirt. The fanny pack was strapped around her middle. Timing was perfect. She trudged in just as Travis was finishing with the second seat.

She shook her head and muttered, "Are we really gonna ride those dinosaurs? They look older than dirt."

Travis let the remark slide for a moment. After taking one last turn with the wrench, he straightened up and scoffed. "Hey! Don't knock it 'til you've tried it. I learned to ride on a bike just like these. It was my dad's when he was a kid. They only have one speed, but they'll do fine for where we're going. And yeah, I know the tires are pregnant-looking. But you know what? They'll work great on gravel. About the only problem will be pedaling uphill. We might have to get off and walk."

C H A P T E R    S I X T E E N

Max was up and at 'em early.

It had been a sleepless night. He couldn't help but worry—that despite having retrieved his motorized toy, the McLean kid might have called the cops.

Maybe it was best to disappear for the day.

Like every morning, Lucky got fed first. The mutt wasn't much to look at, but it was his best friend. Truth be told—the dog was his only true companion.

Other than Madge and Bernie Olson, the elderly couple who ran the out-of-date tavern-store, Max had almost no human contact. And thank God for the Olsons. They were good enough to collect his mail, sparse as it was, and box up grocery goods several times each month.

But then, they were the last of the original residents—former neighbors who knew Max's history. They knew about the fire and sympathized with his loss of family and farm. Better yet, they were tight-lipped. Both knew how to keep secrets.

Max returned his thoughts to the dog. Unlike many people he'd dealt with, Lucky never criticized, laughed, teased or stared. The dog gave love and loyalty without asking much in return.

Mutt fed, Max slurped a bowl of cold cereal. Setting the dish in the tiny sink, he peered through the trailers one clear window.

It was still drizzling. Boughs and branches at the edge of the clearing bent low, their lush summer foliage weighted with water.

But that was okay. Nasty weather meant he'd have the lake to himself. He'd be free to motor over to the island. Check the stash, camouflage the black bags with a fresh coat of vegetation. Hang out where he was safe from snoopy pests— especially those with badges pinned on their chests.

Yup. That's what he'd do.

Max limped over to the miniscule closet. He pulled out a hanger holding a well-worn rainsuit. Like much of his wardrobe, it was camo-patterned. But its colors were different. Instead of leafy blobs of green, black and muted gray, the shapes were vertical stripes of brown and yellow—imitation marsh grass.

He'd come across the raingear the previous fall. It'd been shortly after the duck hunting season. The suit had been rolled into a ball and then left to the whims of nature. The raingear may have been trash to the slob who'd tossed it, but to Max it was a treasure. It was one less thing he had to spend money on.

Not that he had much cash to spread—just the meager income from a monthly disability check. And those dollars had to be closely guarded. Winters in Minnesota were long and brutal. The Airstream was no place to spend December through March.

During those cold, snowy months, Max had to move to town, rent a room in a run-down hotel. He needed a place where he could lie low, looking forward to returning to his own slice of solitude.

The man slipped into the rainsuit. He'd shortened both the legs and sleeves, but there was nothing he could do about the girth. The top was several sizes too large. The rubberized fabric draped his small frame like a child playing dress-up.

*He didn't care. It kept him dry.*

*Returning to the kitchenette, he tucked a few snack bars into a small pack, added a bottle of water, and concluded he was good to go.*

*He stepped outside and closed the door. He'd have to find a way to secure the lock. Isolated as he was, he hadn't worried about it before. But now, with teenagers prowling about, he'd have to make a fix. Maybe have Bernie order him a hasp and padlock.*

*But that would have to wait. Today, and maybe even tomorrow, he'd disappear like a rabbit down a hole. Let things cool down. Not take any more foolish chances.*

*"Come on, Luck," Max called. "It's time we get a move on."*

\* \* \*

By early afternoon Buddy finished the preflight checklist. Removing the ropes that held the ultra-light to the dock, he shoved until his beloved little plane's pontoons floated free. Then, nimble as a mountain goat, he hustled to catch the ultra-light before it bumped the dock posts. Guiding *Johnny* to the end of the pier, he set one foot on a step pad and pushed off.

The wind was from the west-northwest, blowing away from shore. That meant when the engine started, he'd have to taxi out a ways. Once there, he'd make a one-eighty.

Such was the beauty of a floatplane. Unlike a land runway with only two compass points, water meant you could always point the aircraft's beak into the breeze. And that was vital. Taking off downwind was possible only if there was enough time and distance to give lift to the wings.

There'd be no downwind takeoffs today. Judging by the manner in which the tree tops swayed back and forth, it'd be blustery on the opposite shore. He'd play it safe, taxi near the middle and check the conditions. If the gusts appeared too strong, he'd return to shore and tether *Johnny* to the tree—maybe take a nap.

The engine sprang to life with a turn of the key. For the controls to function, the ultra-light needed thrust. Without the propeller churning, *Johnny* was merely a push toy for the wind.

The young pilot nudged the throttle. The motor revved and the floats began to plow ahead. After a moment of hesitation they began to rise. He fed the engine more gas. The pontoons became twin kayaks throwing up spray.

Nearing the halfway point, Buddy eased off the power. He gingerly tapped the left rudder. *Johnny* responded by slowly turning its nose the same way. This was the tricky part. Being crossways in the wind could prove hazardous to one's health.

*Johnny* was a featherweight. It wasn't designed for sideways maneuvering. The pilot had to make certain a gust didn't catch the outboard wing. Without warning the fabric covered appendage could lift. The opposite wingtip would dig water. A strut could break . . . or worse. The pilot might suddenly find himself swimming with the fish.

The half-circle was complete. Twice Buddy had to make quick corrections or risk flipping. Heart pounding and breathing hard, he studied the surface. There was no doubt about it—it was definitely breezy. Wave curls were maturing into whitecaps.

Crunch time—fly or remain earthbound? He decided to go for broke. Once airborne, the breeze shouldn't be much of a factor.

Or at least that's what the young aviator thought.

Sitting tall, the recently licensed pilot planted both feet on the pedals. Swallowing a gulp of air, he shoved in full power. Already in motion, the little seaplane hiccupped once and surged forward.

Pontoons rose to bounce over wavy water. Buddy kept his eyes glued to the airspeed indicator. Twenty . . . thirty . . . as the needle crept past forty, a sweaty hand pulled back on the stick.

With a shudder and a waggle, *Johnny* leapt skyward.

\* \* \*

"Ha! Thought you could beat me, huh?" Travis panted.

The bikers had huffed and puffed the length of the runway. Pedaling a one-speed bike through grass was a workout. After reaching the lane, both stopped for a breather.

"Beat you? I didn't realize we were racing. Besides, it was about time I let you beat me at something." Jess bantered back.

Travis took note that her breathing was not nearly as labored as his own.

"Besides, we've got a long ride ahead of us. Didn't anyone ever teach you about pacing? You don't want to use up all your energy on the first lap. Ya gotta save something for the long haul."

In truth, Jess had tried to keep up. Unlike their foot contests, this time Travis's leg strength proved superior. Plus, this was the first time Jess had ever ridden offroad. She'd grown up in the city. All her riding had been on concrete or blacktop.

On the other hand, Travis had done most of his pedaling on unpaved paths or gravelly dirt roads. Although it was obviously tiring, he made wheeling through grass look effortless. But Jess wouldn't nourish his ego by conceding defeat. She'd wait until the day was over. The bike-hike had just begun.

Riding was easier on the hard-packed, tree-lined lane. The two pedaled side by side, swapping jokes and trading good-natured insults.

"Say, Jess. Do you know where they take sick ships?"

Jess took her eyes off the road long enough to shoot Travis a sneer. "No, Trav. I don't have a clue. Where do they take sick boats?"

Travis swerved to dodge around a rock. Back on track, he said, "Simple. Where d'ya think? They take 'em to the dock. Get it?"

Jess groaned. "Yeah, I get it. That's one of the lamest riddles ever. Where d'ya hear it? From your little sister?"

"Probably." Travis suddenly went still. "Whoa! Hear that? Sounds like Buddy's up with the ultra-light."

The teens coasted to a stop. Now that they were tucked well away from the wide-open runway, wind wasn't a factor. The overhanging forest lane was a wonderful breeze-breaker. The dense foliage softened gusts to a gentle draft.

Travis did notice that the tree tops were jiggling like small children waiting in a long line. He frowned. With only a couple of flying lessons under his belt, he certainly was no expert. But he did have experience with wind and water.

He'd paddled large lakes in the Boundary Waters near his home. One didn't venture out in a tippy canoe on a gusty day. Not unless you were either clueless or wanted to get wet.

"I hear him. It sounds like he just took off." Jess said, turning her head to better catch the engine noise. "What'd ya think?"

Travis looked skyward. There wasn't much of a view. Like Jess had discovered days earlier, much of the sky was blocked by the leafy canopy.

He turned to Jess. "What I think is that Buddy's taking a chance. My instructor told me I had to memorize a saying. It goes something like this; 'there are old pilots, and there are bold pilots . . . but there aren't very many old, bold pilots.'"

Jess made a face. "Huh?" Then she smiled. "Oh, I get it. What you mean is that pilots that take too many risks wake up dead. Right?"

"That's right. Breezy as it is, I doubt we'd go up in the Cessna on a day like this. It's small, but it's a real plane, not a super lightweight. Maybe we'd go if the wind was steady, but it's not. One minute it's ten, the next it's twenty or more."

Jessie's expression turned serious. She stared down at the gravel where she worried a small rock with her shoe. After a moment she looked up. "Are you telling me Buddy's asking for trouble? That he shouldn't have gone up today?"

Travis took a turn at kicking a stone. With a flick of his boot he sent a large pebble skittering into the bushes. "Yeah, that's exactly what I'm saying. But whatever, now that's he's up, we better get a move on. We'll need to get close to that hermit's property, ditch the bikes and scramble through the woods to the lake.

* * *

"For sure," Jess replied, preparing to pedal. "There's no way we'll see Buddy's wing-waving from here."

Buddy was having serious second thoughts. Climbing above the tree-line had been a rude awakening. The first part of the takeoff had been routine, actually quite short. With the breeze at its nose, the ultra-light hadn't used much watery runway.

Once off the surface, Buddy flew low, building speed. Approaching his own shoreline, he pulled back into a steep climb.

Big mistake!

All went well for the first fifty feet of altitude. But then, as *Johnny* rose above the forest wall, conditions changed in a millisecond.

The ultra-light suddenly bucked and twisted like a bull out of the chute. For an instant, Buddy actually thought the lightweight was going to be tipped on its back. Thankfully he recalled his instructor's mantra: "keep it straight and level . . . small control corrections . . . steady as she goes."

Easing the stick forward lowered the nose. Breathing easier, Buddy held it there, still rising but at a slower rate. Meantime the airplane continued to waggle and jerk about like an out-of-sync carnival ride.

Never in his training had Buddy experienced such turbulence. Within seconds, his heart rate raced off the chart and his hands and armpits went sweaty. Flying *Johnny* today had been a huge blunder, he realized after the fact. Now that he was up, he'd have to attempt a slow, wide turn—actually he'd have to make two turns.

The first turn was due right now. This one-eighty wouldn't be quite so risky. He'd be circling to go with the wind.

As he nudged the control stick to the left, the right wing raised and the opposite wing dipped. Caught like a leaf in a whirlpool, and much sooner than expected, *Johnny* swung into the bank.

Buddy eased the controls to a nearly neutral position. Wind power did the rest. The ultra-light's nose continued soaring south in a wide go-round. Buddy concentrated on keeping the plane horizontal. He did so by gently prodding both stick and rudder to complete the half-circle.

Ahead and below loomed the wrinkly waters of Pike. The turn was complete. *Johnny* was speeding southeast.

Hopefully, now that the breeze was at his back, the roller-coaster ride would smooth out and give him time to plan the landing. But the biggest challenge was yet to come—the second one-eighty—the roll to place the nose into the wind. The same gusts that pushed tube and fabric around during turn one would fight equally hard to resist turn two.

But it had to be done. What goes up must come down.

* * *

Travis made the decision. The best route to Pike would be where they'd found the four-wheeler. The game path was in a hollow. It was also near the edge of the "No Trespassing" signs. And the trail probably meandered to the water's edge.

As soon as they arrived, they'd pushed both their bikes into the forest. Fifty feet in they hid them in a patch of ferns. From there, they proceeded on foot.

While wrapping the sweatshirt around her waist, Jess inquired, "How far do you figure it is to the lake?" Despite the temperature, each had removed their outer garments. The mix of nonstop pedaling and being out of the wind had caused both to perspire.

Travis had shed his well-worn windbreaker before stepping off the road. The green jacket was draped around his neck like an old woman's shawl.

"Can't be far. No more than a quarter mile. It'll just seem longer because we're in the woods. But you're the one who studied the map. What'd you guess?"

Jess adjusted the sweatshirt so that it hooked above the fanny pack. "Hmm . . . help me out. The map showed squared parcels of forty acres each. So how long would one side be?"

Travis hitched up his jeans and smirked. "You're getting to be a regular country gal, aren't cha? Forty acres? Do you even know how big an acre is?"

Jess swung a shoe into the leaf duff, spraying litter on Travis's boots. "Uh-uh. But I'm sure you're about to tell me, smart guy."

Travis jumped back in feigned surprise, nearly colliding with a tree. "Hey! Knock it off. You're gettin' my fancy walking shoes dirty."

He playfully kicked leaf litter in Jessie's direction and then said, "You really wanna know? Too bad, cause I can't tell you. I'm not certain. But I do know that eighty-acre parcels are generally a half by a quarter mile in size. So I guess that means this piece would be a quarter mile on each side, and half a mile long."

He paused, frowning at his city-raised friend. "So, does that make me a 'smart guy' or just a dumb old back-woods bumpkin?"

Jess grinned back. "A little of both, I'd say. So tell me in city-speak. About how many blocks would it be?"

"Not all that many. If you figure there are about ten blocks to a mile, then the math is easy . . . two and a half. But the thing is, when you're in thick woods, it usually seems twice that far. I remember when they did some logging near my home. The trail I used to walk to a nearby lake always seemed so long. But when the trees were gone, and I could actually see the water, it didn't seem half that far."

He lifted his ball cap and scratched his head. "Like my math teacher says, 'go figure'."

"What I figure is that if we're gonna catch a glimpse of Buddy over the lake, we better run."

"Wait!" Travis blurted. "Listen! Hear that? He's coming this way right now. That means he'll probably fly past and then make a wide turn. But you're right. If we hurry we might catch him when he flies over from the other way."

\* \* \*

With a gale-force wind blowing from behind, Buddy had never flown so far, so fast. It'd taken less than a minute to sail over Pike. The forest was zooming under the pontoons in an emerald haze.

Buddy forced his nervous eyes to focus on the tiny GPS screen.

Yikes!

The display indicated a groundspeed of over ninety knots—more than a hundred miles per hour! The ultra-light was zooming at a speed reserved for full-sized flying machines.

Depending on the conditions, *Johnny's* safe maneuvering speed was either side of seventy knots. Despite the throttle being backed off, the airspeed needle wiggled between sixty-five and sixty-eight.

Buddy did the arithmetic. Ninety knots groundspeed minus sixty-five airspeed equaled twenty-five. That meant he had a twenty-to thirty-mile-per-hour tailwind.

He was in trouble!

The wings wouldn't bend or break as long they were told to fly straight and level with the wind. But sooner or later he'd have to reverse course. And at this groundspeed, it'd be more than risky . . . it could prove suicidal. The safe crossways wind limit to turn was seventeen knots.

Before the last turn, the fastest he'd ever attempted was fifteen. Much like the one-eighty just executed, that turn had proved to be a nerve-tingling experience.

What to do . . . what to do?

Buddy chanced a downward glance. At such velocity and the low altitude, the ground was a green blur. He couldn't help wonder if Jess and Travis had witnessed the flyover, waiting for the all-clear signal.

Uh-uh. Not gonna happen. He had bigger fish to fry than spying on a hideaway hermit.

He'd be too busy saving his own skin. The number one rule being . . . whatever else happens, fly the airplane.

Buddy trained his eyes ahead. The shiny surface of large oval lake reflected off in the distance.

An idea seed formed, sprouted and took root. There might be a way out.

It meant he had to stay on this course for a while. In the meantime, he'd have to slow *Johnny* as much as he dared. Then, just as plane and pilot darted over the big lake's beach, drop below the tree-line. If the forest there cut the wind as it had on Pike, he should be able to pull it off.

The key would be getting low enough before soaring too far out. There'd only be the one opening, the one chance. If he muffed it, he'd have to keep flying with the wind—hope to find safe harbor further down the line.

The next few minutes would be a guessing game. How much power could be reduced without sinking too low?

He made the first of many tiny tugs on the throttle knob.

Ground school had taught that being pushed from behind had little effect on lift. The key to staying air-borne was speed through moving air, not speed over the ground. Only the air surging over the wings mattered. And the pace of that flow was critical.

Right now he was caught between a rock and a hard place. If he were to bank too steep, too fast—the outer wing could snap like a twig. Even if it held together, the ultra-light could be flipped over in a heartbeat.

But on the other hand, if the turn was too shallow, too slow, that could also spell disaster. Wings lose lift, stall and in an instant, spiral down . . . goodbye aircraft . . . goodbye pilot.

The airline captain wannabe had never felt so stressed. Not even on his first solo. Conditions that special day had been ideal. Bright, sunny, a gentle breeze directly down Bob's runway. Plus, he'd just completed three perfect touchdowns before the instructor cut him loose.

Oh, if only she was here now—her calm voice in the headset, telling him what to do . . . when to do it.

But that was not to be! He was licensed and on his own—supposedly able to make safe decisions. He had dug and fallen into this hole all by himself. He'd have to climb out the same way.

While nudging the stick aft to keep the nose up, Buddy backed off a few more prop ticks. The method seemed to be working. Groundspeed had dropped to seventy-five—better—but still too high.

The airspeed indicator had fallen to a smidge over fifty. Because his airplane wore floats, its stall speed was around forty. The number was higher than that of its ultra-lights with wheels instead of pontoons acting like anchors.

Things were happening faster than Buddy had ever practiced. The oval lake that just moments before had seemed so distant loomed dead ahead. He nudged the throttle back another millimeter. The altimeter followed suit. As *Johnny's* snout dipped, the green haze seemed to rise up.

But of course, that was an illusion. Treetops were stationary. *Johnny* was sinking . . . maybe too fast? Maybe what was needed was more power—not less?

Uh-uh. Groundspeed's still too high. He'd have to bleed off a few more knots.

How? Think of the all the possibilities.

Timeout—back up. It was taught in basic flying 101. Trade speed for altitude, you idiot!

Buddy eased back the control stick—one eye trained on the forest streaming below the floats—the other eye glued to the instruments.

The nose lifted ever so slightly. The needle dropped another three knots.

Abruptly silver-blue replaced muted-green as water raced below the floats.

Time had expired. This was it!

Buddy lowered the nose. Fifty feet . . . forty feet . . . thirty.

He nudged the stick aft. Speed over the waves—sixty. True airspeed—forty-five. Now or never. He had to turn. Any farther and he'd sail beyond the protective wall of the woods.

What he couldn't do was lose another foot of altitude. He didn't have any to spare.

With one hand clutching the throttle, Buddy tapped the left rudder. In unison, he nudged the stick.

A big time whoa! Blue-skinned water rose up. The inboard wing was losing lift. More power—fast!

This was far more dangerous than the one-eighty on Pike. That first half-circle had been done in two dimensions—with floats flat on the lake surface.

The second roll had been into the wind at altitude—and with a slower groundspeed—scary but doable. This turn was a novice's nightmare.

Pushed to the limit like an athlete in the heat of competition—or a soldier in the midst of battle—brain, nerves and muscles tend to act on their own.

Time ceases to exist.

Ball players assert that when they're fully immersed in the game, they can see the rotation of a curve ball. The same thing has been reported by goaltenders . . . pucks float as if in slow motion.

So it was with the fledgling aviator on that windswept

day. An adrenaline rush took the youth to a place he'd never been before. If adrenaline had been jet fuel, the teenager had enough to circle the moon—twice. Scientists call it survival mode—fight, flee or die.

Skeptics call it blind luck.

For a few minutes anyway, the panicked lad's hand-eye coordination would have rivaled that of the most seasoned test pilot. Reflexes went into automode. They responded to every challenge. For each twist, jerk or dip the wind dished out, Buddy tossed it back. And then, just like that, the fight was over.

He'd won this battle. *Johnny's* beak was pointed into the wind.

Drained of adrenaline, Buddy went weak.

*Max couldn't believe his eyes! The McLean kid! Flying his toy waterbug! Was the fool truly crazy or did the idiot have a death wish?*

*It was so blustery Max was leery of crossing back over in the skiff. He might be a little left of the centerline, but that didn't mean he was stupid. All it would take was one wave washing over the stern.*

*Splash! Fill! Sink!*

*No, he could take a shower at home. For now he and the pup would stay put. Motor back when the wind puffed itself out. In the meantime, he'd mess around with his collection of odds and ends. Refresh his mind to why he took them in the first place. Then before leaving, layer on a fresh cover of green.*

\* \* \*

The trek to the lake went fast. Travis had no trouble following the game trail. Hoping to snatch a glimpse of Buddy on the return flight, he'd hustled. Jess shadowed him every step of the way.

Travis slowed before breaking out the of thick timber. An opening in the trees offered a clear view of water. His eyes roamed across the lake's wind-roiled surface.

They scoured one island and then the other.

Nothing unusual.

Facing Jess, he placed a finger to his lips. Then he crept forward, senses alert. No barking, no speech—the only sounds were those of the wind rustling through the tree limbs and the slop of whitecaps washing up on the beach.

After completing a second scan, he whispered, "Let's follow the bank. If we stay behind wood-line we'll be out of sight."

Jess nodded, hugging herself with goose-bumped arms. The gusts coming off the lake were air-conditioned. Before taking a step, she undid the sweatshirt sleeves. Jess didn't give a hoot what Travis thought. She was freezing.

She wasn't the only one to chill out. Trav shivered in silence. He was happy to see Jess gave in. He could put the windbreaker on without being called a sissy.

Zipped up, they moved on. After a few dozen quiet footfalls, Travis eased behind a large basswood. Peering around the thick-barked trunk, he studied what looked like a boat ramp. Draped alongside its weathered timbers was an earth-toned tarp.

He pointed at the empty ramp. "Guess we didn't need Buddy after all."

Jess squinted. "Why I didn't think of it. It's so plain . . . no boat . . . no hermit. That means it's okay to show you his shanty. You think? You're not going to believe the artwork. Actually, it's totally awesome."

Jess took the lead. She pulled up after taking only a few steps. Spinning about, she said, "Jeez—! We forgot all about Buddy. Shouldn't he have gone over by now?

Travis slapped the side of his head with such force his cap flew off. "Am I dense or what? I was so worried about bumping into the knick-knack man, I forgot why we're here."

After picking up the cap and snapping it back on, he eyed the sky. With exception of a few fast-moving clouds, it was clear.

"Heck, yes. He should have passed by here and be long gone by now."

\* \* \*

Buddy was worried he had more on his plate than he could digest.

Unlike the downwind leg, fresh air gushed through open doors with the din of a Kansas twister. Added to his woes, the ultra-light was being whisked about like a leaf caught in whitewater.

And what a difference in groundspeed! The very wind that added thirty knots now subtracted the same. Terrain that blurred below at ninety-plus appeared nearly stationary. Gravel roads and small open fields never noticed going east, now stood unmoving as objects on an aerial photo.

He didn't dare push in full power. The airspeed indicator was showing a safe sixty. Or at least he hoped it was safe. Any faster and unseen gusts could stress the planes wings beyond their breaking point.

Yeah, like they weren't already being tested, he mused. He was well aware that bent wings flew about the same way as a bird without feathers.

It was time to do some mental math. Buddy glanced at his watch. He'd been up for twenty-five minutes.

Five of those minutes had been used lifting-off and turning with the wind. And just now he'd spent another ten brawling with the headwind. That meant it'd taken only ten minutes to reach the oval-shaped lake.

He stole a look at the GPS. The numbers kept changing—flashing between thirty and thirty-five.

Holy-moly! Barely a third of the groundspeed going the other way! It'd take at least thirty minutes to reach Pike!

Could that be right? The four-wheeler would be faster.

Arithmetic was suddenly put on hold. Without warning a gust grabbed an aileron. With his mind in math-land, Buddy jerked the stick sideways.

Wrong response! Like a newbie at the wheel of a car, he'd overcorrected. His reaction was ill-timed. The gust had already blown past. Already relieved of extra lift, the port wing wrenched skyward, the right dipped toward Earth. The ultra-light rolled into a diving bank.

By the time *Johnny* was back on track, Buddy was huffing like a steam engine.

"Ditch the math—stay on path," he panted. "Don't be insane, fly the plane!"

\* \* \*

"Okay, what now?"

Jess shrugged her shoulders. Instead of talking, she continued to study the trailer. With its hodge-podge of peeling paint, the metal box appeared as pathetic as the first time she'd laid eyes on it.

The teens were watching from the birch clump used on her solo escapade. Except today Jess didn't feel threatened. If anything, she felt a smidgeon of pity for anyone forced to live in such a sad little dwelling.

A question had been bouncing around her head since the shoe caper. How could a person—a grownup—choose such an out-of-the-way place to call home?

Why, she wondered, did someone so talented have to hide at all? Was the man an outlaw? A breaking and entering specialist? No, she didn't think so. The trailer defined simplicity inside and out. Surely a master burglar would have scads of modern gizmos.

Could he possibly be a pervert? Wanted in three states for crimes against underage victims? Would that be the reason for the mask? A disguise?

Nah, that didn't seem likely. His diminutive size and wobbly walk would be easy to recognize—mask or not.

What then?

Lying awake the night before, asking the same questions, she pondered one possibility. Was the fellow ashamed of something? The mask could be the clue. Could he have bizarre birth defects—three eyes and four ears?

Travis's voice broke her reverie. "Well? What do you wanna do? Stand here til we grow roots or sneak down and take a peek?"

As if awakened from a dream, Jess blinked her eyes twice. She punched her summer pal playfully on the shoulder. "Lead the way, Daniel Boone. I'll be right behind, ready to run."

Travis padded softly to the edge of the clearing. Once there he stopped. Jess had followed close behind. The two stood side by side, peering at the out-of-place travel trailer. After a pause, Travis whispered, "I don't know, Jess. It doesn't seem right."

"What doesn't seem right? Do you think he's in there?"

Travis shook his head. "Uh-uh. It's not that. I think if he was around, the dog would have barked."

"Well, what then?"

"I don't think its right that we go inside. Once we do that, we'd be no different than he is. After all, we're already trespassing. If we sneak inside, you could add breaking and entering to the charges."

Jess reached out with a finger. She tickled Travis on the nose. She let the finger linger for a second, and then as if realizing what she was doing, pulled it away.

"You are a Dudley Do-right, aren't cha? But I hear what you're saying. To tell the truth, I felt cruddy after I went in. It was like I was violating a private space."

"Exactly," Travis said, scratching the spot where her finger had touched. "I can't fault you for looking inside the first time. You didn't know anyone actually lived here. Plus, the door wasn't locked."

He took a deep breath, considering the situation. "But then, up where I live, we hardly ever lock up. Not unless we're going to be gone overnight. Things are different in the country. You trust your neighbors. Besides, like my dad says, locked doors only keep the good people out."

Jess sauntered to a tree and leaned against its textured skin. Shoving her hands in the pockets of the sweatshirt, she tipped her face in a questioning manner. "Okay then? What'd ya wanna do? Hang out in the woods near shore? See if we can get a good look if the guy motors back in the boat? Or forget the whole thing and head for the hangar?"

Travis shuffled sideways. Drawing alongside Jess, he gave her an unexpected hip check, nearly knocking her over.

"Hey!" she said. "What was that for?"

"Just because," Travis smirked. "Just because I wanted to. Besides, you touched me first."

Travis jumped away, knowing Jess liked to get in the last lick. When he was at safe distance, he nodded toward the trailer. "I said I didn't think we should go in. But we've already come this far. I think I'm tall enough to look in that window. What harm would it cause if I took a free peek?"

* * *

Buddy was becoming a basket case. He had only planned for a fifteen or twenty minute spin—tops. He hadn't bothered topping the tank. There was no need.

*Johnny* was a sipper. The fifty horse engine got great mileage. Or expressed in airplane lingo—burned only four gallons an hour.

He'd stuck the measuring stick in the tank before takeoff. It read over half full . . . more than he'd need for a turn or two around the lake.

Another number problem. The tank held ten gallons. So he'd lifted off with about six gallons—enough for ninety minutes in the air.

But there could be a glitch. Was the reading even accurate? *Johnny* was angled up on the beach? Had gas flowed toward the filler opening . . . or away from it?

How much had he used before this takeoff? How many times had he'd flown over to Bob's and back? Two? Three? And had he topped the tank after taking Jess for a ride? He didn't think so.

What he wished was that he'd installed a gas gauge. But he hadn't. Besides, they weren't always reliable. It was the pilot's duty to make certain the tank held enough for the flight—plus an emergency reserve.

After the fiasco with the four-wheeler, he better not run out. Jess and Travis would have a field day teasing him. But right now, that was the least of his problems. Anyway, without entering the right numbers, doing the arithmetic was pointless.

Another dreadful thought. Even if he'd lifted off with six gallons, not all of it was usable. When the tank was down to the last gallon, the fuel strainer would begin to suck air. The engine would sputter . . . cough . . . lose power . . . shut down.

And right now, bouncing and clawing against an unseen enemy . . . that time could be fast approaching.

A smidgen of relief—Pike finally appeared on the horizon.

Any other day he would have seen the L-shaped waterway long before now. Uh-uh, not today, not on this flight. He was flying lower than a tall hotel.

Early on he'd discovered the higher he went, the slower the pace. So he'd dropped the nose, leveling off only a few hundred feet above the trees. So far it'd proven to be a good move. The GPS flashed an occasional forty.

The downside was that it was downright dangerous. If the engine suddenly died, there'd be only scant seconds to find a field. Because right now the fat water boots were a liability. The only liquid below was a collection of scum covered ponds; each mini-marsh ringed by tall tamaracks.

No thank you—he'd pass on putting down in a puddle.

\* \* \*

"See anything?" Jess asked.

"It's a little murky, but yeah, I can. Man! You didn't exaggerate. It's like I'm peeking out through the window, not in. It looks that real."

Travis was standing on a cement block, hands cupped around his face, nose to the grimy glass. He'd tried stretching tall on tip-toes. The angle was wrong. All he could see was the ceiling mural. But that cloud, painted sky had been enough to kindle his curiosity.

Appetite aroused, he moved one of the steps from in front of the door. Its added height was perfect. By shielding his face, he could peer straight in.

That creek's so realistic I'd swear the water's gonna spill into the room. And the trees . . . the leaves look like they're moving."

After a minute of open-mouthed gawking, he hopped down. Facing Jess, he said, "Did you want to have another quick look? I can stack that other block on top this one."

She shook her head. "Nah . . . I already had my tour.

166

Remember? But if you've seen enough, I think we should get moving before we're busted."

"But first you better put that block back where it belongs."

Travis laughed, picking up the crude doorstep. In an out of character attempt to showoff, he clutched the block with one hand. When he stood upright the heavy slab dangled perilously against his leg.

Grunting softly, he started toward the door. His heel caught a high spot and Travis dropped to one knee. The block sailed out of his hand, crashing against its stoop mate, shattering into odd-shaped pieces.

"Oh-oh! We're toast." Jess gasped.

Travis pushed to his feet, staring down at his creation. "Dammit anyway!"

Jess ran a hand through her hair and laughed. Aren't you full of surprises! I didn't think a Boy Scout like you even knew how to swear.

Feeling his cheeks flush, Travis clenched his teeth. He bent and started brushing litter from his jeans. When he stood, he said, "Boy Scout, huh? Is that the way you see me? Some kind of do-gooder? Holier-than-thou?"

Jess threw up her hands in surrender. "Chill out. I was just surprised to hear you get angry. Actually, I'm kinda glad you did. Now I know you're human like the rest of us."

"Whatever. Right now we've got a problem."

He knelt to inspect the damage. "No way can I piece this thing together. The guy's gonna know he had visitors."

Jessie's stepped close to the trailer. Then she dropped flat to the ground and peered underneath. When she pushed up, she failed to hide a smug smile.

"What?" Travis asked.

"Just never you mind. Busy yourself picking up your puzzle. Hide the pieces in the woods, scatter leaves on 'em. While you're doing that, I'll see about rounding up a replacement."

Spinning on her heels, Jess darted around the corner. Reserve blocks were stacked along the back side. But when she turned the second corner she found more than blocks. An old bike leaned against the spotted aluminum skin. Outfitted with a handlebar basket, the ancient bike rested alongside a two-wheeled cart.

The picture cleared . . . the tire tracks that led her here in the first place. The man didn't drive a car. He used a two-wheeler to bring home supplies. But from where? She'd have to study the wall map one more time.

Travis gathered the pieces in a pile. He pitched the rock-sized remnants as far as he could throw them. The larger slabs were stacked on top one another. By using both hands as a basket, he managed to move the stack in one trip. After dumping the load in a depression, he kicked forest litter over the top.

When he returned, Jess was kneeling near the door. She'd rounded up a substitute, had tamped it into place and was hard at work rubbing soil across its surface.

Travis laughed. She was living up to her Canadian nickname. . . Jess was definitely "Something Else."

Padding close on footfalls camouflaged by rustling tree tops, Travis dug for his deepest voice. "What d'ya doin here?"

Jessie's heart skipped a beat and then seemed to jump into her throat. Thinking she'd been discovered, she rose and spun in one fluid motion. As she swung about, the fistful of soil let loose in an airborne attack, hitting Travis in the face.

"What the heck did you do that for?" He sputtered, spitting dirt.

Scowling, Jess stood up and placed a hand on a hip. With an air of indignation, she spat, "Cause you deserved it! It serves you right for sneaking up on me."

Travis brushed a hand across his face. For sure he'd need another shower tonight. Then he began to laugh. "Sorry. You're right. I guess I did."

Unable to remain miffed, Jess smiled and pointed to her handiwork. Between giggles she gasped, "Yeah, you did. But check out what I was doing before I was so rudely interrupted. I added a bit of local color to the front step . . . made it match the old one."

Travis reined in his laughter. "Clever. Let's hope the guy buys it."

Jessie's expression suddenly turned somber. She stared up at the leafy canopy. Tucked in the woods, away from the lake, not much wind touched the forest floor. But that wasn't true for the tree tops. As if dancing to their own beat, they swayed back and forth.

"Funny, huh? Buddy should have flown over by now, don't cha think? Or didn't we hear him 'cause of the wind?"

Travis glanced skyward. Because there were so many mature trees not much blue was exposed, except for straight up.

"Jeez, Jess. I wasn't paying attention. But you may be right. Unless he came right over this property, we probably wouldn't have heard him. It wouldn't have been like before, you know . . . when he was flying with the wind. The engine noise was being blown our way."

Travis looked in the direction of the lake. He couldn't help but worry. Buddy had no business flying today.

But he was, and there wasn't a thing anyone could do to help him.

After a pause, he went on. "We wouldn't have heard him

going against the wind until he passed right overhead. And this close to the lake, getting ready to put down, he'd have chopped the power. Right now I'd say we take your advice and get outta here before we have company."

# Chapter Eighteen

CHAPTER EIGHTEEN

Max saw the ultra-light before he heard it. At the time he was lounging along shore near his boat. With thick weeds and rushes filling the inlet, both he and the skiff were well hidden from prying eyes.

He hadn't lingered long with his treasure bags. Only enough time to throw on a fresh layer of leaves. He hadn't even looked inside. Why bother? He knew what each bag held.

For some unexplained reason, the ill-gained contents had lost their appeal. The items inside held no real value, they were mostly worthless junk.

No, he thought—there was a cause. He'd been discovered. His secret was out. There'd be no more midnight forays . . . no more after-hour visits . . . no more sneaky snacks.

The more he thought about it, the more relieved he felt. Because in the back of his brain, he knew all along that the thievery had to end. Sooner or later he'd make a mistake, trip up, get caught. Or worse, enter a cabin and have an unexpected greeting from Mr. Colt or Mr. Winchester.

Max let those thoughts slip away. Right now he had an airshow to watch—a pontoon-clad water bug bouncing and scratching against the gale-like wind.

Pike Lake loomed straight-ahead. He was going to make it!

But then again, the island-dotted lake had lingered on the horizon for nearly a half hour. Although the airspeed indicator read sixty, progress over the ground had dwindled to a snail's pace—a scant twenty-five mph. That could only mean that the wind was gusting harder now than when he took off.

There was no other option than to keep the nose straight into the wind. The little aircraft wouldn't tolerate any sudden maneuvers. Besides ripping a wing or breaking a strut, the gusts could easily flip it on its back.

The young pilot focused on flying. Working the stick and rudder had become automatic. Hands and feet responded to changes in altitude and attitude like a high speed computer.

Despite the nippy air whooshing through the cockpit, Buddy's underarms were drenched. "Worry-sweat" his instruction had called it—perspiration caused by high anxiety.

"Worry sweat, right!" Buddy muttered."

"More like a nervous breakdown!"

Like many who find they've panicked—and with no one to talk to—he began mumbling to himself. "Okay, Pike's only a couple minutes away. What's the plan? Power over the shoreline—drop to lake level—fly above the waves until I'm near the dock? Yeah . . ."

Buddy's mumblings were cut short by an engine hiccup. That was followed by a cough, a sputter, and then except for wind noise—silence.

His fear had been realized . . . fuel starvation!

Pike was so close. On any other day it'd been a no-brainer. Glide over the lake, point into the waves, put down and paddle to shore.

Uh-uh. Not now. Ground speed was so meager would he even reach the water? Dang it all! Why hadn't he flown higher? Altitude above was useless. The only distance that mattered was that to Mother Earth.

"Gotta trade speed for lift . . . pull back ever so slight . . . easy . . . easy. Oh cripes! Airspeed dropped . . . but that's okay . . . gained a few feet of sky."

"Ahh, if I can make it over those trees . . . darn but they're tall . . . oh man! No wonder! It's the hermit's place . . . tallest trees in the county."

Big breath.

"Pull back . . . whoa! Too much! Too much!

"Gonna make it! Gonna make it!"

"Come on *Jonathan* . . . glide like an eagle . . . we're almost there . . . just a few more yards."

Too late, Buddy grasped that the coast wasn't clear. He hadn't seen it . . . a giant Norway pine that long ago had stopped feeding its highest boughs. Now a needle-less nearly invisible gray, one fat arm stuck out like a cop directing traffic—warning to go round, go round.

"No time to turn. Pull back! Pull back!"

With a cracking screech, the control stick was nearly wrenched from the youth's grip. The ultra-light skipped skyward like a pebble flipped across calm water. Patchy clouds and blue sky filled the windscreen.

In a reflex move to correct, Buddy jammed the stick forward. *Johnny* answered. The nose dropped and after a small correcting tug, leveled.

Eureka!

The view ahead remained blue. But now it was bluish water, not a cloud-dappled sky, that Buddy was staring at. He'd made it!

The next challenge was to plop down before the wings lost lift, stalled, dropped like a boulder.

How high was he?

Buddy leaned left. He craned his neck, chancing a downward glance. No problem. It was a good forty to fifty feet to the surface. The landing was do-able.

He stared ahead. The flight path was directly at the second island. Good. Both wind and waves would be tempered by its shoreline.

A delayed image suddenly flashed across his mind. An already overworked heart shifted into a second overdrive. The float—something was wrong with the float!

Buddy leaned left again. He forced himself to look directly below. What he saw made his stomach lurch. It wasn't the bent wheel housing that set off a new set of alarm bells. It was the float itself, or what remained of it.

The glancing blow had split the pontoon in two. So wide open he could see whitecaps through the crack.

"What now?"

He'd have to set down at an angle. Hold the broken float off the surface until the left wing lost all its lift.

But what if the other leg was injured? He had to check.

Buddy tilted to the right and peered over the side. What he discovered made him wish he hadn't bothered.

The top of the pontoon appeared normal. Even the retractable wheel was up and locked in position. It was what was fluttering kite-like behind that overloaded Buddy's circuits. Still attached, but flapping violently in the breeze, was a slender piece of the pontoon's belly.

The fiberglass must have turned brittle. Instead of flexing, the thin skin had shattered like a frozen eggshell.

Why, oh why, had they installed used pontoons? Floats that had been long retired, somebody else's cast-offs?

The answer was easy—to save money. New floats carried a price tag nearly equal to the cost of the airplane itself. At the time, that was something he couldn't afford.

So much for taking the cheap route! When he needed them most, they were about as useful as shoes without any soles.

No doubt about it. He was in trouble.

The only way out was to keep the wings flying—close the gap to the island—pitch the nose up just before impact. If the broken floats didn't catch and flip the ultra-light, he'd have a few seconds to bail out . . . swim to shore.

"Ten feet . . . five . . . keep flying . . . keep flying! Just a little lower . . . pull back now!"

The wings lost lift as cracked glass and ivory-tipped water were about to meet. Yanking back on the control stick was a fruitless endeavor. Like a seagull diving for dinner, Jonathan's beak plunged headfirst into Pike's choppy waters.

Despite being cinched tight, the sudden braking propelled Buddy forward like a cannon ball. The impact ripped a safety belt bolt from its mooring. Unrestrained, the young pilot flew over the front seat. His red-haired skull cracked sickeningly against the windshield.

But Buddy never heard the impact.

His lights had been extinguished.

* * *

Jess coasted to a stop. Breathing hard, she braced the bike between her legs and then turned to face Travis. "Well, at least we got some exercise. I hate to admit it, but you were right. These old bikes work just fine on a dirt road."

Travis grinned. "You have a paper and pencil?"

Wide-eyed, she gasped, "Why? You gonna take notes or draw me a picture? Don't tell me. I think I already know. You're going to put it in writing that I beat you back to the airstrip."

Travis remained perched on the bike seat. His long legs allowed his feet to touch the ground. "Notes. I wanna get it on paper that you admitted I was right about something."

Jess threw her head back and laughed. "Oh, you're right about a lot of things. It's just that I don't always tell you. Don't want your head to outgrow that beat-up old ball cap."

Travis twisted the handlebars back and forth. After a moment he nodded toward the runway. "Speaking of growing . . . it looks like we better trade the bikes for lawn tractors. The grass could do with a buzz-cut."

"But first, as long as we're this close, shouldn't we check on Buddy? Seems funny we never heard the airplane come around."

Travis shook his head. "Nah. He probably decided it was too windy to be up fooling around. No doubt he made a wide turn while we were in the woods. Yeah, in this wind we wouldn't have heard him."

Jess propped on one leg, preparing to pedal. "Okay then. I'll race you to the hangar. Winner gets first pick on which tractor to use."

Before Travis could protest, she pushed off. He waited until she cleared the brush line before following. He wasn't worried. The runway was nearly half a mile long. That was more than enough space to catch up.

Once he'd closed the gap, Travis purposely lagged behind. He was savoring every moment. It was obvious Jess was tiring. Pedaling on a hard surface was one thing. Biking through the grass was hard work. But despite the difficulty, she was giving it her all. That thought brought a smug smile to his lips. She sure was "Something Else."

He couldn't help wonder how Jess would react to the nickname. It was probably best to keep it under the radar. No sense creating storm clouds on such a sunny day.

The wide hangar door grew closer with every pedal turn. It was time. Like a cowboy using stirrups, Travis stood on the pedals. Then he pushed down with all his might. The old bike shot forward like a stone from a sling.

The route Jess pedaled ate more energy than her rival's. The middle of the runway was hard packed from years of takeoffs and landings. Travis purposely stayed close to its centerline.

He waited until they'd drawn even before cutting across. It was time to make his move. Pumping with all the strength his legs could muster, he angled toward the big door.

There was a sudden snapping noise much like the report of a small rifle. At the same instant, the pedals offered no resistance. Pushed past its limit, the rusty bike chain had thrown in the towel.

# Chapter Nineteen

C H A P T E R    N I N E T E E N

*From the way it was wallowing, Max was certain the ultra-light was going down. And not just anywhere! It looked to be heading for the center of his cove. But at the last second, just before reaching the shallows, the noisy little bug nosed over.*

*With a splat and a splash, the front half of the plane plunged below the surface. Then like a giant bobber released by a monstrous fish, it popped up—completely altered. The wings had been folded back along the fuselage!*

*For a moment, Max just stood and stared. He was about to flee into woods when the contraption settled deeper into the water. How could that be? It was a pontoon plane.*

*Max stayed put, wondering what would happen next. A minute passed, two minutes. Something was wrong. The crazy McLean kid hadn't bailed out.*

*Why not! Was he hurt?*

*Or worse?*

*How could that be? The little plane wasn't going that fast.*

*Come on kid, climb out! Climb out!*

\* \* \*

Jess set the soda can on the counter. She ran a hand

over her lips and in a playful tone said, "Too bad you had to use the little tractor. That big one is more fun to drive and it cuts three times as fast."

Travis refused to take the bait. He took another sip of soda. Then he held the can out and pretended to read the label.

Undeterred, Jess threw out a second cast. "Serves you right for trying to cheat."

That set the hook.

"Cheat! How'd ya figure I cheated? All I did was pedal down the middle. Actually it was farther than where you rode."

"Right . . . like you can't remember Uncle Bob telling us to stay off to one side unless we're mowing."

With one last gulp Travis drained the can and dropped it to the floor. Displaying a look of annoyance, he smashed it with the heel of his boot. "Yeah, really. Like anyone would be landing today. It's so windy, my hat blew off twice when I was mowing. Lucky it didn't hap-pen when you were around the way you drive, or it would have been history. It'd been chopped into a thousand little pieces."

Jess smiled. She so enjoyed teasing him. "History, huh? That'd be no big loss. From the looks of it, that cap is older than you are."

Travis reached up and removed the well-worn ball cap. He turned it around so he could trace the Twins logo lovingly with a finger.

Just then the phone rang. Both listened as its loud bell clanged once, twice, three times. Jess was about to hop off the stool when the ringing stopped.

"Guess they picked up in the house." She eyed the wall clock. "Which reminds me, Aunt Betty said supper would be ready at six-thirty. We better go before Uncle

Bob comes looking."

In fact, Bob was just about to come out as Travis opened the entry door. A worried expression was written all over his normally cheerful face. Deep furrows etched his weathered forehead. His lips were pressed together tightly as if in grim thought.

"Oh, good. I was just coming out to chat with the two of you. We might have a situation . . . a very serious situation. Let's go in the kitchen. We need to talk."

The elder turned back down the photo-framed entry hall. Jess glanced at Travis and shrugged. Travis shook his head as if to say, "I have no idea."

What was this all about? Were they in trouble? Had the strange fellow reported them for trespassing?

Travis made an "after you" motion, then followed Jess into the dining area. When they turned the corner, Bob was already leaning against the serving island. The table was set. Betty was sitting on the padded bench below the bay window, staring out at the lake. Both teens thought it odd she didn't turn to say hello.

Jess gazed at her uncle. The short walk hadn't erased his worry lines. He nodded toward the chairs, indicating the kids should sit.

Bob waited until both were seated. "Now then . . . I need to ask a couple of questions. But before I do, I want to remind both of you not to draw any hasty conclusions. Okay?"

Travis and Jess glanced at each other with questioning eyes. Where was this headed?

Bob cleared his throat with a pronounced *a-hem*. "No doubt you heard the phone a few minutes ago. That was Mrs. McLean. She wanted to know if Buddy was flying home for supper or eating with us."

Bob shifted his gaze toward Betty for a few seconds then

refocused on the kids while running his fingers through his silver hair. "I didn't know what to say. I told her we'd be in touch shortly. Obviously the ultra-light isn't at their cabin. And just as clear, it's not parked here."

He paused while his eyes darted back and forth between the teenagers. "So the question would be, 'Where is it? And more importantly, 'Where's Buddy?' I need to know when and where you last saw him."

Jess gasped. Travis gulped.

Travis found his voice first. "We saw him when we were on our bikes. It must have been around two-thirty. He was flying over Pike heading east. Are you saying Buddy never flew home this afternoon?"

Bob nodded grimly. "That's the way it appears. Now before we jump to an unhappy ending, there could be good reason for it. Once he was up, he may have decided it was too risky to turn back toward home."

Bob paused, studying the wagon wheel light fixture hanging above the table. One of the bulbs had gone dark. A sign? He went on. "Instead . . . and this is what I'm hoping . . . is that he set down on a smaller lake to wait it out. That he's going to stay put until the wind drops."

He trained his stare on Jess and then on Travis. "You both know 'bout that . . . a lake that offered some protection. Remember, like we did with the Cessna in Canada?"

Jess shivered at the memory.

Travis flashed on the close call in the boonies. Bob, with all his experience, had his hands full aligning the larger, more stable floatplane to the wind.

After a pause, Travis asked, "Doesn't Buddy have a two-way radio? So he could have talked to an airport?"

"He does. But as low as he flies, I doubt a hand unit would broadcast far enough to be heard. Besides, the little airports around here are 'uncontrolled'. No control towers. Chances are, even if he did send a message, nobody was listening."

Aunt Betty turned away from the window. "Robert, I think it's time you call the Civil Air Patrol. Start an air search immediately. It'll be dark in a couple of hours. What if that sweet young man is injured . . . lying helpless in the woods . . . waiting for first-aid to arrive?"

Bob glumly agreed. "Like usual, you were reading my mind. The number is posted on the wall in the work-shop. I'll phone from there. Meantime, maybe you should grab a quick bite with the kids. Once I call for help, I think we need to make a trip to the McLean cabin. Explain to Dorothy in person."

Betty shook her head. "I'm too upset to eat. I'll pull the Buick around while you're making your calls. Now that the doctor has given you a green light to drive, you can drop me off and come back here."

She rose on nervous knees and shuffled to the stove. Pulling the door open with an oven mitt, she removed a casserole. She set the steaming bowl on the range top. Then she turned to face the teenagers. "Looks like it'll be just the two of you. There's enough hamburger hot-dish for a couple meals. Jess, I'd appreciate that when you're through with supper, you'll cover the bowl, stick it in the fridge."

"I had a bad feeling all afternoon . . . Your fool friend had no business taking *Johnny* up today." Travis mumbled around a mouthful of food.

Jess had only picked at the spoon-sized mound on her plate. "He's just as much your friend as mine, she replied, setting down her fork. "And if you had a bad feeling, how come you were so convinced that he looped around and landed?"

She lowered her brow and made a face. "Jeez! How can you even eat? I'm worried sick about Buddy."

Travis finished chewing. He took a big swallow of milk. After gulping it down, he said, "Well, duh! I am too. But that doesn't mean we shouldn't eat something. How are we going to help if we get sick 'cause our bellies are empty?"

Jess picked up the fork and began separating the hot-dish's plump noodles away from the hunks of meat. "Help? What can we do? We'd just be in the way."

Travis loaded his fork and shoveled the food into his mouth. After chewing and swallowing, he said, "I been thinking about that. My guess is that the air patrol will be using Bob's strip as home base. 'Specially since he's already got a two-way radio setup. Don't ya think?"

Shrugging, Jess herded a few more kernels of burger around her plate. "So what?"

"Search planes will be coming from miles around. Once it's too dark for an air search, some of those pilots are probably going to bunk in the loft. You could help Betty with food. You know . . . serve coffee . . . do dishes . . . stuff like that."

Jessie's dark eyes blazed as their lids narrowed. "Oh, you want me to play nursemaid and waitress, huh? And what, pray tell, did you plan for yourself? Wait, don't tell me. Let me guess. Since you're a boy, you get to ride along and be a spotter. Right?"

Travis felt like he was shrinking in his chair. Either that or the room was growing.

"No . . . I just thought since you don't really like to fly, you'd want to stick around and make yourself useful."

Jess had to grant him the point. Some of her fire faded. But just the same, it irked her that boys so often assumed what a woman's role should be.

"Well, you're sort of right about the flying part. I don't like it when the air's all bumpy. But there're lots of other things I could do besides wash dishes, ya know."

Travis breathed easier. It was his mistake. He knew Jess well enough by now not to make any sexist suggestions.

"Of course there are. You're great at reading maps. Maybe you can help whoever works the radio. You know . . . like plot and track flight patterns."

The compliment helped cool her off. "Thanks. But I'm sure the pros have a system worked out. Probably some type of grid."

Back to breathing normal, Travis wolfed down another mouthful. The room returned to its original size. After sipping and swallowing, he shared a thought. "I'll bet, since he can't legally fly, your uncle will be working the radios."

Travis nodded in agreement to his own remark. "But remember, he gets tired talking too much. He'd probably appreciate you spelling him from time to time."

The teens froze as an airplane roared overhead. Travis hurried to the living room's rear window. Pulling the curtain aside, he stared at the runway. A small high-winged aircraft was about to make its final approach. He watched as it aligned with the runway then let the curtain fall and returned to the kitchen.

"It's my instructor, Pete Paulson. By air, his strip's not all that far away. I'm gonna run out meet him . . . fill him in on what's going on."

* * *

Minutes later the Cessna 150 was airborne again. But unlike his flying lessons, Travis was now sitting in the right seat.

Pete hadn't bothered shutting off the engine. As he taxied up, he spotted Travis standing outside the hangar. Gunning the plane around, Pete opened the side window and beckoned Travis to go around the tail.

Travis darted to the right side door, sucking in dusty

propwash for the effort. Pete had already leaned across to release the latch. After a push-and-shove contest to keep the door from blowing shut, Travis scuttled inside.

The rangy, raw-boned pilot pointed to the headset looped over the co-pilot's yoke. Then he pushed in the gas. The Cessna was rolling before Travis had the muffs over his ears.

"Can you hear me all right? If not, turn up the volume. The knob's on the side of the earpiece."

"I hear you fine," Travis replied, looking left toward the pilot.

Although younger than Bob, Pete had to be closing in on seventy. He was a lanky, slim fellow whose narrow face often wore a severe expression. After being introduced, Travis discovered that the man's hawkish appearance belied his sense of humor. Instead of criticisms, Pete made his student laugh with his witty observations. Travis didn't expect to hear any of the man's amusing chit-chat during this flight, however.

"I'm surprised you're not gonna to wait for a few other air patrol pilots."

"Actually Trav, I don't belong to the Civil Air Patrol. Besides, it'll take awhile for them to get here. That's why Bob called me first . . . told me our young pilot friend is missing. Said I should hustle over and pick you up. He also said you're probably the last one to see him."

Pete broke off conversation as he swung the plane into the wind. It was closing in on evening. Gusts had relaxed to flag-flapping rather than flag-ripping velocity. With the plane's nose pointed down the runway, the pilot sat up straight. He eyed the gauges, added ten degrees of flaps and pushed in full power.

Because it was a grass strip, he lugged the yoke toward his chest. It was a control input that would transfer weight off the front wheel and place more on the mains. With a jerk and a wiggle, the two-seater began its rollout.

Pete was all business. As momentum picked up, he eased the yoke forward. Keeping an eye on the airspeed indicator, he tugged again. The nose tipped skyward along with the fuselage and the passengers.

Several seconds later the pilot pushed the yoke forward, leveling the aircraft several feet above the freshly mown grass. Free from Earth's friction, the airspeed needle surged past sixty. Pete pulled the yoke one more time, lifting the nose above the horizon.

Travis took it all in. He wondered if he would ever be able to make piloting look so matter-of-fact.

Business behind, Pete continued the conversation. "About the air patrol coming in . . . we'll be losing light if we were to wait on 'em. There'll be time to talk . . . either by radio or in person later at Bob's. Right now I need you to fill me in on where to look first."

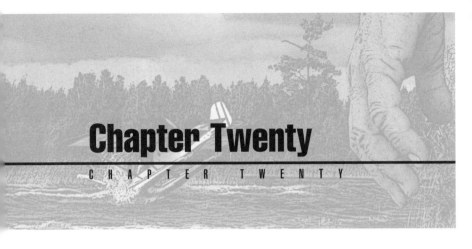

# Chapter Twenty

C H A P T E R   T W E N T Y

*He had to do something.*

*Nuisance or not, the kid didn't deserve to die.*

*Max hobbled to the boat, moving faster than he had in years; with one herculean heave the skiff was floating free. Then he slogged into the shallow water, shoving the dinghy ahead. It'd take too long to put the trolling motor down, turn the boat around.*

*By then it might be too late to even bother.*

*The airplane wasn't that far from shore. It was sinking just beyond the inlet. The lower part of the cockpit was already taking on water. Unfortunately for the McLean lad, the bird had nose-dived on the deep side of the drop-off.*

*Drop-offs were one of the unique features of Pike Lake. Along some shorelines a person could walk out the length of a football field. The water wouldn't even reach their chest. But beware. For when it did go deep, it plunged nearly straight down . . . forty, fifty, sixty feet or more.*

*This island inlet area was a classic example. Shallow and weedy, it averaged only a couple of feet deep. Even out past the rushes and rice stalks, the depth was no more than double that.*

*Then all at once it plunged—cliff-like—to over seventy-five feet. It was a delightful distance if you happened to be a coldwater fish. Not so great if you were a handicapped fellow of pocket-sized stature, trying to rescue someone from a sinking aircraft."*

*Max wasn't at all certain he could be of any help. He didn't even know how to swim.*

\* \* \*

Miffed at being dumped, Jess let the screen door slam with a bang. She was crossing over to the shop when her uncle's Buick raced up the drive. Because of the mild stroke, the senior hadn't been behind the wheel for a while. But you couldn't tell it from the way the car fishtailed around the hangar and skidded to a dusty stop.

Leaping out, Bob started shooting questions machine gun style. "Were there any calls? Did Pete fly in yet? How 'bout Travis? Did he go up with Pete?"

Jess tried to keep up: no, yes, yes. They left about five minutes ago. I'd a thought you woulda' seen 'em take off."

She held the side door open. Her uncle nodded and hurried into the shop. As he passed, Jess made an alarming observation.

The doctor had just given the go-ahead to resume a regular routine. But the situation with Buddy was anything but normal. Although it was no fault of his own, Bob would feel responsible for whatever happened to Buddy. Bob appeared two steps away from a 911 call.

His complexion was ashen. Looking like creases on the trunk of an old tree, deep wrinkles furrowed his forehead. Added to the mix, she could hear every breath the old man inhaled.

Jess had witnessed the result of stress overload during the Canadian fiasco. The first stressor was a line of dark-bellied storm clouds that had pushed the floatplane around like a feather in the wind.

Then a lightning strike had fried the Cessna's wiring.

Even so, Bob managed to set down safely on an isolated wilderness lake. The party of three teens and one adult thought they'd escaped disaster. Not so. The third blow came while they were setting up camp—*whoosh!* A small but potent tornado flipped the floatplane bottom side up.

Before they knew what hit them, they were stranded in the middle of nowhere. The ordeal had been too much for the veteran aviator. Never mind that the storm had been an act of God. Her uncle felt to blame for everything that took place—the gusty clouds, the lightning, even the tiny twister.

He said it was poor piloting on his part. That he should have reversed course at the first hint of troubled weather. Sure, like he could have predicted the future.

But nevertheless, the man carried a boxcar of guilt for placing three young lives in harm's way. All the fretting taxed his reserves. The stroke came while he was sleeping. Overnight her beloved uncle changed from an active go-getter adult to a candidate for a senior center.

The good news was, Bob fought back. He said he wasn't ready to push up daisies. Although hobbled with slight balance and speech problems, in a matter of days he was thinking clear as spring water. And more importantly, during the past couple weeks, his physical appearance had returned to near normal.

Now Jess was frightened that this episode with Buddy could undo Bob's recovery.

Jessie eased the door shut. She followed her uncle over to the corner section of the workbench. Several years earlier, Bob had installed state-of-the-art radios in the floatplane. Never wasteful, he'd saved the old ones.

It was a simple winter project to create a communications corner. When futzing about in the shop, he'd often tune in one or both of the two-ways. That way he could monitor the coming and going of local pilots—see who was going where, when.

Bob sat on a stool and then reached across the bench. He switched on both radios. Then he turned toward Jess, his face a roadmap of worry. "We've got our work cut out for us, Jazzi. I'm going to need you to help with the talking. Think you're up to it?"

"I'm not sure, Uncle Bob. What do I have to do? I don't know much about airplanes."

The senior shot her a weary grin. "That's not important. Until the pros take over, for a while this setup will be the nerve center."

He sucked in a rasping breath. "Let's hope we won't need trained help. Let's keep our fingers crossed that Buddy did what I said earlier. That he set down . . . that he's waiting on the wind to go down. But in the meantime, Pete, along with another pilot friend of mine will be doing a flyover. Trouble is, their airplanes have only one radio."

Jess arched her brow. "I don't get it. Why would they need more than one?"

"Fair question. One's all you need to broadcast and receive. But the deal is, Buddy might be trying to call out. We can't be certain what frequency he'll be using. There are several different numbers just for the regional airports. Plus, when a pilot has a problem, there's a couple more. One frequency is for emergencies and another is to talk to Flight Service.

Jess thought about this. She recalled a similar conversation in Canada. "Remember when we talked about an emergency radio called an ELT? The one that sends a signal after a plane crashes? I'd said it sounds like some kind of sandwich. Seth and Travis teased me. They said a sandwich is called a BLT, like the jerks didn't think I knew that."

She hesitated, trying to recall what the initials stood for. "I remember now. It's called an 'emergency locating transmitter,' right?"

Bob nodded. "Jazzi, your memory beats any computer. You're absolutely right. But why do you ask?"

"Well, does Buddy have one of those gizmos on *Johnny*?"

Bob grimaced. "No, my dear. He doesn't. It'd be nice if he did. But I don't believe it was required on a plane that small. Remember, as a rule of thumb, ultra-lights usually only fly around their home base. They're designed for local fun, not long trips."

Chatter burst from the speaker.

"Birch Lake . . . Birch Lake . . . Bob Ritzer at Birch Lake . . . do you copy?"

The senior keyed the microphone. "This is Bob. We copy loud and clear. Who we talking to? Over."

Bob made a head gesture, indicating Jess should listen up.

"Hi, Bob. It's Jerry from Aitkin. I was at my hangar when Pete caught me by cell phone. I passed the message along to Wally at the maintenance bay. He was going to call a few other local fellows. Over."

Bob indicated with his eyes for Jess to watch as he keyed the mike. "That's terrific. Pete just took off a few minutes ago. He stopped to pick up a young friend who saw the McLean kid fly over Pike. Tell you what. Why don't you switch over to 122.8? I think Pete's probably tuned in to that frequency. It might be the one Buddy would use. I'll keep the radios tuned to both. Over."

The amplifier erupted with a high-pitched, screeching squeal. Jess threw her hands over her ears. Bob knew the cause of the commotion. It meant two pilots pushing talk buttons at the same time. He waited for one or the other to let off.

"Repeat . . . this is Pete Paulson in Cessna three-six-two Charley x-ray. Welcome aboard, Jerry. I just changed frequencies and caught the tail end of your call. Travis and I are about four miles east-southeast of Pike at two-thousand. Nothing so far. Over."

Bob cleared his throat and keyed the mike. "Now that you're in touch, why don't you both switch over to an air-to-air frequency? That'll clear 122.7 and 122.8 for incoming broadcasts. When they come in, I'll tell any other pilots to do the same. Over."

"Roger, Robert. Six Charley-x-ray switching to 131.5. Over."

"Ditto for Three-Bravo-Whiskey. Over."

Bob set the microphone on the bench. He reached in a pocket and pulled out a red-and-white checkered hanky. After wiping his brow, he stuffed the cloth back in a pants pocket.

"Well, Jazzi? What d'ya . . . think? Can you listen for calls coming in? And if any do, are you up to telling them to switch over to the talk number?"

"Sure, Uncle Bob. But why me? You know more what to say."

The senior slid off the stool. "I have some phone calls to make. I called a pal who helps with the Civil Air Patrol. But I think, to be safe, I ought to notify the sheriff. If Buddy's still missing come morning, he'll want to organize a ground search. Question is, where to begin?"

* * *

Pete completed his radio chatter. "Okay, Jerry. We'll go as far as Big Round and loop back. Maybe the kid put down along the lee side of the lake. If we don't see him, we'll make another pass toward Pike. We'll stay on the north side of a direct flight. You can work toward Round on the south side. Over."

Travis stared through the windshield. A large egg-shaped waterway emerged in the distance. Too big, he thought, to offer any relief for the ultra-light. Buddy probably would have chosen to set down in a small lake, one not so windswept.

The youth glanced at his watch. They'd been up for fifteen minutes. No sign of the amphibian or the foolish pilot that flew it. But then, except for a series of scum-covered ponds, it was mostly lowland forest below. If Buddy had crashed, and *Johnny* had slipped through the canopy, the wreck would be impossible to spot.

Travis was jarred from his musings. Pete was speaking. "Well, Trav . . . any thoughts on where we should look next?"

"Huh? Well . . . I was just thinking about that. Do you really think Buddy might have landed on that big lake? Wouldn't it have been even rougher than Pike?"

"Probably. The only other scene I can come up with is that he continued to fly with the wind. There are some smaller lakes scattered near the interstate. And if that's the case, he could be on any one of them. But that's another thirty or forty miles from here. That's too large an area to cover before dark."

Travis leaned left to scan the airspeed indicator. The two-seater was sailing over the landscape at ninety-five knots. He crunched the numbers. One hundred knots equaled one hundred fifteen miles per hour. Adding the tailwind, they were going at least one hundred twenty mph.

He checked his watch again—seven thirty.

"We have at least an hour before the sun sets. It would-n't take that long to get to the interstate, circle a few of those lakes . . . would it? No more than fifteen or twenty minutes?"

Pete glanced over at his co-pilot. "Atta boy! You're able to crunch numbers in your head. Good. That's a must if you want to pass your test. But here's a lesson you gotta plant in your noggin. Flying is not like driving a car. We're not planning to land once we get there. The same wind that's pushing us at warp-one will be in our face when we turn about. Speed over the ground will be cut darn near in two."

Travis felt his face flush. It was a stupid mistake. Of course it'd take twice as long to fly home. Plus, circling a whole bunch of lakes would gobble even more time.

Embarrassed, he stared through the side window, hoping not to see blue on white below.

"Hey. Don't feel bad. I'm impressed that you were able to work the numbers in the first place. But here's one more bit of advice to store away. This little bird ain't no military jet. We don't have the luxury of a fuel tanker tagging behind. And there aren't any gas stations up here. So remember . . . never, ever, fly farther than the clock allows."

When Travis didn't reply, he added, "Let's hope Buddy remembered that lesson. It's one that's taught to every pilot from day one."

C H A P T E R   T W E N T Y - O N E

*Pulling Buddy from the ultra-light had been chancy. Twice the dinghy had nearly come close to capsizing. Fortunately, one of the plane's pontoons hadn't completely filled. It remained afloat enough to hold Max's weight.*

*After rowing to the ailing aircraft, a quick look showed the reason why the kid hadn't bailed. The lad was slumped across the front seat like an oversized pillow. An ooze of bright red trickled from an apple-sized welt on the boy's forehead.*

*For a moment Max thought the young man might be a goner. To his relief, he noted up-and-down movement of the teen's chest.*

*That meant the kid was breathing.*

*Not dead, just unconscious.*

*While Max stood staring, the pontoon burped a bucketful of air. The float settled deeper into the water. If he didn't want the kid to drown, Max had to get him out immediately.*

*But how?*

*While pondering this dilemma, Max felt the fuselage settle a few more inches. Time was running out.*

*The little man knew he wasn't strong enough to lug the hefty teen out of the cockpit. Could he float him free?*

*Max noticed the life vest tucked in the bow. A Coast Guard-approved model, it was designed to keep a person afloat, face up.*

*It was a tug of war but Max managed to get the vest on Buddy. Water was already lapping at the bottom of the window opening.*

*Max positioned the skiff so the cockpit's door could swing out. Then he looped the free end of the anchor rope through the preserver's padded collar.*

*Max's heart stutter-stepped when at touch of a hand, Buddy's body had twitched. A groan gurgled in the boy's throat, seeping out through an open mouth.*

*Max froze, certain the teen was coming around. But Buddy was down for the count. His body went slack yet again. Just then the pontoon gushed a final gasp. The fuselage began dropping like an out-of-date elevator—slow but sure.*

*Max frantically tied the rope to the dinghy's seat support, making certain there was slack. He tipped down the trolling motor and twisted the control. Then he pointed the boat toward the shallows, a small blue whale chasing close behind.*

\* \* \*

Buddy awoke to a world of pain.

This couldn't be Heaven. It hurt too much. Besides, Heaven was supposed to be bright and clear, ringed with white angelic clouds. The world he could make out through half-opened eyelids was on the shady side of dusk.

One thing was certain. He now knew what the expression "rode hard and put away wet" meant. Every fiber of his being seemed to be seeking attention. The loudest to sound off was an aching temple. With each beat of his heart, it felt as if someone was tapping his skull with a hammer.

Buddy struggled to sit upright. Then he forced his eyes

fully open—they seemed to be the only part of his body not screaming foul. No, that wasn't true. Although his ears were ringing, they didn't hurt. They vaguely recognized the din of a distant airplane.

His eyes told him that he was in a forest near the edge of a lake. But where? And how did he get here? Sitting up had been a mistake. All at once he felt dizzy, light-headed, as if he were going to faint. He eased back down and let everything go limp.

Strange. Was his head resting on a cushion?

Before he could muster the effort to check, a wave of nausea washed over. He barely had time to turn his face before throwing up. He lay his head down again, exhausted.

Never had he felt so tired.

"Sleep. I need sleep, he thought." "I'll feel better when I wake up."

As is common for someone who has suffered a concussion, Buddy drifted off.

* * *

Pete poured himself a short cup of coffee from the pot gurgling on the shop's workbench. Then he stepped over and eased into the recliner. He'd set the Cessna down shortly after sunset. As on their downwind leg, neither he nor Travis had caught a clue of the ultra-light's whereabouts.

Cradling the mug in his hand, he said, "Don't want to drink too much of this stuff this late. It tends to keep me awake."

He turned an eye on his copilot. "The way my wife says I snore, that might be a good thing for you, huh? Are you certain that you don't mind me sharing the loft?"

Travis was perched on a stool, fiddling with a survival tool. Jess was leaning up against the wall, studying the

**197**

map. Bob had joined Betty at the McLean cabin. Upon hearing the news, Buddy's dad had dropped everything and raced up from the Twin Cities.

He'd been lucky not to get a speeding ticket. Less than two hours after receiving the call, he pulled into the cottage drive. Unfortunately nothing had changed. His son and the airplane were still missing. In this instance, the saying "no news is good news" didn't seem appropriate. Mr. McLean felt certain that if Buddy had set down to wait out the wind, he would have been in contact by now.

Bob hadn't said so, but he felt the same way. He had driven over to console the McLeans. During the short drive, he came up with a dozen reasons why Buddy hadn't been in touch. But in his gut, he didn't believe a single one of them.

* * *

Pete took a sip, made a face, then set the cup up on the bench. "Who made the brew?"

Jessie turned away from the wall. "I did. Why? Did I make it too strong?"

"No. It's fine," Pete fibbed, not wanting to step on the girl's feelings.

He stared at the ceiling while scratching a whiskered cheek. "Well, maybe it's a tad potent for this time of day. But come five a.m. it'll be just the ticket to get my motor started. Travis and I need to lift off before sunrise."

He reached for the cup and took a second sip. This time after swallowing, he grinned. "You did great. It's sure better than the sludge I make at the hangar."

Jess knew the man was trying to be polite. She'd never made coffee before. So if it was a little stout, big deal. If the guy didn't like it, he could darn well make his own. Jess was irritated that her prediction had come true. Travis was going to take part in the search. At first light,

**198**

he and Pete would be flying to the Aitkin airport for a flight briefing. Because the runway there was hard surfaced, air patrol passed on using Bob's grass strip. Plus, Aitkin had a fuel pump.

Meanwhile, Jess was supposed to stay put and listen for radio calls. Yeah, like there'd be any. There'd only been one radio transmission earlier in the evening. Some guy named Jerry wanting to talk to her uncle. And now, with the action shifting elsewhere, why would anyone bother calling here? It wasn't like Bob could take the seaplane up and help. Currently it was a pile of parts waiting to be bolted back together.

Steamed at Travis, Jess returned her gaze to the map. She'd thought they were pals, if not more. But oh, as soon as something more exciting came along, he'd dropped her like a hot potato. Well Travis Larsen could go ahead and take to the air. He could take a flying leap back to the boonies where he belonged.

Sensing the girl's mood, Pete shifted his attention. "Well, young man. If we're going to get briefed at daybreak, we should probably hit the hay. What d'ya think?"

\* \* \*

Jess awoke to light streaming through the blinds. She pulled the pillow overhead and closed her eyes. All at once she threw back the covers and sat up. It had just dawned on her sleepy brain— she'd overslept.

Springing from bed, she stumbled to the window. A quick peek at the lake confirmed her suspicion. Under a clear blue sky, lightly rippled water sparkled with a coppery sheen. That meant the sun was already up.

Darn it! She had things to do and places to go.

Jess wrestled into her jeans and sweatshirt then raced to the kitchen.

Empty.

A note lay on the counter. It said that her uncle was dropping Betty at the McLeans'. Then he'd be going on to Aitkin. The note went on to read that all communication would be handled at the Aitkin field. That there was no need for her to sit in the workshop monitoring the two-way. The day was hers to use as she pleased.

That was what she was hoping would happen. But first she needed to fuel up with a bowl of cereal and a glass of juice. Then after that, stock the fanny pack and check the cellphone's battery.

Thirty minutes later Jess was one chore away from leaving. She entered the shop and went straight to the workbench. She reached across and removed a thin-bladed screwdriver from its clasp.

Moving over to the map, she used the blade to pry loose thumbtacks. She rolled the map into a cylinder, dug three rubber bands from her pocket and then slid them around the paper tube.

Moments later she was free-wheeling down the run-way's centerline. No wonder Travis had caught her so effortlessly, she bristled. Pedaling was much easier on the hard-packed middle than slogging along through thick grass near the edge.

Jess kept the wheels rolling when she reached the gravel lane. She slowed only enough to negotiate the turn. Then it was back to full speed ahead.

She crested the first rise and received the first surprise of the day. While coasting the grade between Birch and Pike, an automobile appeared over the opposite crown. Topped by a bar of red lights and several antennas, she knew in an instant—a squad car. It was too late to turn around. For certain the driver had spotted her. Besides, she really had no reason to hide. She was merely biking on a public road.

The white Crown Victoria slowed to a crawl, then braked to a standstill. The driver's door opened. A deputy, clad in two-toned brown, pushed up and out. After adjusting a wide, black belt laden with police gear, the portly man raised his hand.

Jess wasn't certain if it was a greeting or a command to halt. Whichever, she thought the best policy would be to make small talk. Drawing close, she pasted on a smile, raised her own small hand in greeting, all the while letting the wheels slow by themselves. She jumped off just as her ride was about to tip.

She walked the bike close to the car. Deciding to take the lead, she chirped, "Good morning. You surprised me. I've never seen anyone on this road before."

"Yeah, likewise. 'Cept it's not all that great a morning. If you haven't heard by now, there's a search-and-rescue operation taking place. One of the cabin kids chose to fly a little airplane in yesterday's high winds. The darn fool never returned home."

Just then the hum of an aircraft could be heard in the distance. Jess and the deputy craned their necks. Moments later a low-winged Piper roared over.

"Anyway," the deputy drawled, nodding toward the tail of the disappearing aircraft, "for a time this morning you're apt to have company back here. Besides air-planes overhead, there might be a few four-wheelers motoring about. They'll be checking out old logging trails and fire-breaks."

The man grasped the edge of the open door, ready to be on his way. As he lowered his ample backside into the car seat, he barked, "Go ahead and finish your ride. Just make certain if you see anything out of the ordinary that you tell an adult. Got it?"

"Yeah, sure," Jess muttered, upset at man's dismissive manner. Right—like she wasn't capable of communicating about a downed airplane. The guy hadn't even asked who she was, or why she was riding here in the first place.

Without comment or eye contact, Jess climbed on the bike. She thrust down on the pedals—making the rear wheel spit gravel—some of which rattled off the squad car's rear fender.

She was more than happy to be rid of such a pompous big-shot wannabe. A picture of the man's ample waistline developed in her head. A smile dimpled her smooth cheeks. Deputy Do-Right had probably been called in early, missed breakfast. The man was no doubt late for a date with a doughnut.

First on Jessie's agenda was what she mentally labeled a deer trail hollow. She'd chosen the spot for a couple reasons. Most importantly, it was the last place she and Trav had witnessed *Johnny* fly over. And she was familiar with the lay of the land.

After arriving, Jess walked the two-wheeler into the woods. Once the bike was hidden, she tugged the fanny pack around to the front. It was time to break out the bug spray.

Although she was getting more at ease being alone in the forest, she'd vowed never to become pals with its host of winged invaders. After dousing on a thick layer of insect repellent, Jess began the trek toward Pike.

* * *

Eight airplanes and sixteen sets of eyes took to the sky as an orange smudge smeared the horizon. The wind was down to a puff blowing from the northeast. Visibility was ten miles or more—nearly severe clear. If ever a day was designed for man to fly, this was it.

Pete and Travis had been second in line to lift off. Pete was already familiar with the terrain east of Pike. He was asked to repeat the previous day's route. Only today he'd do things differently. First, he'd be flying slower and lower. And second, unlike the evening's wide return flight, he was to use tight spacing on the back track.

The idea was to cover every square foot between Pike Lake and the freeway some thirty-odd miles to the east. If no sign of the ultra-light revealed itself, all planes would regroup at Aitkin. After refueling, new territory would be assigned.

"So tell me, Travis, did my snoring keep you awake?"

Travis answered without taking his gaze off the landscape. "Not at all. I got used to hearing far worse in Canada. For a time after Bob had his stroke, he slept day and night. Talk about your nose trumpet."

A patch of white caught the teen's attention. "I just spotted something. Maybe we should do a go-round, check it out."

"Will do. Get a fix on a particular tree or some other identifying feature. Pick something nearby that I can circle."

Pete nudged the throttle to ensure the Cessna carried enough airspeed to perform a steep bank. Slow, sharp turns were dicey, especially so low to the ground. There'd be little time to recover from a stall.

Satisfied, he pushed a bit of right rudder while cranking the yoke into the turn. As the wings tipped, he asked, "So what's your mark?"

"I picked a lonesome pine with a dead top. It's about a football field south of where I saw a flash of white."

The Cessna continued to wing about. Pete stared past Travis until the tree came in view. "Got it! You say the thing you saw was about a hundred yards on the other side? I'll straighten out and tip the wings just before we fly over."

"Well? What d'ya think?"

"I think we wasted fuel," Travis mumbled into the mouthpiece. "It's a deer stand. The hunter left behind his makeshift chair—an overturned white bucket.

Sorry."

Pete eased the aircraft back on course. "There's nuthin' to apologize for. You did better than good. You did great. Give a holler if you spot the smallest thing out of the ordinary. That's why we're up here."

# Chapter Twenty-Two

C H A P T E R    T W E N T Y - T W O

Max winched the dinghy up on the rollers and covered it with the tarp.

The forest was coming alive. Birds chattered from high branches, frogs croaked along the lake and cicadas strummed from unseen perches—hoping to be heard.

The man paid no heed to Mother Nature's woodland orchestra. Max's concern was the amount of light reflecting off the lake. As if triggered by a dimmer switch on the uptake, the glow was intensifying minute by minute.

He didn't have much time. The sun would be up soon, and with it a new set of problems.

The good news was that the McLean kid seemed to be doing okay. It was just a bad bump on the head, a trickle of blood and a minor concussion—nothing more.

Max had spent most of the night on the island. He'd been there, spying, when the teen first awoke. What a relief that had been!

But soon the woods would be overrun with strangers stumbling about. How would he explain pulling a kid from a sinking airplane and not reporting it?

Cripes! He'd already done more than he could talk about.

*The last thing he wanted was to be the center of attention. All he desired was to be left alone, to paint in peace.*

*Leaving the boat cushion was a slip-up for certain. And the water bottle, blanket and breakfast bars were also major mistakes. Each would raise eyebrows—encourage local constables to haul Max in for a hotseat grilling.*

*Now that he was confident the lad would come around—either be found or signal for help on his own—it was time to do a vanishing act. He needed to pack a few supplies, roll up an earth-toned tarp to use as a shelter—and head into the bush until things cooled down.*

\* \* \*

Jess traipsed along the lakefront, eyes searching for clues, her ears tuned for any incoming aircraft. She made certain to stay inside the wood-line, out of sight from both sky and water. Better to remain unidentified. If she were spotted, searchers would soon be swarming about like bees in a garden.

One deputy a day was more than enough—thank you.

Now that she was here, she felt foolish. What did she expect to find? That Buddy was alive and well—cuddled up by a campfire, chanting silly riddles and nonsense rhymes?

How dumb was that image?

That she would discover *Johnny*, tethered safely between trees, all in one piece?

Foolish—foolish—foolish.

Jess suddenly stopped. The drone of an airplane was coming her way. She spun about to face the woods, looking for a place to hide.

A hundred feet farther in, a mammoth pine towered over its neighbors. Its green boughs would rule out anyone looking straight down. The tree's broad base was more than ample to screen her slender frame.

Jess broke into a jog. Reaching the pine, she dropped behind its sturdy trunk. Within seconds of curling herself into a ball, the airplane roared overhead. As quickly as it arrived, it was gone.

Jess uncurled herself and got to her feet. After brushing off the pine needles that had attached themselves to her pants, she tipped her head to look straight up. This had to be the oldest tree in the county. The thing was enormous—wider than a round table in a Caribou Coffee cafe back home. And maybe because it was so tall—the crown was so far from the roots—a few of the top boughs had died.

Kind of sad, she mused. It was sort of like the saying "better be careful what you wish for?" Continually seeking sunbeams, the branches had perished in the very rays they'd sought.

Her neck muscles began protesting the odd viewing angle. Jess lowered her gaze and then twisted her head from side to side. What looked to be a white scrap of paper caught the corner of her eye. It's probably a paper cup or a flap of cardboard, she thought, trudging over to retrieve the item.

At first Jess was uncertain to what she was staring at. She turned the wallet-sized object over and over in her palm. Suddenly the answer struck with the impact of a bat hitting a ball out of the park. This was a piece of fiberglass—the exact color of *Johnny's* floats. And because the fragment hadn't been layered with needles, it had to be a recent deposit.

Jess dropped to her knees and scoured the area, searching for more pieces. At first glance she saw only a brown carpet of typical forest litter.

Then she focused forward, in the direction of Pike. Straight ahead lay another small sample!

She dashed over and snatched the scrap with a trembling hand. Yes—definitely the same material! She squeezed the splinter as a lump formed in her throat.

For if the fragments did belong to *Johnny*—where was the airplane? And more importantly—where was the would-be airline captain?

Could both he and the aircraft be in the water? It didn't seem possible. A person might sink. But even with a damaged pontoon, *Johnny* should have stayed afloat. A dreadful thought jumped to the front of the line. What if both pontoons had been split open? Would *Johnny* have stayed above water?

Not likely.

The lump in her throat seemed to have super-sized.

Jess dug in the pack and fumbled for the phone. She pulled it out, flipped up the cover and started to push the power button. Her finger touched the key-pad and froze.

What was the big rush? If the mental picture held true, rescue time had already run out. She didn't want to be in the area when the search team invaded. So what would it matter if she waited a few minutes before making the call? Besides, what if she was wrong? Two tiny pieces wasn't proof of anything.

Jess brushed a bug away from her face and was surprised when her fingertips stroked a wet cheek. Sniffling, she started plodding toward Pike. She'd make the call and then head for the hangar. But first she needed a moment to gather her wits.

Stumbling to the rock-and-pebbled shoreline, and not caring a hoot whose property it was, Jess made a right turn. Then she meandered along the water's edge, her mind a jumble of wild thoughts. Up ahead an old aspen had tipped toward water. The fallen tree invited her to sit.

Jess walked over to the windfall and then plopped on its trunk. She'd use the phone in a minute or two. But first she wanted to examine the evidence one more time.

She opened her hand to display the two fragments. One piece was the size of a drink coaster. The smaller sample wasn't any larger than a wallet photo. Was this enough proof something dreadful had happened?

Jess reviewed the facts. *Johnny* wore two large floats. If one was damaged, the second one would keep the ultra-light from sinking.

But what if both had holes?

That seemed more than unlikely. It seemed impossible. They'd have to be struck at the same time.

She turned sideways to stare into the forest. She could still make out the mammoth evergreen. And then the frame filled. That tree could have been the cause. The tall pine had a huge bare branch poking out parallel to the beach. Its silver-gray tint would be barely visible from above.

Oh, my God!

Buddy had probably planned on dropping down onto the lake as soon as he cleared the tree tops. For some reason he must have cut the approach short. The floats could have skipped off the invisible bough, cracking not one, but both. From there *Johnny* might have sailed far enough over water to do a cannon-ball.

Jess clenched the proof in a balled fist. A shudder shook her shoulders, a sob choked her throat. Then she closed her eyes and whispered a stuttering appeal. "Buddy . . . wherever you are . . . I hope you're happy. I know how much you loved flying. I didn't know you all that well, but you seemed like a nice guy . . . maybe a lousy poet but a great friend. I can only wish when you get to Heaven they fit you out with biggest wings available."

There was no sense putting it off any longer. The call had to be made. Jess unzipped the fanny pack and dropped in the evidence. She fumbled around the water bottle until her fingers reclaimed the cell. After flipping it open, she pressed the power button.

Who should she call first? The airport or nine-one-one?

Pondering the decision, she gaped vacantly at the hour-glass island. After a moment she let her gaze drop to the keypad. Suddenly, as if yanked by a chain, her head snapped straight up.

What had caught her eye? She refocused across the open water. There! Something was on the point where she and Travis had beached the canoe. It was a big, blue something. And it was waving.

Jess slammed the phone shut. The call could wait. After she knew Buddy was okay. Right now she needed a boat.

Her first thought was the Grumman. The canoe was sitting on shore at the McLean cabin. She'd have to bike around. No, forget that. It'd take too much time. Maybe she should phone right now. Let the grownups do their thing.

Wait. There was another way. And it was close—just a short trek along the lake. She could only hope that the hermit and his mutt were tucked in the trailer. With a bit of luck it wouldn't take long to launch. And once out on water she'd be safe. What could the guy do about it? Swim after her?

She didn't think so.

Jess began to trot, waving her hands overhead, hoping Buddy would notice.

He spotted her immediately. A bellow tracked across the water. "Jessie! Hey, Jessie! I could use some help. I was gonna swim across . . . but there's too much darn kelp."

Jess couldn't help laughing out loud. The guy didn't know when to quit. She dropped her arms, shook her head and raced on.

The first delay was figuring out how to release the cable winch. After a moment of frustration, Jess tugged the dinghy a few inches farther on land. She gained enough slack to unsnap the clip. Pushing the boat down to the water was effortless. Set on rollers, all it took was one big heave. Gravity did the rest.

Another minor delay occurred figuring out the boat's trolling motor. It turned out to be quite simple. Rotating the handle clockwise increased the power. Turning it counter-clockwise did the opposite.

The noiseless electric outboard propelled the skiff faster than Jess would have imagined. Unlike yesterday's wind, the morning breeze had barely enough vigor to rumple the surface. Soon, the gap had been closed.

As the boat neared the point, Jess eased off the power. Impatient to be picked up, Buddy paced back and forth. The flight suit displayed dark blotches where water had yet to dry.

Drawing close, Jess saw the angry bruise on her friend's forehead. It looked like a dandy. But the weirdest item was a blanket. Cardinal red, it was drooped around Buddy's broad shoulders like a Superman cape.

Hadn't she seen a similar blanket in the Airstream? Interesting.

She'd have to ask Buddy about it. He could fill in the details when they were high and dry.

But other than sleep-hair, a doozey of a bruise and a half-soaked, one-piece Elvis suit—her friend didn't look any the worse for wear.

Before the bow could even grind gravel, Buddy sloshed out to grab hold.

"I don't freaking believe it! How did you even know I was here? And where's your pal? Wow! You just stole the junkman's boat. And what's with all the airplanes today? Why aren't those guys working . . .?"

"All right, already! Please just shut up and climb in. I'll fill in the holes later."

Jess had Buddy do the dialing. While she steered toward the McLean cabin, he phoned home. The

**211**

exchange was a mishmash of nervous laughs and meek apologies. Finally he ended it by saying, "I think the phone battery is about to die. See you at the dock."

Next he punched in the number on Jessie's note. Once connected, it took a few minutes for Bob to come on line. Buddy waited patiently. He wanted to be the one to inform his mentor that he was alive and well.

By the time Buddy switched off the call, the skiff had rounded Loon Island. Jess pointed the prow toward the cabin. The entire McLean clan stood on the beach, awaiting its arrival. Buddy wondered if they were a welcoming committee or lynch mob—ready to hang him for making such a foolish flight.

Jess hung around the dock only long enough to endure hugs and pats on the back. This was Buddy's carnival. Let the family celebrate a life not lost.

She was growing antsy. The dinghy had been borrowed without permission. She didn't want to be hollered at by a hermit. The best policy, she decided, was to return the skiff pronto, before the fellow even knew it was missing. She'd cruise straight across, tug the boat on shore, retrieve the bike and race nonstop to the hangar.

Jess informed her aunt that she was leaving. At first Betty protested. After all, Jess had saved the day. But after Jess explained the situation, her aunt relented. Jess promised she'd pedal straight home and call when she got there. By then Travis might have returned. The two could ride over later in the day, when the hoopla had died down.

Jess felt strange motoring off on her own. It felt especially weird when Buddy's family trundled out on the dock to wave goodbye. With one last gesture of her own, Jess cranked the electric motor full power. Without extra weight, the skiff skipped over ripples. What would have taken thirty minutes or more to paddle was halved by battery power.

Fifteen minutes of piloting gave Jess time to reflect.

First on the mental checklist was the red blanket. She'd queried Buddy about it, but he said he was clueless. For that matter, he was oblivious to most everything.

The last thing he remembered was *Johnny* suddenly bouncing skyward, sailing over open water and then losing lift. The events that followed were sheets of blank paper.

He couldn't recall swimming to shore—didn't know how he got there. He had no idea what happened to his airplane—if it sank or floated away. After stalling out, the next thing he recollected was waking up at first light this morning.

How the blanket came to be draped over him was a mystery. He sort of remembered, but wasn't certain, of waking up the evening before. But that seemed more like a dream than a real memory.

The motor began slowing as she rounded Loon. The battery charge was on its last legs. By the time the boat was in position to beach, its speed was a turtle's pace.

This was the scary part. Before touching land, Jess shut off the motor. Then she sat still, looking and listening. Finally satisfied no one was around, she cranked the control to full power. The timeout had given the battery a chance to recoup a little juice. The dinghy spurted forward with just enough thrust to beach the bow.

Jess became a whirlwind. She scampered to the front and jumped out. Next she grabbed the bow plate, then lifted and tugged. With a rock-scraping screech, the boat slid forward far enough to stay put.

Satisfied it wouldn't drift off, Jess turned south and started sprinting along the shore.

There was a fat-wheeled bike to collect and a three- or four-mile ride to pedal.

CHAPTER TWENTY-THREE

He'd have to rough it for at least a week, maybe longer. There'd be a need for more supplies than he could tote on his back. Besides, he really didn't possess a decent pack. The solution was the cart.

Max didn't want to have to use it, but he saw no other way.

He wheeled it to the door and began loading provisions. Canned goods, a pot, pan and silverware, several moth-eaten wool blankets—he wished he owned a sleeping bag—several gallon jugs of water, a change of clothes, two lengths of rope, a hatchet and a tarp all went into garbage bags. Once filled, he snuggled them into the cart's box-like bin.

What else would be needed for an extended campout? As Max mulled over what to bring, he realized Lucky had run off.

Dang dog!

Max scanned the clearing, hoping to spot the errant mutt chasing a chipmunk. No sight of it though. But cripes, the sun was climbing higher. Already shafts of sunlight filtered through the canopy, casting yellow highlights on the forest floor.

Max experienced an uneasy chill. Searchers would soon be out and about. If not here at the camper, most certainly driving up and down on the road.

He had to get a move on. An aircraft engine hummed in the distance. Things were starting to shake loose. Several low-flying airplanes had already roared over, an event that rarely happened—especially on a weekday.

Bug lotion, he'd definitely need bug lotion. Max stepped inside and hurried to the closet. He threw open the door and realized he'd forgotten to pack the rainsuit. He pulled it off the hanger, then bent down to pick up the can of bug repellent.

Going out again, he stashed the suit and spray into one of the big bags. Then he stood brooding. Max tingled with that strange sensation a person gets when they go off knowing they've forgotten something.

But for the life of him, he couldn't think of what it was.

Time was wasting. Max closed the door, wishing he'd ordered a lockable hasp weeks earlier. There was nothing he could do about it now.

He brought the silent whistle to his mouth and blew it. Lucky never went too far away. The mutt had the nose of a bloodhound. The dog was sure to find him.

Feeling edgy, Max clutched the hitch in his good hand. With a last look at the place he called home, he began trudging into the woods, the two-wheeler at his heels.

He had a specific spot in mind. A pond created by a beaver dam. It'd be a perfect place to hide out. Right now he needed to sneak to the game trail, check for traffic and cross over into the bigger woods without being noticed. Once there he'd continue trekking until he came to an old logging road. Hopefully he'd be a mile or more in before search teams ventured about on their ATVs.

By then he should have put enough distance between himself and the lake to avoid any questions. He knew in his heart he hadn't done anything criminal. But dreadful past experience told him to get out of Dodge while he had still had the chance.

* * *

215

Like fog in the wind, the nervous tension slipped away. The jog along the lake and the hike to the bike had proved uneventful. Besides, Jess considered, how dangerous could the hermit be? Who else had the opportunity to give Buddy food, water and a blanket? The man couldn't be all bad.

It was pretty strange that he hadn't notified a single soul though. The least he could have done was ferry Buddy to the mainland. But he hadn't. That fact bothered Jess.

So why hadn't he made the effort?

Had one of her first impressions hit the bull's-eye? That the fellow was wanted by the long arm of the law—that he needed to stay out of sight?

Or did Buddy's suggestion ring true? On the night of the Honda rescue, Buddy said that all the hermit wanted was to be left alone. That maybe he was a true loner and was frightened of human contact.

Breathing hard from the run, Jess placed her shoulders against a tree, then lowered herself to the leafy carpet. She'd catch her wind before wheeling the bike to the lane. Once there, it'd be nonstop until arriving at the hangar.

She wondered, now that the search had been called off, if Trav was on his way home. It wouldn't take long in an airplane, probably less time than it would take her to pump the pedals. No, that wasn't quite right. It wasn't his home. This wasn't where Travis lived. His house was way up north, near the Canadian border.

Anyway, Pete probably had other things to do. Certainly he'd want drop off his student pilot before heading home himself.

But then, why did she even care where or what Travis was doing. With all the activity this morning, she'd misplaced the anger. Recalling how Travis had taken flight without so much as a "see ya later," some of the earlier irritation resurfaced.

In one fluid motion, Jess jumped to her feet. She grabbed up the handlebars and started stomping toward the lane.

She spat words to herself. "Get over it! Get over it, girl! Why do you care what a kid from East Deer Tick chooses to do? It ain't like he's your boyfriend or anything."

Minutes later, Jess approached the road. She laid the bike in tall weeds, her head poking out past the brush-line. The narrow cut appeared empty. Good. There was no one to bug her, grill her with questions.

Picking up the two-wheeler, she pushed it onto the gravel and prepared to hop on. Looking down, as a smile played her mouth, she realized she hadn't been the only traveler on the trail. A host of heart-shaped deer tracks imprinted the soft-sandy shoulder. One set was large, the other tiny. Probably a doe with its fawn, she thought.

She cast her eyes across the opening. No tracks showed in the road's gravel-packed middle. But she could see more imprints on the opposite side. Apparently, despite her presence, deer were still frequenting the game trail. She liked that her scent hadn't frightened the gentle creatures elsewhere.

Jess threw a leg over the center bar, placed a foot on the pedal and prepared to push off. She hesitated, gazing at the opposite shoulder again. More than hoof prints entered the woods. There were also line-like tracks—too skinny to have been created by a four-wheeler.

Jess slid off the seat and walked the bike across. The marks were familiar. And she knew what laid them down—a two-wheeled bike cart—no doubt the one stashed behind the Airstream.

The imprints looked fresh. So recent it was damp where the tires had pushed aside the soft sand aside. She wondered if the tracks were made coming or going. Unlike deer prints with pointy double toes, tires didn't leave clues of the direction of travel.

A crow cawed, momentarily startling her. She swung her gaze back and forth, checking for vehicles. Empty.

Returning her stare to the tire prints, she realized something was missing. There were two side-by-side tracks, not three. The cart wasn't being towed by a bike. That meant the man was on foot. Like deer prints, boot soles point forward.

Jess cocked her head and listened for human activity. Hearing only birds and cicadas, she leaned the bike against a bush. With a last nervous scan up and down the lane, she stepped onto the game path. Unlike the route leading to the lake, the vegetation hadn't been crushed by ATV wheels.

It appeared the narrow trail had been trampled daily by four-footed travelers. Deer had come and gone so often their sharp hooves had cleaved the topsoil. A thin brown line meandered around aspen and birch, disappearing where it snaked over a slight rise.

How far did she dare go? And the question was—why? Because she was curious, that's why, she told herself. She wouldn't go far, not like the day she found the travel trailer. She'd keep the road in clear view.

It didn't take but five steps to learn the direction of travel. Embossed into soft soil was a boot print. The same size track she'd found the first day. Toes pointed into the forest, not out.

Why was the hermit, artist, thief, or whatever he was heading into the woods? Jess stood gazing down at the diminutive boot cast. She took a step forward to place her own shoe alongside. They were nearly identical, the imprint being slightly longer than her own.

Jess spun about and dashed to the bike. She slid back

the binders holding the map tube tight to the handle bar. Then she dropped to one knee, unrolled the thick paper and placed it flat on the ground.

Using a finger, she traced the route from the airport to the "No Trespassing" property. Then she backed her finger a few inches and held it there. This, she thought, is where I am right now. She slid her finger toward the top. And this is where the tracks lead.

Other than a couple of dotted lines depicting abandoned logging trails, and a few spots of blue representing ponds, that part of the map was featureless. No farms, no buildings, no roads.

So what's the attraction? Did the guy have another horde hidden away? Maybe a second trailer, this one *really* tucked away in the woods?

It might be fun to find out. Jess thought of Travis. He loved putting his tracking skills to work. Maybe this afternoon they could bike back here and take a nature hike.

Then she remembered. She was supposedly miffed by his sudden departure. Jess rolled the map and secured it to the bike again. A grin creased her face. Yeah, like if she told him how rude he'd been, he'd fall over backward saying "sorry." Travis might be a lean, mean tracking machine, but when it came to girl skills, the kid was clueless.

* * *

With a gentle breeze and bright sun, the day warmed. Halfway home, under a blue sky just beginning to add white frill, Jess stopped to shed the sweatshirt. Even so, dressed in jeans and T-shirt, by the time she parked the bike, beads of sweat glistened on her forehead.

Entering the workshop, she made a beeline for the fridge. Although the shop was cool, she held the refrigerator open to savor its cold air.

She was bent at the waist, head inside the big white box, a can of soda pressed to her temple, when the shop's interior door swung open.

"Whatcha doin'? Trying to air condition the whole shop?"

Jess hadn't heard Travis enter. Startled, she shot up straight, ready to launch the soda can.

"Oh, it's just you," she said, lowering the container. She closed the door, traipsed across to the recliner and flopped down.

Travis hopped on a stool, a puzzled look on his face. "What d'ya mean . . . 'It's just you?' Who were you expecting . . . a reporter from the New York Times? A camera crew from the cities?"

Jess took a long pull of cola, swallowed, and then asked, "Why do you say that? What's a reporter got to do with anything?"

Travis slid off the stool and then trudged across the room. He opened the refrigerator and peered inside. "Good thing I prefer root beer. I think you just nabbed the last cola. You better put some more in after awhile. It's supposed to warm up into the eighties tomorrow."

Jess took another swig, and then set the can down on the floor. "Hey buster. You didn't answer my question. Why would I expect a camera crew?"

Travis popped the top on a can of root beer, brought the can to his mouth and swallowed several gulps. He lowered the can, sporting a toothy grin. "Yeah, like you don't know."

Jess sat straight in the chair, then stomped a foot. "Know what? What are you jabbering about?"

He finally caught on. She really didn't get it. "Everyone's calling you a hero. Or should I say heroine?"

It was Jessie's turn to look perplexed. "What'd I do? All

I did was borrow the trailer guy's boat, ferry Buddy to his dock."

Travis shook his head, a shaggy mane in need of trimming. "You did what a squadron of airplanes and army of ATVs didn't do. You found Buddy."

Jess frowned. "People think I'm a hero? Why? It wasn't like he was lost. And I didn't really do much. I just biked around to that game trail we used the other day. Buddy's the one that spotted me."

She hesitated. "Hey, I shouldn't even be having this conversation. I'm mad at you."

Travis had returned to the stool perch. He did a quick double take—head back, chin down. "Mad? Why would you be mad at me? What did I do?"

Jess pushed up and out of the recliner. Then she marched over and stood so her face was directly in front of Travis. "I thought we were partners in this trailer guy thing. So naturally, when Buddy came up missing, I thought we'd be partners in that, too."

She paused for effect, placing a hand on her hip, one foot tapping the concrete. "But no . . . first chance you get to take off and partner up with someone else . . . poof . . . you disappear."

This was all news to Travis. He didn't know what to say, so he said nothing at all. He merely gulped. The tension grew. Except for the tick of the clock and the hum of the fridge, the room fell quiet. Jess continued staring, eyeball to eyeball, one foot tapping a soft, near-silent beat.

Travis broke off eye contact, suddenly counting ceiling tiles instead. Jess knew she'd made her point. She took a backward step, cracked a smile and broke the impasse.

"You know, I would expect you to go up with this Pete guy. Thing is, you never even asked me to tag along. Or for that matter even uttered a simple 'see ya later.' You just ran off."

"Jeez, Jess," Travis stammered. "I didn't think you'd want to go. Besides, Pete's plane is pretty much a two-seater. There's a child seat in the rear, but I didn't think you'd want to sit in it. I'm sorry. I didn't think you'd care."

"Are you really, *really* sorry. Or are you apologizing just to get on my good side?" she asked.

Releasing a breath, Travis flashed a sheepish grin. He looked directly at Jess and admitted, "A little of both, I guess. But then I'm not the big shot hero, ahh . . . heroine, here. You're the one whose mug will be on the front page of the local paper."

"Not if I can help it. Right now I need to call Aunt Betty, let her know I'm home. Then, my tall shaggy-haired friend, I have an idea how we can spend the rest of the day. That is, if you can fix that bike chain you broke when you tried to cheat me out of first place."

\* \* \*

After scrounging through one of a dozen spare parts bins, Travis came up with a repair link for the bike chain. While he was fixing his ride, Jess fixed them a couple of sandwiches and packed a few snacks. By the time Bob drove in with Betty, the teens were ready to roll.

Their next task was to persuade her aunt and uncle. Aunt Betty thought Jess should hang around and give the reporters a chance to do an interview, take a few pictures.

Bob looked worn out, in dire need of a nap. But knowing his young pal was alive and well was written all over his face. He kept breaking out in a grin.

The old man wasn't so certain Jess needed to stay put. He knew she didn't relish being the center of attention. His Jazzi was a go-getter, a doer, not a braggart. If the lass chose to be elsewhere when deputies or reporters stopped by, so be it. They could catch the facts without splashing her picture across the front page.

After congratulating Jess on a job well done, he said,

"Sweetie, remember the note I left? It said the day was yours to do whatever you wished. If you want to spend the afternoon with Trav, I say go ahead. Your aunt and I can answer the door—give whoever stops by the details on what happened."

"He means how brave you were," Betty said, glowing with pride. "But I think my old coot of a husband is right. If you don't want your picture in the paper, go ahead, run along. Enjoy the rest of this beautiful summer day."

# Chapter Twenty-Four

C H A P T E R      T W E N T Y - F O U R

Max strung a rope between a pair of poplars. On aching legs he hobbled to the wagon. He opened a bag, reached in and tugged out the tarp. The plan was to drape the vinyl over the cord, then secure the four corners—instant shelter.

He'd been careful about choosing this particular campsite. After striking the abandoned logging road, he'd followed it a mile or more before veering off. He knew the overgrown trail brushed one end of a beaver pond. He'd left the cut just as it started a southerly curve around the marshy side.

His goal was midway to the north end. From that vantage point he would hear any passing ATVs. The riders would be busy steering around the swamp grass, saplings and rotting logs. No way would they spot this crude shelter. Unless they were to stop and circle the pond on foot, he was out of harm's way.

Once the tarp was in place, he returned to the cart. This time he pulled out blankets and a roll of thin plastic. By then he was breathing hard and needed a rest. Other camp chores could wait. Tugging the tiny cart over and around the scratchy brush, bumpy stumps and windfalls had proved to be a grueling task.

Max dropped to his knees in front of the opening. He unrolled the plastic and spread it out on a layer of leaves.

*Next he flipped open one of the blankets, which he laid on top of the moisture barrier. It was almost time for a snooze.*

*But first Max let his eyes roam over the pond. In the center, budding up like a fat brown igloo, stood the mud-and-stick mound of a beaver lodge.*

*He let his gaze drift along shore. The tree-chewers had been hard at work. Looking like giant "pick up sticks," trees of all sizes littered the gentle slope. A few stalks still clung to green sprouts. Recent cuttings, Max mused. Others had been trimmed of all their branches, which were no doubt impaled in the pond's soft bottom—snack food for the frozen months.*

*He stared across the water, imagining how an earth-toned tarp would appear to prying eyes. Unless one stopped, trekked to the water's edge and knew where to look—nearly invisible.*

*Max crawled inside the open-ended cover. He stretched out, relaxed his aching bones flat to the blanket and closed his eyes.*

*A sharp bark sounded in the distance. The man smiled— Lucky. Although the dog was missing an ear and part of a leg, his nose was still a wonder to behold.*

*Max nodded off, knowing in a matter of minutes he'd have welcome company.*

\* \* \*

Jess unrolled the map and spread the chart flat. As she had done several hours earlier, she placed a finger on her uncle's airport.

She nudged Travis with an elbow. "Pay attention. I realize you know how to read a map. Probably better than me. But by tracing the route over to here, you'll get an idea of how big these woods are."

Enjoying the close contact, Travis returned the bump. "Don't have to look. I already know. It's four miles to the next road."

The teens were shoulder to shoulder, resting on hands and knees. Today's ride had been peaceful. In what seemed like no time, they'd reached the site of previous visits—the hollow with its now-familiar game trail. Now, under a bright blue sky, a warm breeze rustling the leaves overhead, Travis recited a few simple jokes. Jess tried not to laugh, but they were so corny she couldn't help herself.

The one that caused her to giggle the loudest was the line that went; "Did you hear the one about the skeleton who rattles into a bar and orders a beer and mop?"

She'd waited for the punch line before picturing the image. Then she laughed so hard, tears trickled down her cheeks.

Jess pushed up so that she was resting only on her knees. "How d'ya know that? You haven't even looked yet."

Travis lifted so he was again the taller of the two. "Pete and I flew over here a half-dozen times, coming and going. It's mostly flat-land woods."

He nodded at the shadowy forest. Because the land had been logged sometime in the last decade or two, the new growth was thin-stalked and closely clustered. Compared to the burly stalks filling the "No Trespassing" property, the trees here resembled runway models—thin and willowy.

"Back in a ways there's a few ponds, nothing big. Up to about the size of a football field. And the road beyond really isn't much of anything. It's just like this one."

He nodded again. "Just a skinny cut through a sea of trees . . . no houses . . . no farms or fields . . . mostly scrawny second-or third-growth aspen."

The crunch of rubber on gravel wafted from the far side of the rise. Travis jumped to his feet. "Come on, let's get off the road. Nobody needs to know we're here."

He swept up the Schwinn and at a fast trot, rallied it into the dim forest. Jess followed right on his heels.

Twenty yards in, both dropped their bikes. Then each scrambled behind a bush.

A white Ford adorned with a gold star rolled by. Jess recognized the driver. She'd met the man shortly after sunup. It was the rude officer, or as she'd tagged him in her memory—Deputy Doughnut.

Travis spoke first. "What d'ya think that's about?"

Before Jess had a chance to reply, Travis held a finger to his lips—indicating she should keep quiet. Jess listened. Another car was coming. Decorated exactly like the first one, the cruiser sped by trailing a dust plume.

As if the deputies had super human hearing, Jess whispered, "I have an idea where they're headed. I bet they're going to pick up the trailer guy. By now Buddy's probably been questioned. No doubt he mentioned the blanket and food. That probably raised a few eyebrows. The cops will want to know who, when and why."

Eyes still focused toward the road, Travis stepped around the shrub and across the path. Standing next to Jess, he said, "I don't get what you mean. Buddy's safe at home. *Johnny's* at the bottom of Pike. But until the McLeans secure an okay from the state, that's where the plane will stay . . . at least for the time being. I don't see why the sheriff would be involved."

Jess stood and adjusted her bulging fanny pack. Weighted with sandwiches, water bottles, the phone and bug spray, it had a tendency to slip down on her narrow hips.

Satisfied, she lifted her face as if worshiping an unseen sun. The overhead foliage was too dense for rays to penetrate. She sniffed the air, taking in the dank odor that reminded her of a musty basement.

After a long moment, she lowered her gaze and asked, "What time is it? With all that's gone on today, it seems like it should evening by now."

Travis glanced at the watch strapped around his left wrist. A month ago, the timepiece had been a gift for his fifteenth birthday. But with a water-stained band and scratched crystal, it looked years older. The worn-out appearance was a result of the Canadian adventure. It'd been in and out of the lake a dozen different times, been slept on, and on several occasions, dropped on a sandy beach. Travis thought that it was a triumph of modern technology that it even worked.

"Hmm, let's see quarter after two"

"Really? I figured at it was at least four, maybe later."

Travis reached up and ripped a twig from an overhanging branch. Stripping the leaves off, he stuck the stalk in the corner of his mouth. He grinned and said, "Then you'd been wrong, wouldn't cha? And I could mark it in my the notebook."

* * *

"What time is it now?" Jess asked, worming the fanny pack around to the front.

"Five after three. But Jess, both of us can't be using this watch. It'll be too hard on it, break the main spring or wear out the battery."

"Ha! Keep it up and you'll be drinking pond scum."

After unzipping the pack, she poked a hand inside and pulled out a water bottle.

The trackers were resting on the weathered surface of a windfall—an old poplar that long ago had shed its thin bark.

Off to their left, through a jungle of sumac and buck-thorn, Travis could make out the shimmer of water. He didn't need the map to know where they were. This pond was familiar.

Thinking Buddy may have attempted an emergency

landing, he and Pete had made several fruitless passes around the pond's perimeter.

Before they'd sat down, following the trailer man's route had been, as Travis had put it, "a piece of cake." Impressions made by the two-wheeled cart were as easy to read as a first grade textbook.

The only confusion came where the man had left the overgrown logging trail. The teens had been trekking at a brisk clip—nearly a jog. Neither would admit that a slower pace might be more appropriate. So they'd passed by the man's detour.

Not until Travis realized there weren't any wheel prints did they stop. And when they did, through the trees, Jess had caught a glimpse of something shiny. When she pointed it out, Travis bent low, peered around tree trunks and saw it, too.

They'd held a conference. Jess thought they should back track, and pick up where they'd last seen the wheel marks.

Travis wanted to stay on the trail a little longer—at least to where it wound around the water. He reasoned that if the man was planning on hiding out, the guy wouldn't set up shop right on the logging cut. Anyone coming by, whether on foot or four-wheeler, would spot his camp in a heartbeat.

Travis had further reasoned that the man would veer off, but not go far. The cart would be a bugger to pull through untamed woods. He ended his side of the disagreement by saying, "at least that's what I'd do."

So they trekked another hundred yards. When Travis was certain the trail bordered the marsh, he called a timeout.

Jess uncapped the container and took a long drink, draining the bottle almost to the halfway mark. She wiped her mouth with the back of her hand, and then recapped the top.

Travis looked on with envy. "Please tell me you brought more than one."

With deliberate movement, Jess tucked the bottle into the pack. "If I did, what's it worth to you?"

Travis thought it over. "I'll report the time every fifteen minutes and on the hour. You won't even have to ask."

"Deal," Jess smirked, pulling out a second bottle. "I'm kinda of hungry. What d'ya say we eat our sandwiches?"

Travis nodded. It didn't take long for the hungry teenagers to polish off the food Jess had made. Finished with the late lunch of peanut butter and jelly sandwiches, Travis got up to stretch. "Are you about ready?"

Jess stood and readjusted the pack. "Ready for what?"

She trained her gaze toward the tangle of thorny brush sprouting between the logging cut and hints of unreachable water. "Please don't tell me we're gonna try going through that maze. We'll be lucky not to lose an eye."

"Nah. I think we should back track until we hit higher ground. Then head for the far side of the pond at an angle. From what I can tell, this is the marshy end. I'm guessing that across the way trees grow right to the water. Hop up on the trunk and look over the top of the brush. You'll see a slight ridge where the land rises. Betcha that's where we'll find the hermit."

After fifteen minutes of stop-and-go picking their way without a path, the teens stood at an opening. Evidence of the flat-tailed water rats' work was everywhere. A helter-skelter jumble of downed aspens lay on the ground. Near their ragged bases, broken points of tooth-pocked stumps poked through clusters of fresh green sprouts.

Travis nodded toward the beaver lodge. "I've never seen one that size. It looks big enough to rent out rooms."

Jess was digging in the pack for bug spray. Both had

shed their outer sweatshirts. Before leaving home, she'd swapped the white one for a red, half-sleeved jersey.

Jess found the can and sprayed a liberal dose on her forearms. "Don't the bugs get to you?" she asked, holding the can behind her neck. She closed her eyes and pressed the release. A mist of spray enveloped her head.

"Yuck! For sure I'm washing my hair tonight."

Travis laughed, "Was that a joke? Do the bugs bug me? Yeah, they do. But I try to ignore 'em unless they're really bad. You know, when they swarm around my head in clouds and I start inhaling 'em."

Jess dropped the can in the bag and wiggled the pack around to her side. "What about the bites? Don't they hurt and swell up?"

Travis removed the Twins cap and ran a hand through his unkempt hair. "Sometimes . . . if they happen to nip the right spot. But most times I don't even feel 'em. I guess it's my thick elephant skin. They don't bother my dad, much either. Or maybe we just don't taste as sweet as you."

Jess didn't know where that remark was headed so she changed the subject.

She fixed her gaze on the pond. "You're right. That lodge is a lot bigger than the one where we camped in Canada. But don't beavers like to block up running water? You know, like a creek or stream?"

Travis shuffled closer to the jumble of trees. "Yeah, I guess when they have to make a pond to store food for winter. But this spot would be like prime real estate to a beaver. The pond's already here. And with all these tender trees," he said waving a hand in both directions, "it's beaver heaven."

He started toward the water, moving left and right around stumps and logs. Jess picked her way after him, careful to look where she stepped. The closer they crept to the shoreline, the more jumbled the logs and branches became.

Finally they were close enough to see the entire pond without trees and brush blocking their view. Travis hopped up on a log. He jumped down just as quickly. "I was right! The guy's right over there," he motioned, pointing at the woods near a second cut-over area.

"He made a tent with one of those camouflage tarps. It looks like he's taking a nap."

"You're kidding, right? Let me see."

Nimble as a gymnast on a balance beam, Jess mounted the windfall, tiptoed to its highest point and stretched tall. After taking a quick glance she jumped down, nodding.

"I saw him. His cart, too. Come on, let's get closer. I want to get a good look at his face."

CHAPTER TWENTY-FIVE

*It felt, oh, so good to relax, to nod off. The all-night vigil with the McLean kid had sapped Max's reserves. Not that he ever had much to spare in the first place.*

*He'd just nodded off when Lucky came shambling into camp. Happy to be reunited, the mutt performed a face washing. Max was awakened by a slobbering kiss.*

*As he was swiping dog drool from his cheek, it struck him. He hadn't packed a mask.*

*Well, it was too late now. No way was he going to hike back to the Airstream. Besides, he was well off the beaten path. There was no need for a cover-up. The only eyes would be those of birds, squirrels, chipmunks and—maybe if Lucky didn't bark—a beaver or two.*

*Wild creatures never took offense to his blemished features.*

*It was only humans that gawked in sympathy or turned their heads in disgust. And he'd learned since leaving the city, he didn't need other people's pity.*

*Max scratched the dog behind the ears. Then in his fire-scarred voice, the man whispered a few comforting words. He lay back again and closed his eyes, knowing Lucky would warn him if they had uninvited company.*

*Max had just drifted off when he was startled awake. Was the shriek real, or had he been dreaming?*

*He lay still, straining his ears. Had there been a friendly yip—not the warning bark Lucky used for strangers?*

*Whatever, he'd have to check it out. Rolling over, Max crawled out from beneath the shelter. He slowly pushed to his feet. It took a moment to regain his balance. Once certain he wouldn't topple, he stared toward the pond. Everything looked the same—greenish, algae- tinted surface, big almond-colored mound—cattails circling the shoreline.*

*Looking left he almost had a heart attack. Kneeling on one knee—no farther than fifty feet away—was a girl.*

*Willowy build, short black hair, sand-colored skin—it had to be her! The snoop who'd caused him to transfer the treasures.*

* * *

The plan was to creep in from behind using the woods as cover. And if they were discovered, run like a storm wind toward the afternoon sun. It'd be the quickest way to hit the logging trail.

Once they backed away from the beaver cut, visibility became limited. Being a young forest, what the trees lacked in size, they made up for in numbers. Patches of bushy plants competed for sunlight. Jess was content to let Travis lead the way.

The fact there were no unique features to follow didn't seem to bother him. He moved through and around obstacles as if he had a GPS implant.

Left here on her own, she'd probably have a panic attack. This wasn't anything like the island adventures. By comparison, surrounded by water, those forested knolls were safety zones.

The lane they'd hiked in from was more than a mile to the west; the next road nearly three to the east. So it was no mistake Jess followed on his heels—so near,

Travis could hear her every breath.

He didn't mind. In fact, he enjoyed showing off his trekking skills. This little section of flat terrain was child's play compared to the wilderness where he lived. There a person could hike for days without running across another living soul. As long as the sun didn't fall out of the sky, he knew which way to go.

What did bother Travis was that they were spying on the man. For whatever reason, it was obvious the guy wanted to be left alone. They'd discussed it earlier. How bad could the man be? Although the hermit hadn't notified anyone, he had watched over Buddy—even left food and water.

Jess had described the big bump on Buddy's forehead. She said *Johnny* had gone down in deep water. That Buddy didn't remember swimming to shore. Add it all up, and the masked man might be the real hero. It was possible that the fellow had saved Buddy from a watery grave.

So why was Jess so enthused to catch an "up close and personal" look? Cripes, just days earlier she'd been scared out of her gourd by the guy.

Travis didn't know the answer—didn't have a clue.

Reaching the crest of a slight rise, the young outdoors-man stopped. He raised an arm and pointed.

All Jess saw was a jumble of moss-covered rocks scattered about in room-sized cavity.

"What?"

"We're not the first to stand here. You're looking at remains of what used to be somebody's home. It was probably a one-room cabin dating back to the early logging days."

Jess shuffled closer to the bowl-like depression. Stunted saplings sprouted randomly from its center.

"Really? Once upon a time somebody actually lived here? Out in the middle of nowhere?"

**235**

Travis clumped alongside, then stood with his hands in his pockets. "Yep. It's hard to believe but back in the eighteen hundreds, there were little cabins all over this part of the state. What's more amazing is much of northern Minnesota was once a sea of pines. Trees so tall that you'd swear they touched the clouds."

Jess pictured the old sentinel standing guard near the edge of the "No Trespassing" property- the evergreen that Buddy's ultra-light had clipped. The tree was humongous, towering over its neighbors like a skyscraper.

Jess turned to face Travis. "So where'd they all go?"

Sensing a chance to impress her, Travis continued matter-of-factly. "The lumber barons cut 'em down, almost every cotton-pickin' tree."

Peering straight into her brown eyes, he said, "You see, back then settlers could get free land. But they had to promise to clear it, build a cabin and live there for a period of time. It was called homesteading."

He was getting in the swing of it, recalling one of the few history lessons that'd held his interest.

"The trees were too large for any one family to tackle. So what the timber companies did was have settlers lay a claim, sign up with the government."

He hesitated and looked skyward. A small cloud had covered the sun, erasing the forest floor of all shadow. It soon passed, and the woodland took on light.

"Lumberjack crews would come in and harvest the wood. If the settlers built a shelter, stuck around for a few years, the land was theirs to do whatever."

He paused again, this time to check if she was listening.

Jess nodded for him to continue.

"Of course the land was lousy for farming, although most folks tried anyway. Mostly the homesteaders were left with fields full of giant . . . stumps."

Travis pulled his hand from his pocket and looked at his watch. "It's ten after three. We better get a move on if we want to make it home in time for supper."

Jess was impressed but she didn't say so. Instead she beat around the bush. "Thanks for the history lesson, Mr. Larsen. Maybe I'll read up on it when I'm back in school. In the meantime, how much farther before we bump into 'you know who'?"

After a few more minutes of zigzagging, they broke out in the second beaver cut. It was a duplicate of the one they'd left a little earlier. Aspens lay this way and that, quarter-sized wood chips scattered around pointy stumps.

Travis had purposely overshot the campsite. He hadn't wanted to break out of the woods directly behind the man's shelter. That wouldn't have allowed a safety zone.

Travis put a finger to his lips and then pointed. He bent close to Jessie's ear and whispered. "The guy's right over there, on the far side of this opening."

Jess rose up on tiptoes. At first she didn't see it. The camouflage cover blended well with the background.

After a moment she nodded, then relaxed. "Got it. He's still tucked under the tarp. All I can see are his feet. Come on, let's get a little closer. I want a get a better look."

Travis stood his ground. "Nope. This is as far I'm going. If he wanted company, he wouldn't be hiding out. Besides, I don't get it. A few days ago you were scared stiff just to be in the same county. Now you want to sneak up on the guy."

Jess gazed at the ground, toeing soggy wood chips. When she looked up, there was a set to her jaw.

"Hate to admit it, but you're right. That day, when I lost my shoe, I thought I was going to die.

"But that was then and this is now. I've given it a lot of thought. The man's not a threat to us. If anything, it's the other way around. For some reason he's terrified of people. And I think he wears a mask because he doesn't want anyone to see his face. I'd like to know the reason why."

Jess studied the chewed-over opening, seeking the least-littered path to close the gap. There looked to be two possibilities. One route would mean circling near the pond and then sneaking toward the tent. The snag in taking that approach was she'd be out in the open. There would be no easy avenue of escape.

The other possibility was to follow the woodline along the edge of the cut. If discovered and she had to bolt, she could run into the woods. But that course also had a drawback. The shelter was much closer to the woods than the water. Her approach would have to be as quiet as a church mouse during the pastor's silent prayer.

Jess pondered for a few seconds and then made the choice. She pursed her lips and shrugged her shoulders. Without further discussion, she began a meandering track toward higher ground—treading softly around gnawed branches.

Travis stood quiet, watching her walk away. He didn't approve of what Jess was doing. They'd found the guy, why not leave it at that? If later they learned that the man was a fugitive, they could pass the info on to the sheriff.

All of a sudden Travis became aware of where he was—out in the open—an easy mark. If Jess snapped a twig or kicked a rock, the man could wake up. He'd stick his nose outside to find out what made the noise. Travis wet his lips and whistled a bird-like "wee-up, wee-up."

Jess stopped mid-stride and spun on her heel. Her face contorted in "what d'ya want?" expression. Travis pointed at his chest, then toward the forest. He dangled two fingers in a walking motion.

Jess got it. She pointed at a spot behind the tent. Then she wiggled two fingers fast to designate running.

Travis nodded and trotted toward the woods. Jess had indicated that he should come around from behind, staying in the foliage. Once she got a good look, she'd meet him there.

The whistle was barely audible to a human ear. But to the dog, the "wee-up" was loud as a foghorn. The dog recognized its origin—humans.

Lucky rose up on three legs, hop-stepped past his sleeping master and stuck his snoot out of the tarp.

The mutt caught a whiff of a visitor near camp. He started to yip the alarm bark, but cut it short. The odor was familiar—the nice human on the island—the game of tag with the tennis shoe girl. Rather than woofing out a full warning, Lucky yipped lightly and bounded toward the scent.

Jess figured she'd come about as close as she dared. The tarp was scarcely a softball pitch away. She was near enough to hear the man's gruff snores. Good news—the man was sleeping.

The problem being she wasn't in line with the opening—couldn't see inside. To get a good peek, she'd have to sneak more to the right.

From where she stood, that wasn't possible—unless she crawled over the sprawling branches of a chewed-over aspen. That would be risky, make too much noise. The guy would be startled and wake up.

She turned to check the area at her rear. There was a path of sorts. She'd need to retreat a few steps, pussyfoot around the dropped tree, then avoid tripping on its stubby, tooth-chiseled stump. Heart pounding with excitement, Jess started padding alongside the tree trunk. Rustling sounds suddenly came rushing from behind.

Jess whirled about, emitting a frightened shriek. She threw up her hands, ready to fend off man or beast. The breath she'd gulped was expelled in relief. It was only the three-legged dog.

Breathing easier, Jess dropped to one knee. As the multi-colored mutt tottered close, she held out a palm as a peace offering. Lucky wobbled to a stop, stretched out a burr-infested neck and extended a pink tongue.

Jess let out a second soft sigh, realizing that the dog hadn't barked. How great was that? She extended the palm over the dog's head and started scratching.

Lucky thought he'd died and gone to dog heaven. He dropped flat and closed his eyes. Jess was so focused petting the dog she neglected to keep an eye on the shelter.

With the angry bellow of a thunderclap, a booming voice hollered. "It's you again! Why can't you stay away, leave me alone?"

Petrified, Jess sprung to her feet, ready to run like a deer. Yet she didn't move. She remained fixed in place. At first glance Jess thought the guy was wearing a Halloween disguise. But then she grasped it wasn't a mask at all.

One side of the fellow's face looked normal—graying sideburns, beard stubble, tan cheek.

The opposite half was a nightmare. That side bore grotesque scars. Looking like melted plastic, reddish-orange ropes of scarred flesh curled from the man's forehead down to his neck.

Another clue fell into place. He wasn't dangerous. He hid out because he was ashamed to be seen.

The man yelled a second time. "Are you satisfied? Or would you like to take a picture? Now that you know I'm a freak, just go back to wherever you came from and leave me be."

Jess felt herself flush. She'd been staring, probably with an open mouth at that. How rude!"

She had to say something, anything to let the poor fellow

know she meant him no harm. "Ah, ah . . . I'm so sorry. Really I am. It's just that my pal and I know what you did. You saved our friend. We just wanted to say thank you. We think you're a brave man, a hero."

Standing so near, Jess could gauge the man's size. The faded jeans and an oversized flannel shirt had probably been purchased in the teen department. Both hung loose on his pocket-sized frame.

Jess experienced another wave of guilt. Besides having to endure the humiliation of a disfigured face, the man's size was probably also an issue. Dripping wet, he couldn't weigh much more than she did—one hundred fifteen. Both Travis and Buddy would tower over the guy like a pair of redwoods to a stunted birch. For that matter, she was at least his height, maybe an inch or two taller.

The man fired a third barrage. "I don't what you're talking about. You've had your fun and laughs. Now scram!"

He started to turn and then remembered his dog. "Lucky, get your tail over here! You are a sorry excuse for a watchdog."

The dog got up grudgingly. With baleful eyes he stared up at Jess. He turned to look at his master. Reluctantly, with stubby tail tucked tight, he started a slow hobble to the one who provided food and shelter.

The initial shock of seeing the man's face was past. Sympathy replaced fear and apprehension. Jess wanted to console the guy, convince him she meant him no ill will. "Listen, I know what you must think. That I'm some sort of teenage delinquent. But really mister, it's not like that at all."

Max didn't acknowledge Jessie's words. Except for turning sideways to hide his scars, the man hadn't moved. "Come on dog! Get over here. Now!"

Fearing a scolding, the closer he got, the slower Lucky limped. Stopping an arm's length away, the dog lowered its head and dropped to its haunches.

Growing desperate, Jess tried another tack. "You probably won't believe me. But I think I can help you."

Max had heard enough. If the girl wouldn't get out of his space, he'd get out of hers. What the brash teenager didn't need to know was that he had more to fear from her, than she did from him. But that was something Jess had already sensed.

Max flashed on his weekly forays into vacant cabins, pilfering odds and ends. And then there was yesterday's fiasco with the McLean kid. He didn't need a dialogue with Miss Snoopy. The less she knew—the better for him.

"Ha! You're nothing but a teenage busybody. Go mind your own business."

Using a much friendlier tone, Max spoke to the mutt. "Come on dog. Let's take a hike. Maybe when we return, we'll have some peace and quiet."

Jess picked up on the change of voice. Ragged as Lucky looked, it was apparent the fellow loved the animal. And it appeared the dog shared the feeling. Probably the only warm receptions either ever got.

She was ready to depart, but would make one last stab. "Look, I peeked inside your Airstream. Sorry, but at the time I though it was empty. Anyway, I can't believe what you did with an artist's brush. You're marvelous, so talented. I could help get you discovered."

Max turned to face the cheeky teenager. Even from a distance, Jess could see she'd overstepped the man's patience. His hideous-looking scar tissue blossomed red with anger.

"Discovered! Why the damnation would I want to be discovered? Haven't you been listening? Or are you just stupid?"

With that Max turned and began a weaving shuffle

toward the beaver pond. Lucky seemed confused. First he looked at the retreating form of his master. Then he stared at the kind human who scratched behind his ears. With a last look that implied, "sorry, he's the one who feeds me," the dog followed in his master's footsteps.

Realizing she'd made a terrific blunder, Jess yelled down the slope. "You should want to get discovered because you might become rich. You might have more than enough money to fix your face."

Oh Jeez! She'd done it again. She'd said more than she should have. Jess added a few more syllables, hoping to soften the intent. In a loud "trying out for cheerleading" voice, she yelled, "I mean that's only if you wanted to do something about your scars. Because I don't have a problem with the way they are now."

Jess stood and stared as man and dog tottered toward the pond. After a moment of soul searching, she turned and headed for the woods. She'd made a fool of herself. Hopefully Travis hadn't caught the exchange.

# Chapter Twenty-Six

C H A P T E R     T W E N T Y · S I X

*Help him get discovered! Money to fix his face! What stars shone at night in this girl's world? It was crazy talk.*

*Loony!*

*Phony as a three-dollar bill!*

*Yet, what if it was possible? He'd perused enough art magazines to know that every once in awhile a starving artist hit the jackpot. Some rich dude discovered the artist's renderings, then was willing to pay big dollars to hang the work on his wall.*

*Yeah, right. The odds were better buying a lottery ticket.*

*What was the likelihood the girl came from big bucks? The chance was about the same as finding a pot of gold at the end of a rainbow—none to zero.*

*Kids from wealthy families don't go to the likes of Pike over summer break. They mingle with their own kind at some fancy resort. The kind with a couple of golf courses, horseback riding, speedboats to rent so they can hassle fishermen with their fifty mile per hour wake.*

*So why did she even mention such a possibility?*

*Was she mocking him?*

*Being mean?*

*Max didn't think so. She may be misguided but she sure sounded sincere.*

*At least he'd told her the truth. She was a busybody, a snoop.*

*Who needs her kind?*

*Good riddance.*

\* \* \*

Jess didn't say much on the return ride. Travis had pushed for details. She stuck to the basics.

She said she'd gotten only a glimpse of the fellow. The man appeared to be about her size. And that he probably wore a mask because one side of his face had scarring.

Travis said he had heard shouting. What was that all about?

Jessie's respond was that the man had yelled at her. Said she should scram, go mind her own business.

Travis knew more than a few syllables had been exchanged. Rumbles of loud talk had filtered to his hiding spot. Trouble was—he couldn't understand all the words. And right now Jess was reluctant to share. The girl was in a funky mood.

Why, he wasn't certain.

Jess was feeling more than a little remorse. On the ride home her mind was a racetrack. Thoughts kept chasing around and around like cars on a speedway. And every now and then, one would crash.

Before actually meeting the man, she'd viewed it as a game, a sport to speculate about. Why did he wear a mask? Steal odds and ends? Was he a scofflaw or a true hermit? Was the guy really crazy or just a little loony?

One look had changed the score. How dare she intrude on the unfortunate fellow's solitude! It was more than rude. Her behavior had been offensive, just plain nasty.

Jess flashed back on her own experience of entering a new school. She'd suddenly been tossed into what seemed a sea of fair-skinned blondes. With her jet-black bangs and sand-colored complexion, she stuck out like a cola stain on a white dress. She detested every minute, didn't want to go.

Yet she'd come to realize that the problem was her own paranoia—self-induced worry. At the time she would have sworn the other students were staring at her. That they were talking behind her back—making jokes at her expense.

She'd been wrong. Most of her classmates couldn't have cared less. But for a while it had seemed real.

Compared to the disfigured fellow, her incident had been trivial—a fly speck on an otherwise clear window. What must he feel every day when he checks himself in the mirror?

That is, if he even dared to look.

And it wasn't only facial scars. He walked with a limp, held one hand in a claw-like curl. Obviously, more than his face had been damaged.

Then there was his diminutive size. He was too elfin to ever physically confront tormenters over the age of fourteen. So it made perfect sense that he chose to live tucked away in the woods.

But surely something could be done to improve the facial scarring. Plastic surgeons work wonders. She'd seen before-and-after pictures in a magazine. A woman's face had been disfigured by a car fire. Over time doctors had grafted new skin. Although the lady would never be the same, the results were amazing. With the aid of cosmetics, she no longer had to hide. She could go out in public without people staring.

Picturing the woman sparked another thought—the mar-velous talent the man had with an artist's brush. Jess was no critic, but in her mind, the guy was a genius.

Until now, she hadn't asked her stepmother for a single favor. Nothing. But that was about to change. Tonight, when she was alone, she'd make the call. She'd explain to her stepmom what she'd stumbled across. If her father's new wife really wanted to connect, she'd listen.

It'd be a good test of her stepmom's sincerity.

Once the call was made, she'd pen an apology and a promise. Bright and early tomorrow, pedal back to the man's trailer and stick the envelope in his door.

Jess was lost in her thoughts—the ride home was only a blip in her memory.

* * *

The teens put the bikes away, then sauntered into the shop for a soda. They weren't alone.

Buddy was perched on a stool. Although he still sported a cherry-sized lump, he'd abandoned the crud-covered Elvis outfit. He was decked out in fresh blue jeans and a hockey jersey. Even his normally unruly red hair was slicked down.

A rather plump woman occupied the recliner. The lady was outfitted in oversize black slacks and a flowery blouse. A reporter's notebook rested flat on her ample lap. At the sound of the door closing, both heads swiveled about.

Seeing Jess, Buddy practically tripped over his shoes. He took several giant strides across the concrete, threw an arm around Jessie's shoulder and swept her across the room.

"This is the friend I was telling you about . . . the one who rescued me. She's the one you should be interviewing."

Jess was dumbfounded by the unexpected shoulder hug. She stood like a toy soldier—hands dangling at her hips, mouth open in a fly-catching mode.

Travis had a different reaction. Where the impulse came from he had no idea. The normally easygoing teen felt the sudden urge to form a fist. Gritting his teeth, he forced the feeling back in its hole.

Then he went straight to the fridge, brushing past Buddy without a word. Reaching in, Travis clutched up two cans of pop and slammed the door. He stomped to the workbench, set the cans on the surface and slid onto a stool.

The reporter's antenna detected teenage tension. Either jealousy had raised its head or this lanky boy was plain impolite. Irregardless, the woman picked up the notepad, put a pretend smile on her painted lips, and got to it.

"Now then, Jessica," she said in a girlish voice. "As I understand it, you got up early this morning to go out and search. What made you look where you did?"

Jessie's mind was elsewhere. Her brain was mulling over the bear hug. Having her formal name announced snapped her to the here and now. "Excuse me. Would you repeat the question?"

Pen poised, the woman sighed. "I said, what made you look on the east side of Pike Lake? Did you have a dream? You know . . . like a vision?"

Jess glanced at Travis. Spotting the soda can, she saun-tered over and picked it up. Then looking at Travis, she rolled her eyes, "can you believe this?"

She leaned back against the rim of the workbench. Staring at the woman, Jess said, "I'm sorry. But I didn't catch your name or why you're asking me these questions."

The journalist was caught off guard. She hadn't expected such a grownup statement from such a slip of a girl. A blush blossomed on the reporter's cheeks.

Buddy broke the standoff. "Sorry. My fault. I should have introduced the two of you."

He nodded at the woman, then with a slight bow and an arm wave said, "Rose, I'd like you to meet my friend, Jessica Ritzer."

He turned to face Jess. "Jessie, this is Rose Gardener. Rose writes for several local papers. She's here to do an interview with you, maybe snap a photo. Is that okay?"

Jessie's lips pursed together so tight her mouth nearly disappeared. After an expectant moment when the only noise was the tick of the old clock, Jess glared at Buddy. "Aren't you forgetting someone?"

Jess shuffled sideways to be closer to Travis. Slouched on the stool, he remained as mute and still as a statue.

Jess playfully tapped Travis on the shoulder. She returned her gaze to the reporter, mulling over the woman's name. Rose Gardener? How weird was that? Stifling an urge to giggle, Jess said, "It's nice to meet you, I think. This is my friend, Travis Larsen. You should know that he was one of the first to fly over in an effort to locate the ultra-light."

Shifting her stare, Jess fixed her brown eyes on Buddy.

"Last night, long before an official search could get off the ground, Travis went up with his flight instructor. They flew back and forth hoping Buddy had set down some-where safe. Actually, if you want to know the whole truth, Travis chose not to go up in the ultra-light yesterday. He thought it was too risky. Turns out he was right."

Jess paused, giving Buddy time to chew on her words.

"Anyway, when Travis heard that Buddy hadn't returned home, he hooked up with his coach. The two of them flew until dark and then again at first light today. "

Displaying her own version of a belittling smile, Jess faced the woman. "So you see. . . I really didn't do much. I just started looking where we'd last seen the plane fly over. It's kind of like that expression. You know . . . the one about being in the right place at the right time. I'd call it dumb luck."

Jess threw Buddy a charity smirk. Refocusing on the reporter, she added, "Besides, if I hadn't spotted him, somebody else would have. The most he would have missed was a meal."

The interview was soon over. Ms. Gardener said that she had more than enough material. Would Jess mind having her picture snapped? Jess said only if Travis was included.

Buddy hitched a ride back home with Rose. Once the photos were snapped, both of them climbed into her Blazer for the short drive to the McLeans'.

Travis looked at his watch. Much had happened since rising early that morning.

"It's after six. We better get in the house before Betty sends Bob out lookin' for us. He's gotta be drained. I know I am."

Stifling a yawn, Jess agreed. "Me, too. It's been quite a day and it's not over yet."

* * *

Supper finished, Travis headed for the loft. He was looking forward to reading a Gary Paulson novel until he nodded off. Tired as he as he felt, it'd be an event that wouldn't be long in coming.

Bob was equally exhausted. The past twenty-four hours had been most demanding for one recovering from a stroke.

Oddly enough, conversation over the dinner table had been minimal. Aunt Betty was overjoyed with Buddy's safe return. But she didn't press Jess for a detailed account.

Bob asked if the teenagers had enjoyed their afternoon bike ride. They said they did but didn't go into details.

Travis asked about *Johnny*. Would it be raised anytime soon? Bob said probably in a week or two. Because the gas tank was empty, pollution wasn't a problem. Buddy's dad was going to make the arrangements.

Did Buddy get checked out by a doctor? He had—the lad was lucky—only a slight concussion. Other than avoiding strenuous activity for a few days, he was given the all-clear.

At the word strenuous, Jess chuckled.

When the others gave her a confused look, she laughed, "Yeah. Like strenuous would be a problem for him."

No further explanation was necessary. Each had a small chuckle at Buddy's expense.

Strangely enough, neither senior said anything about the real hero. There was no speculation on who delivered the food and water or possibly even pulled Buddy from the water.

The teens also kept mum about the passing patrol cars. Maybe, once the deputies discovered the man wasn't home, they'd forget the whole thing. As Travis had mentioned at the time, why should they care?

"No harm, no foul."

\* \* \*

Jess and her stepmom had their first pleasant, extended chat. After small talk, Jess described what she'd run across. Would the art gallery be interested?

Definitely. Her stepmom volunteered to make the drive any day the artist chose. Besides, she gushed, they'd missed Jess at home. After viewing the paintings, the two of them could go out to eat.

Jess composed the letter slouched over the outdated desk. The same surface she'd written Travis a few weeks earlier. But she found it hard to put her thoughts down on paper. After several false starts, she let the words flow as if she were talking.

The note opened with an apology. It moved on to say that discovering the secret stash had been accidental. But not to worry, she and her two friends hadn't told a soul.

She explained about that first hike on the dirt road, and how curiosity got the better of her. That she hadn't meant to invade his space. For that she was truly sorry.

And then she got to the meat of the matter.

On the day she peeked inside, she'd caught a glimpse of a wildlife painting. Jess wrote that it was more than terrific. And although she herself was not an expert, she knew someone who was. It just so happened that her stepmother was a curator at a large gallery.

Twice a year they featured "new" talent. Renditions of wildlife were extremely poplar in the Midwest. And that once an artist was discovered, original canvases often sold for thousands of dollars.

Jess wrote that if he didn't want to, he wouldn't even have to show himself. The paintings could be arranged inside. At the appointed time, Jess would lead her stepmom to the Airstream. If she liked what she saw, they could communicate by mail.

It could be a win-win. He'd have an opportunity to sell his wonderful work.

The gallery would gain access to new talent.

What did he have to lose? If interested, he could tack a reply to the power pole.

She'd bike by each day to check.

CHAPTER TWENTY-SEVEN

*Max woke to a gray dismal day. Every bone in his body hurt. Sleeping out on damp ground was for youngsters. Most certainly it was not something an over-the-hill adult should do.*

*Crawling out of the shelter, he stretched and yawned, letting his eyes roam. Although the temperature was mild, the ceiling looked low. Tatters of metallic clouds drooped over the forest. A thin layer of ghost-like fog shrouded the pond. For a time he stood quiet, framing a mental photograph.*

*It'd make a great painting. He'd place the beaver lodge just left of center; one tree-cutter squatting on top—a second swimming with a branch in its mouth. In the foreground, he'd place a turtle resting on a log.*

*The difficulty would be blending muted greens with the dreary sky. But he enjoyed a challenge. What else did he have to look forward to?*

*Max yawned again. He hadn't slept well but it had little to do with the leaf-litter mattress. Hard as he tried, he couldn't shake the snoopy girl's sass. Money—he could charge money for his paintings?*

*And then there were the words about fixing his face. Wasn't he too old? Besides, hospitals were for the rich . . . or those who had good insurance.*

He had neither. All he had was the land—a measly eighty acres. The lakeshore property was the last remnant of what once had been a huge family estate. He'd rather suffer in poverty than part with it. So he survived on a measly monthly disability check.

But what if what she said about big dollars held a smidgen of truth?

He could save the money . . . let it grow. Maybe by the time he hit fifty-five, have enough cash to afford a skin graft.

Lucky barked at a beaver, breaking Max's train of thought. Right then and there he made a snap decision. One sleepless night on the ground was enough. He'd pack up and sleep in his own bed tonight.

* * *

Max first spotted the footprints in a low swale. They were good-sized, larger than his palm. Interesting enough, they were embossed on a twin set of shoe marks. Apparently the girl hadn't hiked in by herself. Probably the kid with the cap tagged along to hold her hand. The tracks weren't from the McLean lad. They were average size, not gunboats.

Whatever, the footprints ran both ways—in and out. But that was yesterday's lesson. No one would prowl the woods this early. He'd be home before the snoops finished breakfast.

On the higher, dryer ground the tracks vanished. He didn't see another sign until cutting the game trail. He also discovered how the teens found him so easily. The cart had laid down a set of matching wheel prints. The twin lines would have been as easy to follow as train tracks.

Oh-oh! Fresh bear tracks were embossed on top of the deer cleaves and people prints.

Max brought the whistle to his lips. Although seldom dangerous, bears made him uneasy. Lucky wasn't a big dog, but what he lacked in bite, he made up for with bark. And black bears didn't like being yipped at.

*They usually turned tail, pointed their snouts in the other direction. The key word was "usually." Every now and then they'd challenge a mutt. On other occasions, they'd climb a tree and play a waiting game.*

*These prints were probably from the trash-can bear. The bruin could have smelled the pork and beans Max had heated over an open fire. That was all the more reason to be cautious. Such bears often lost their fear of humans.*

*The path all but disappeared as it wound through a brushy thicket. The cart's wheels were set too wide to fit through the narrow passage. Max had to stop and bend the brush to make an opening. The sound of something approaching from behind stopped him in his tracks.*

*Then the animal was on him.*

*Lucky.*

*The dog had his nose to the ground, spike tail quivering like a tuning fork. He was back-sniffing the trail, ready to protect his master.*

*Max grinned. He didn't have many human pals, but he had something better—the love and loyalty of man's best friend.*

* * *

Half awake, Jess waved an arm and thumped the alarm button. Through sleepy eyes, she squinted at the clock—ten minutes to six. If it was going to get done, now was the time.

She forced herself out of bed and stumbled to the window. Outside, the lake was a steel blanket, reflecting gun-metal gray from the low haze overhead. At least it wasn't raining.

Excellent. There was a letter that needed delivering and she was the mail carrier.

It made no sense to shower. She'd be sweating soon enough. After throwing on her jeans and sweatshirt from the day before, she padded to the kitchen. All was quiet. For once her aunt and uncle were sleeping in.

Jess grabbed an apple and then scribbled a note. *Went for a bike ride. Back before breakfast. Love, Jess.*

The tricky part was retrieving the bike. She didn't want to wake Travis. This was her mission. No one else had a need to know.

She'd been able to sneak in and out without a sound. Mere minutes after leaving the house, Jess was flying down the runway. Like she had the day before, she steered down the middle. It was so much easier.

Jess was getting to know the gravel lane like the back of her hand. Compared to pickups and ATVs, the fat-tire Schwinn rolled along like a stealth fighter. Except for crunching an occasional pebble, it was nearly noiseless.

Jess wasn't the first one up. Four times she startled grazing whitetails, once so close she almost had to steer around the animal. Never in her dreams had she expected to become so personal with wild creatures. Each encounter was a thrill, a rush—a snapshot to burn on her mental CD.

Although the bike was silent, the forest was not. Crickets fiddled, crows cawed, and once a distant loon sounded its primal wail. Jess smiled at the sound. The first time she'd heard the eerie call of a loon had been in Canada. Back then, it had scared the wits out of her. She'd thought it was a wolf howl.

Travis and his sidekick, Seth, had laughed. They were quick to point out her mistake. On this morning hearing the now-familiar cry brought back memories. Loons, she'd since learned, were the official state bird. Only fish needed to be on guard. The beautiful two-toned divers were minnow grabbers. Teenagers were definitely not part of their diet.

Jess pedaled nonstop. She braked where the electric line looped over the road. For a minute she straddled the seat, concentrating. Knowing his cover was blown, the man could have returned.

She hoped not.

She didn't feel up to another close encounter. She'd rather wait until the guy had a chance to read the note.

Jess forced the bike through roadside brush. She let it fall on its side. Unless you knew where to look, it would be invisible. After crossing the gravel, she pulled out her cell phone.

She hadn't bothered with the fanny pack. The cell phone, apple and envelope were the only items stuffed into her pockets. But this wasn't about making a call. She was curious how long it took to bike over. The kitchen clock read six fifteen when she'd snuck out. The cell phone's display showed six fifty-five.

Jess worked the arithmetic. A one-way pedal took about forty minutes. Add another twenty dropping off the note. Two hours—tops. Heck, there was good chance she'd be home before Travis was even awake.

She made one last scan down the lane. Seeing nothing of concern, Jess slipped through the brush-clipped opening. Unlike the first encounter, she knew exactly where the overgrown drive meandered.

Breathing easy, Jess jogged at a leisurely pace—mind hectic with activity. What with all this riding and running, she'd be in great shape by the end of summer break. Maybe when the fall term started, she'd sign up for cross-country. But not the girls' division, she'd want competition.

"Wouldn't that be a hoot?" she thought, rounding a curve. "Give the boys something to chase after."

She couldn't compete with varsity jocks. By the time boys were juniors or seniors, they'd reached another level. But against kids her age she had yet to come in second.

Jess was reminded how this woodlot differed from the adjoining forest. The trees were taller—broader at the base—wider at the waist. Unlike yesterday's hike, there was scant underbrush to obstruct her sightline. The woods even wore a slightly different fragrance, one closer to soggy socks.

Ahead the terrain began its drop to Pike. Could she have jogged so far so soon? The first trip had seemed to take forever. But that day she was sneaking, not certain where she was going—or what she was going to find when she got there.

The birch clump featured in her first "I Spy" episode was off to the right. The clump's white paper-like bark stood in stark contrast to its darker neighbors. A little like her, she mused—easy to pick out in a crowd.

It was time to pull up, peek over the hill.

Jess no longer feared the man. But why risk startling the fellow? She didn't need a repeat performance of yesterday's calamity. If the hermit and his dog had already returned, she'd perform a disappearing act.

There was an alternative plan. Pedal back to the deer trail, sneak to the boat. The envelope could be placed on a seat, weighted down with a rock. Sooner or later the fellow would find it.

Jess circled warily behind the clump. She dropped to one knee, all the while keeping an eye trained on the trailer. In the early morning gloom, the metal box appeared lonesome, abandoned. From its forlorn appearance, it was hard to imagine the amazing talent it contained.

For five full minutes Jess stared and listened. No movement, no sounds. Not even the chatter of a squirrel telling her to go away.

She stood, sucked in a breath, then took one last look around. It was time to deliver the mail.

She picked her way down the slope, watching where she stepped. There was a possibility both man and mutt were sleeping. Why snap a branch or stumble on a rock? Better to tread softly, slip the envelope in the door and disappear.

Gazing down at the ground, Jess didn't see the creature until the bruin bounded into the clearing. By then it was too late for her to cut and run. Even with its weak eyes, the bear spotted her. The brute stood unmoving, one front paw dangling off the ground, a toothy muzzle pointed at the teenager.

For an instant, Jess was too petrified to do anything but gawk, her feet set in concrete. Then adrenaline kicked in. Emitting a panicked high-pitched shriek, she took the only avenue of escape. Jess bounded to the Airstream, threw open the door and flung herself inside.

* * *

Travis was snoozed out.

He'd nodded off before completing the third chapter. Rolling over, he held out his wrist—six thirty. He'd dozed off a little after nine. He hadn't slept that long since sixth grade.

After a quick shower, the teen slipped into his daily uniform—jeans and a sweatshirt. He pulled on his Twins cap, then treaded into the workshop. As anticipated, it stood empty. Seeing only soda in the fridge, he quietly entered the house.

All was quiet.

Slipping off his shoes, he padded down the hall to the kitchen. The first thing that caught his eye was the note lying on the table. He picked it up and read it.

A furrow creased his forehead. Oodles of unanswered questions came to mind. What was she up to? How come so early? And why go alone?

Travis filled a glass with juice then perched on a kitchen stool. He sat sipping, considering potential answers. By the time he'd narrowed the possibilities, the glass was drained. Whatever Jess was up to, it had to be centered on yesterday's close encounter. Something said or seen when she confronted the trailer guy.

Well she wasn't the only one who knew how to pedal a bike. Travis added a "me too," scribbled his first name and returned the note to the table.

Ten minutes later a second antique bicycle rolled down the runway.

# Chapter Twenty-Eight

C H A P T E R   T W E N T Y - E I G H T

*Max towed the cart across the road. With all the recent foot traffic, the game trail was beginning to look like a cow path. He took little notice. There were more important things to mull over.*

*He'd only been gone the one night. Would the authorities still be looking for him? No doubt—they probably want to play a game of show and tell.*

*Tough!*

*Nonetheless, it'd make more sense to sneak in from the lakeside. See if he had any unwelcome guests. And if necessary, wait 'em out. Hunker down on his property sneak inside after dark—then slip back into the woods before sunup.*

*Yeah. It'd work. He could keep up the routine for however long it took.*

*Probably best not to drag the wagon all the way home, though. At least not until he was certain the coast was clear. For the time being, he'd park it next to the boat. Besides, his gimpy leg was pleading for relief. He'd take a break before checking out the trailer.*

*From the first glimpse Max knew the dinghy had been moved. Only the bow was beached. It should have been up in the woods, tight to the last roller. And the tarp was missing.*

*Whoever messed with it hadn't returned the boat to its proper place. At least the motor hadn't been swiped. The prized MinnKota stuck out from the stern like a hitchhiker's thumb.*

*First the trailer, now his watercraft! Wasn't anything sacred?*

*Some of the rage diminished when he clumped alongside. The tarp wasn't missing after all. The cover had been folded into a sloppy square, then pushed under the front seat.*

*Wait a minute. A boat cushion was resting on the rear bench. The one he'd left with the McLean kid. How'd it get there?*

*Max reached in and tugged out the tarp. He opened it. Nestled inside the first fold was a rolled up blanket and the water bottle.*

*It was starting to make sense. Whoever ferried the teenager from the island had done so with his dinghy.*

*But then why hadn't they put the boat back where it belonged? As he pondered the reasons, he heard a blood-curdling shriek. Now what?*

\* \* \*

Jess peered through the one uncovered window, nervous fingers drumming the countertop.

Unbelievable! What was she doing here? Invading the man's space for the second time? It wasn't what she had planned.

A patch of fur flashed at the edge of her sightline. The bear must be back! Her scream should have been enough to send the critter packing. But it apparently hadn't.

What had Travis preached? Wild creatures are far more frightened of you, than you are them.

As her uncle often joked, "Yeah, sure—you betcha!"

That was easy enough for Travis to spout, but hard to believe when it actually happened. Especially when the brute had a set of big teeth, long claws and weighed more than a sumo wrestler.

The entry door jiggled, followed by scratching. Oh, no the critter was clawing its way in. One swipe from a huge paw and the door would be history, torn from its tiny hinges like tinfoil.

Jess rose up on tiptoes. She leaned over the small basin and pressed her face against the glass. Hopeless. The angle was wrong.

The door rattled a second time. Jess felt the sudden urge to use the toilet. Despite the dilemma, she stifled a panicky laugh. Isn't that what Buddy said about taking his flight test. That he's been so nervous he thought he'd wet his Levis? Now she understood.

The bathroom! She could hide in the bathroom.

Jess scrambled across the small living space. She threw open the closet-sized access, scurried inside and pulled the door shut behind her.

A hazy glow filtered down from a miniature skylight. Like the remainder of the Airstream, the bathroom was the reverse of super-sized. The tiny room provided only two services. A petite toilet stood against one wall. Opposite that was a narrow, rectangular shower stall.

She didn't see a basin. Apparently hand washing and teeth brushing took place at the kitchen sink. What she wished for was a window.

There was another round of door jangling, followed by scraping sounds. Then a dog barked.

The bear wasn't clattering the door. It was the three-legged mutt!

The relief was quickly replaced by a second wave of alarm. If the dog was home, could its master be far behind? The answer came swift and certain.

"Lucky! Knock it off! What d'ya trying to do? Make your own doggie door?"

* * *

Panting like a steam engine, Travis allowed the bike to coast. He braked to a halt and then dumped the two-wheeler at the edge of the right-of-way. The first checkpoint was the deer trail. Jess could have returned to the scene of the accident. She was full of surprises. One could only guess what she had up her sleeve.

There weren't any new hoof marks. To be expected. He and Jess had left loads of scent the day before. Whitetails would tolerate an occasional whiff, but avoid areas drenched with human odor.

But there were fresh tracks. A set of parallel tire prints grooved the sand on both shoulders.

More scuff marks, faint and smeared, marked the soft edge. Some resembled boot prints. Others were round or oval shaped. He couldn't tell for certain, but Travis thought they were paw prints—bear tracks.

He trudged to the Schwinn, then stood scratching his cheek. From their dampish appearance, the tire grooves appeared fresh. They'd been laid down this morning, not more than an hour earlier.

What were they telling him? The most likely answer— the hermit was heading home.

That made sense. Having been confronted by Jess, the campsite was useless. Maybe the guy wanted to restock his wares and relocate somewhere else. Or maybe he was just fed up with being hassled.

Travis clutched the handlebars and began walking the bike uphill. Reaching the crest, he hopped on and began pedaling. There was a second entrance to the "No Trespassing" property.

It wouldn't cost anything but time to look.

* * *

Max hobbled as fast as his gimpy leg allowed. He took

the shortest route, angling through the big timber. Lucky had run on ahead.

First it was a teenaged pilot, then a nosy snoop, and today a damsel in distress. For that's what the scream reminded him of—just like in the movies—a young woman scared silly.

It was probably that busybody. Maybe she bumped into the bear. Good. It'd serve her right. Who did she think she was—admitting that she'd peeked inside the trailer? What a nuisance.

Yet her words echoed in his head, *Money to fix your face.*

Right!

Like that was going to happen.

If it turned out to be the same girl, he'd want some answers. Yet he had to be careful how he asked. He didn't dare push too hard, frighten her.

Ha! Like that didn't happen every time someone looked at him. Max slowed. He wanted to eyeball the Airstream before showing himself.

Maybe she hadn't come alone. What if she'd called the sheriff? Blabbermouthed to the law, spilled the beans about the stash?

A black blur raced along the ridge—the bear. No doubt the one that made the paw prints. At least the brute was lopping away from the camper. Probably with a splitting headache triggered by the piercing scream.

Zigzagging from tree to tree, Max was thankful for his camouflage clothing. The rounded hulk of his home materialized through the early morning gloom. Close enough. He hunkered at the base of a double oak to listen and stare.

No deputies. No teenaged girl. The only sign of life was Lucky scratching the door.

Because they'd cleared camp at first light, Max hadn't bothered with breakfast. The dog hadn't been fed. It was no wonder the mutt wanted in.

* * *

Jess cringed as the door hinges squeaked. The camper's floor shuddered.

Footsteps! The man was indoors!

She felt like a fish in a barrel. She should have taken her chances with the bear. Too late now!

Timing her moves with footfalls, Jess eased into the shower stall. With a shaky hand, she closed the curtain. If it were possible, she would have turned on the spray and washed herself down the drain.

The dog whined. The man spoke. But opposed to the preceding day, his tone was pleasant—mellow.

"Yeah, yeah. I know you're hungry old pal. But hang on. You gotta give me a minute. Okay?"

A cupboard door opened and closed, followed by the clunk of a can on the counter. Then the man's voice again. "Whoa! Where'd this envelope come from? Dang it all! Someone's been in here! Is that what all your whining is about?"

The trailer fell quiet. Jess stopped breathing. She could picture the guy standing in front of the cabinet, paper in hand. A thought struck like lightning, piling on panic. What if the guy was illiterate? What if he didn't know how to read?

The man began to recite out loud. Jess slowly exhaled, unaware she'd been holding her breath.

She hung on every syllable, gasping short mouthfuls of air, rubbery legs quivering. But hearing the letter orally only made her feel idiotic. The words sounded patronizing, snooty.

Who was she to be giving advice to a grownup? The man was definitely not illiterate. He intoned every sentence with the expertise of a TV news anchor. If he had command of the written word, surely he knew the value of art.

Just before the ending, the dog yapped. Nails clicked on vinyl tile, a paw scratched the entry door. Then the dog began barking.

"Hush! What is it? What d'ya hear?"

The trailer tilted ever so slightly. Jess pictured the man doing what she'd done minutes earlier. He was probably leaning over the sink, peering through the window.

Footsteps, the snap of the latch, the hinges repeating their request to be oiled. The camper's wiggle, was followed by a soft thud as the door closed.

* * *

Travis traced tire tracks to where they left the lane. He only went in a few yards. Jessie's bike was lying on its side, veiled in knee-high vegetation. He crossed the road, noting that a sagging electric line did the same.

This had to be the camper entrance—the neglected drive Jess explored on her first visit.

So what possible reason did she have for returning? And so soon at that! It couldn't be about the odds and end stash. They'd known for days that the hermit was responsible. Case closed. Jess had something else on her plate—something she was reluctant to share.

Travis took a last scan, confirming the Schwinn couldn't be seen. Satisfied, he slipped through the opening and paused to get his bearings. Sure enough, bold as black stripes on a zebra, an old cut meandered in the direction of Pike. He pulled his cap tight and broke into a jog.

In a few minutes he slowed to a walk and stopped. Bent at the waist, hands on hips, he sucked wind. Ahead, the stump-filled trail turned a lazy curve before dropping away. The terrain looked familiar—a ridge, a copse of basswoods, a clump of thick-stalked birch. He'd been here before, the day he peeked in the trailer at the mural.

The sound of a dog barking broke his reverie. Travis tensed, ready to run. If the dog was home, no doubt the man was, too.

Cover—he needed to get off the path, find a place to hide. He darted toward the birch cluster. The trees' dull-white covering would blend with his light-gray shirt. Plus, the clump made a perfect observation post. As he recalled, it provided a clear view of the Airstream.

From this ringside seat, it was like watching "News of the Weird"—only more bizarre. The door swung open. First to hop down was a three-legged dog. A rare sight by itself.

Then an impish adult stepped out. Other then being clad head to toe in camouflage, the man appeared ordinary. That was until the guy turned to close the door. Even from a distance, the teen's eagle-eyed vision registered shock.

The opposite half of the man's face was a surreal painting, a live Picasso. Pulled taut over his cheekbone, rivulets of red scarring swirled as if smeared by an angry child's finger paint.

Jess had said the man probably wore a mask because of his mutilation. Talk about an understatement.

Travis now understood Jessie's reluctance to share. She felt sorry for the guy. He did, too. How lonely it must be to have to hide out—to be afraid to be seen in public.

Travis watched as the hermit shuffled behind the camper. The dog acted bewildered. After trailing the man, it returned to the step-block. The replacement chunk Jess had cloaked with grime. The mutt sniffed the ground, then stuck its nose in the air. After a few whiffs it raised its one front paw against the door and began whining.

The man reappeared, pushing a bike with a basket. Seeing the dog at the door, he clapped his hands and whispered. Travis was too far away to hear the words but it must have been a command. The dog stopped pawing, hopped off the step and limped alongside its master.

Travis expected the man to head across the clearing and wheel the bike up the drive. Instead, with one hand guiding the two-wheeler, the other patting his thigh, man and dog shuffled toward Pike.

The next event was two steps beyond eerie. Travis had remained motionless. He wanted to make certain it was safe to move out—that the dog wouldn't catch his scent.

He'd come to find Jess. So where was she? Was she also doing the spy thing? Hiding nearby? Waiting for the man to leave?

A mental picture exploded, paralyzing Travis with dread.

What if? What if he had caught Jess trespassing? But just why she'd be wandering about on the hermit's property, Travis didn't have a clue. But surely being so early in the morning, she was on a mission.

Was the man capable of brutality? Could he have tied her up . . . or worse?

Thoughts went wild, conjuring awful images. Travis was still staring at the trailer when the door poked open. And then to both his surprise and delight, Jess jumped out. She closed the door, glanced around, then began sprinting up the drive.

Travis stayed put until Jess was almost even with the clump. Then he sprung up and waved his arms while whistling softly. Despite not wanting to scare his friend, he did just that.

When her side vision detected motion, Jessie's brain screamed bear—run! Her feet changed from trot to mad dash in an eye blink. Travis had no choice but to pursue her. He darted toward the drive at an angle, hoping to cut the gap by shortcutting the curve.

It would have worked if Jess hadn't been flying like a missile. Instead, by the time Travis scurried through the woods, the only reward was a glance at her backside. But instead of slowing, Travis turned on his own afterburners.

A few heart pounding, lung-bursting moments later, he closed on the last bend. The lane was just ahead. And so was Jess, sprawled flat in the trail's one mud-filled hollow. This time, Travis called out.

"Jess!" he huffed between guzzles of air. "Don't . . . run . . . away!"

* * *

"Jeez, Jess . . . I didn't mean to scare you. How many times do I gotta apologize?"

Wearing a scowl and mud-stained jeans, Jess punched Travis on the upper arm. Unlike the playful taps she usually dispensed, this one hurt. Travis was beginning to think a punching bag would be an appropriate Christmas gift for the girl.

"Hey! Knock it off! That hurt!"

"Good! Serves ya right! You took twenty years off my life. I might as well start smoking again. It couldn't shorten things any more than you did back there."

Travis scuffed a line in the gravel with the heel of a shoe. "Aw, don't go there. And for the last time, I didn't know about the bear. If I had, I woulda' made sure you saw me right away."

When he looked up, he said, "For crying out loud, Jess. I know it's not really my business, but what were you doing? First I see a three-legged dog come out of the Airstream. A minute later, a two-faced man hobbles down. Then, after they take off toward Pike, you come sneaking out."

Travis focused above the road opening. A pair of crows

flapped over the tree-line. When they passed, he lowered his gaze and stared straight at Jess. "Are you gonna tell me he didn't know you were in there? Or did the two of you make up after yesterday's shouting match?"

Jess met the stare with a squint of her own. "I wasn't going to tell you unless my plan worked. But now that you caught me, in the act, I'll try to explain."

It took time for her to finish. When she did, Travis removed his cap, ran a hand through his hair and shook his head.

"Well, I'll say this much. You've got more guts than me. But I guess I have to agree with you. Seeing the man camping out like we did, I woulda' thought the trailer would be empty. Besides, you only went inside because of the bear. Right?"

Fixing his gaze on the ground, he began working the gravel again. "Remember, this whole spy thing started because we were curious about the stash of stolen junk. But you seem to have moved on to something new."

He looked up. "What now? He read your letter. Do we wait for him to post a note, or do we go get it over with? Find out one way or the other about this art thing?"

Jessie's jaw dropped. "What d'ya mean, 'get it over with?' Are you suggesting we confront the guy? Hike down to the lake, see what he's up to?"

"Yep. That's what I'm asking." Travis glanced at his watch. "If we don't stand here all morning, we'll be through with it. Maybe even be back in time for pancakes."

Jess beamed. "Spoken like a guy who thinks with his stomach. Come on. Let's get the bikes and make our approach on the deer trail."

CHAPTER TWENTY-NINE

*Giving the situation a second thought, it was risky to stick around. Probably best to disappear until the water-beetle had been fished from the lake.*

*Reluctantly, Max coupled the cart to the bike. He'd have to push the two-wheeler all the way to the road. From there he'd pedal to Olson's store and load up on can goods. There was another out-of-the-way logging trail farther up Pike Lake Road. Except this time he'd cover his tracks.*

*Max clutched the handlebars and began plodding. If only he could cover ground like Lucky. The fact that it had only three good legs didn't seem to bother the dog.*

*The mutt had already scampered off. He was probably down at the lake, hoping to find a dead fish. In some strange quirk of nature, Lucky relished rolling about in rotting flesh.*

*The only reason Max could fathom was that the stink acted like a cover-up. It allowed Lucky to sneak closer to forest critters. Not that the dog would actually do anything if it did catch one. Like children at play, it was mostly a game of tag.*

*Max yawned. He was bushed, drained drier than desert sand. He wished he could just return to the trailer and sack out for the day. Why couldn't people mind their own business? It wasn't like he'd done real harm to anyone.*

*Sure, he'd snuck into a few lake homes, swiped some odds and ends. But in the big picture, he was owed far more than a couple trash bags of useless junk. The summer cottages were standing on land that rightfully belonged to him.*

*The county hadn't paid one tarnished penny for his birthright. Valuable lake property that would sell for upward of a million bucks in today's market. And then, after the county steals the estate, they sell off a half mile of pristine shoreline to strangers.*

*Some justice!*

*"Failure to pay back taxes" was what the court order read. Yeah—like he'd have cash after growing up as an orphan. Then the moment he turned of age, the county bean-counter demanded years of non-payment—plus interest.*

*Well that didn't happen, couldn't happen—impossible. The only saving grace was that they couldn't take it all. The law said he was allowed to keep one parcel, one bit of property to call home. And he was walking on it right now—eighty acres of prime timber.*

*His ankle ached. His calf complained. If the throbbing kept up, he'd never make it to the road, much less pedal to the store. He needed a break, a few quiet minutes to think this through one more time.*

*The big pine loomed ahead, the giant the McLean kid had clipped. This was Max's favorite spot in the woods. For more than a hundred years, the monarch had rained down needles. The ground circling its massive trunk was a soft mattress, the perfect place to meditate.*

\* \* \*

"What is this, like your third or fourth trip through here?"

Jess let the bike tumble. "You know, I'm not sure. I think it might be the fourth time. Enough so the deer trail is beginning to look like a pathway. Do ya think they'll ever use it again?"

Travis let his bike fall alongside Jessie's. "Who'll use it?

**273**

Oh, you mean the deer? Yeah, they will, after the rain washes away our scent. Whitetails are kinda like humans. They form patterns that are hard to break."

Jess spun around, eyes blazing. "Are you referring to my smoking habit again? 'Cause if you are, drop it. I gave it up . . . haven't even thought about puffing since we got back from Canada."

Travis held his palms up in surrender. "Give it a rest. No. I wasn't referring to sucking on cigarettes. It never even entered my mind. Okay?"

Jessie's features softened. "All right, I believe you. But I guess I've started a new habit, huh? I've been hiking this trail so often I could probably lead ya to the lake with my eyes closed."

"Okay, you go first then. But keep your eyes peeled. Could be that your new pal doesn't plan on playing with his boat. The more I think about it, he's more likely to be heading for another sleep-out."

Jess shrugged and started off, throwing a question over her shoulder. "Why d'ya say that?"

"Well, sometime during the next few days there'll a lot of action out front. Buddy's dad is gonna hire a diver to locate the ultra-light. They'll tie a couple lines on it, mark it with buoys."

Jess stopped mid-stride and spun around. "Mark it with boys? What d'ya babbling about?"

Travis was trailing so close he nearly collided with her. "I'm talking about the kind that's spelled b-u-o-y, not a b-o-y. Think big red bobber."

He stepped off the path and leaned against a tree. "They'll anchor a couple pontoon boats on either side. As little as *Johnny* weighs, they might be able to winch it up by hand. Then it'll be a matter of placing some big inner tubes underneath. Once that's done, it can be towed to the McLean dock."

"Oh. Sounds simple enough," Jess said, starting off again. "And you know about this because . . ."

"I know because I asked your uncle. He's the one that came up with the idea."

They were getting close enough to Pike to catch glimmers of steel-gray water. Jess slowed and pointed to the right. "That big tree Buddy clipped is over that way. Did ya want to see it up close?"

Travis nodded. "Yeah. Why not? How far is it?"

Pursing her lips, Jess took a guess. "You know I'm not good with distances, especially in the woods. But it's just on the other side of the line of "No Trespassing" signs. You know, where the trees suddenly get humongous? So how far would that be . . . half a city block?"

Travis's brow squiggled, wiggling the bill of his cap. "Somethun' like that. Not all that far. Lead on."

\* \* \*

*Max didn't see any reason to push the two-wheeler one step farther. He leaned the bike against an oak. Satisfied it would remain upright, he fumbled his pipe and tobacco pouch from a front pocket.*

*The man had heard the prattle as to why he shouldn't smoke. That it could shorten his time on Earth by five to ten years. Big deal! He wouldn't be missed.*

*Like his brushes and paints, the pipe was one of the few pleasures his dismal life afforded. Besides, it wasn't like he was chomping on cigarette filters and inhaling fumes deep inside. Mostly he just puffed to make smoke.*

*He found the whole process relaxing—packing the pipe, striking a wooden match, watching smoke curl—even the aromatic odor of blended tobacco. Once his back was tight to the bark of the forest king, he'd light up and do some heavy thinking.*

*Max limped forward, each stride a torture test. The lofty*

*monarch loomed straight ahead, standing head and shoulders over its neighbors. It'd been around for more than a century, closer to two. He'd ask the wise old tree for advice.*

* * *

"It's just up there a ways." Jess said quietly, gesturing down the hill. "Pretty awesome, wouldn't you say?"

Travis trudged alongside. He craned his neck trying to peer through the canopy. "Whoa! Not many of those babies around anymore. Imagine, giants like that once covered a third of the state. It's hard to believe most of them were butchered."

Jessie's chin scrunched in good-natured annoyance. "Yes, Mr. Larsen. But you taught that lesson yesterday. Remember, at the outdoor schoolyard across the road, way back near the beaver house?"

Then she smiled, letting Trav know it was a joke. "What? You didn't think I was paying attention?"

Her expression suddenly turned somber. Jess tilted her nose in the air and asked, "You catch a whiff of that? It's the same thing I smelled that first day on Loon."

Travis sniffed the air like a bloodhound and he nodded. "Yeah, I do. It's definitely pipe tobacco . . . the smelly kind. Where do you think it's coming from? We're still a ways from the boat, aren't we?"

Jess placed a finger to her lips. "Yeah. But let's keep it down," she whispered. Then she stood on tiptoes, testing the air like a doe she'd seen at first light.

"It's hard to say. But you're right. It's not coming from down by the boat. It's a lot closer than that."

After taking a moment to ponder, she murmured, "Tell you what. I'm the one who violated the guy's space. Plus, I've sort of met the man . . . even left him a letter. Why don't I go on ahead? You follow behind, but keep me in sight. If I run into him, I'll try my best to keep him calm . . . try to explain that we only want to help."

\* \* \*

*What a relief. It felt so fine to be plunked on his bottom, shoulders snuggled against pine bark. No way could he consider trucking all the way to the store and beyond. Not with only one good leg.*

*Maybe he should set up the shelter right here. Secluded and pine scented, this certainly was a peaceful place. However, it might not be safe haven. Some government know-it-all will probably want to take a snapshot—"The big tree that brought down a water beetle." Then file the photo away in some never-to-be-seen-again folder.*

*Nope, it was chancy to stay put.*

*Max puffed on the pipe, then exhaled. A wisp of whitish-gray spiraled into the air before seeming to dissolve. Setting the pipe safely alongside, he let his lids sag until his eyes were closed.*

*Take a five-minute nap. Fall asleep mulling over the options—not that there are many. Reconsider the letter, reflect on the girl's words—"money to fix your face."*

*Did he dare even let a sliver of possibility burrow in his brain?*

*Probably best not to even think about it. He'd been down that road before, only to have his hopes dashed like a small ship against tall cliffs.*

\* \* \*

Pulse racing, breaths fast and shallow, Jess padded toward the pine. She kept her gaze down, careful not to step on any tell-tale twigs. She entered the opening under the lofty evergreen, then stopped.

Moisture laden, the damp air reeked with burning tobacco. Either the man was nearby or he'd recently passed through.

Standing perfectly still, she tuned her ears, straining to

hear unusual sounds. There weren't any. In the early morning gloom, the forest seemed unusually quiet—much too quiet. Unless something or someone had caused them to scatter, birds should be chirping, squirrels should be scolding.

Which was it? Bear or man?

Jess scanned the pine's massive trunk, noting nothing out of the ordinary. Then she let her eyes wander all the way to the top. She fixed on the long, grayish limb sticking out like a well-muscled arm. Identical to the color of the cloud cover, the needle-free bough appeared innocent enough. It was hard to fathom such a benign branch having nearly claimed a life.

Her eyes lazed back to the bottom. The tree's base was as broad as a double door. Jess had no way of knowing that with a few more steps, a confrontation would take place.

She peered over her shoulder. As requested, Travis had followed several yards behind. He was leaning against an aspen where the forest thickened with a multitude of tree trunks. Wearing a gray sweatshirt, and with the green windbreaker wrapped around his waist, he seemed to blend into the background.

It was a relief knowing she wasn't alone. Jess extended a hand and waved. Travis nodded and gestured in return. Exhaling a more relaxed breath, Jess crept closer to the giant tree.

Had Max not been wearing camouflage clothing, she may have spotted the man's legs poking out. But he was and she didn't. Upon reaching the wide base, Jess looked skyward again. The tree was so lofty, so regal. It was nearly impossible to circle the trunk without looking up at its crown.

Eyes fixed toward Heaven, feet falling silently on a needled rug, Jess shuffle-stepped around the monarch. And then she tripped, falling with an oomph on the forest floor.

Almost at the same instant, Max was jerked wide awake. Startled, thinking it was the bear, he let out a frightened bellow. "Yeow! Scram! Get away!"

Then his pupils focused on the cause of his distress. The girl again! Wouldn't that busybody ever leave him alone?

"Oh for crying out loud! What is it you want now? Can't you read? Or didn't they teach you that yet? You're trespassing on private property."

At the first word, scared beyond screaming, Jess rolled away from the pine. She was about to leap to her feet and let her shoes take the lead, when her eyes made contact with the man's.

What she saw in them tugged at her heart. She'd seen the very same look in little children. The saucer-sized eyes preschool kids displayed when scared out of their minds. So, instead of springing up and scrambling to Travis, she slowly sat upright. Never letting her gaze wander, Jess worked at catching her breath.

Confident she could speak without gasping, she said, "Once again, I must apologize. You must think I'm crazy. A real basket case."

Max nodded, his scarred mouth twisted in either anger or annoyance. Jess couldn't be certain of which. But she went on anyway. "But believe me, Mr. Grogan, I had no idea you were here. Tripping over you startled me as much as it must have frightened you. If you would hear me out, give me a chance to explain, maybe we can part as friends."

The man's lips curled, displaying teeth that could do with some dental work. "Why should I trust you? So far all you've done is make my life miserable. Everything was fine until you came along."

He started to say more but then hesitated. Max wanted to vent his rage but his heart just wasn't in it. The girl was so relentless with her message of hope. She was like the Energizer Bunny—she kept going and going.

So instead of following up with more anger, he barked, "You called me by name. How did you know? Who told you?"

It was hard not to stare at the man's distorted features. But nevertheless, Jess kept her gaze focused on his eyes. The startled "deer in the headlight's" look had faded. It'd been replaced by one of sorrow. She'd seen the same sad eyes on TV, pleading for money. They were the kind of ads featuring starving children clinging to life in some third world country.

Despite the man's artistic talent, did he feel his life was as bleak as those unfortunate little ones? Did the scarring run that deep, both inside and out?

Jess caught a glimpse of grayish-green moving toward the tree—Travis. Without taking her stare from the man, she held up a hand. "Stop—let me handle this."

Speaking softly, she said, "Actually I wasn't certain. I saw a photo that first day . . . the time I looked inside your trailer thinking it was vacant. Anyway, I read the inscription . . . yes; I do know how to read . . . that said something about the Grogan ranch."

Max nodded but remained silent.

Jess went on. "A few days earlier, my Uncle Bob . . . he's the one with the airstrip . . . told me his property had once been part of a huge dairy farm. He said that after a fire destroyed both the house and barn, the land stood empty for years. And that finally the county took it over."

Hearing the word "county" caused Max to sit tall. "They didn't take it over! They stole it! They never paid a penny, not one red cent! By rights all of the land around Pike and Birch belongs to me. It should have been my inheritance."

Then the man did something that more than tugged at

Jessie's heartstrings. It tore the threads off altogether. Max did something he'd hadn't done—refused to do—since losing his entire family in the fire.

He began to sob, slowly at first followed by shoulder-jerking, head-bobbing wracks of weeping.

Jess could only sit and watch, oblivious to the tear tracks staining her own cheeks.

# Chapter Thirty

C H A P T E R     T H I R T Y

*Once the dike was breached, Max couldn't hold back the flow. When tears ebbed, a river of words gushed in their place. He told Jess the whole story. For the first time in his miserable life, Max found the courage to relive that horrible night.*

*Being the runt of the family, and at the tender age of eight, he'd been allowed his first sleep-out. His parents hadn't let him go far, just a little pup tent pitched behind the house. But to one that young, it was an adventure—a dark, creepy-crawly outing he could brag about to his buddies.*

*Max told of waking to the sound of crackling and crashing. Crawling out from under a thick quilt, he poked his head outside. He was instantly engulfed by a sea of warm air. Lighted by flickering orange, the backyard was cast in a ghastly glow. As he turned toward the two-story, panic gripped him with an iron fist.*

*The house was ablaze! Hungry tongues of yellow licked through cracked windows. Like Fourth of July fireworks, red sparks shot from the roof, raining down on the yard.*

*For a time Max, was too panicked to do anything but watch in horror. When a glowing ember landed on the tent, burning through the fabric, he scrambled to his feet. And then he ran. But he didn't run away. Instead, he scrambled around the burning building.*

*It was a warm summer night, and his two older brothers were sleeping in the enclosed front porch. He had to wake them, make them go upstairs, save Mom and Dad.*

*He was too late. The porch was already ablaze. Flames and smoke swirled from the wide window openings.*

*There was another route—the outside staircase leading to the second story. Shrieking at the top of his lungs, Max rushed around the corner. The steps were intact. He raced up, oblivious to heat pulsing from the side wall.*

*As he began banging, the door was whooshed off its hinges in a fiery blast of heat and light. The explosion propelled little Max off the landing like a leaf in a storm. He fell flat on his back, well away from the building. Unfortunately the burning door did the same, kiting through the air, covering the small boy like a burning blanket.*

*The drop had rendered little Max unconscious. While he was under, the fire department arrived in time to save the chimney. Without other wood to feed the flame, the door slowly burned itself out. But the damage had been done.*

*He was scarred for life.*

*Family dead, house in ashes, Max was sent to the Twin Cities. A year later, his one aunt contracted cancer. Then he became a ward of the state, shuffling from one agency to another. It seemed no one wanted a defiant, pint-sized Halloween goblin scaring the other children.*

*Finally, in his teens, Max caught on with a private charity located in Minneapolis. In exchange for nighttime janitorial work, he was given room and board. Like Quasimodo in the Hunchback of Notre Dame, Max turned in thirty years of midnight labors.*

*Only when his scarred leg began complaining did he apply for government benefits. Besides, he figured, he'd put in the years to deserve them. It wasn't like he was being given a free lunch.*

*Once modest checks began to arrive, Max moved north to his acreage. But by then it was much too late to reclaim his birthright. Instead, to quell anger and jealousy, he made midnight entries into vacant buildings. He knew stealing souvenirs was wrong. Yet, resentment still burned in his bones like a slow fuse.*

*He couldn't help himself.*

*He'd wanted to quit for some time. Let the past be history and live in the present. Because Jess had stumbled across his secret, he'd be forced to stop. So even though she was a nosy busybody, he couldn't stay mad at her.*

\* \* \*

Following the confession, Jess introduced Max to Travis. Then the teens helped Max wheel the bike back to the trailer. By this time Lucky had returned. But he wasn't allowed inside. Max had figured correctly. The mutt rolled in a fish and reeked worse than week-old garbage.

On the trek to the Airstream, Jess reviewed the possibility of a gallery showing. She made Max no promises, but said she thought it was a very good possibility.

If Max was agreeable, she'd call her stepmom immediately and have her drive up this very afternoon.

For his part, Travis kept his lips glued. This was Jessie's stage. He did, however, go inside. Once he got a look at the artwork, he told Max they were wonderful. He said he'd seen lesser selling for hundreds of dollars apiece.

The high praise helped Max warm up to the tall teen. For a time, the man forgot about the scarring, forgot about his freakish appearance.

And when Max relaxed, the teenagers did, too. Instead of scar tissue, they saw a human being. A person with doubts and fears—wants and needs—not unlike any other person on Earth.

\* \* \*

"Here's the plan. First Trav and I will paddle to the island and reclaim the bags of whatnots."

Jess found it difficult to look at Buddy. The bump had gone down. But in its place, an ugly black-and-blue bull's-eye had spread across his temple.

"And you, Mr. Lucky-to-be-Alive, are going to be busy doing payback. Put your way with words to work. Use your laptop to write a letter explaining the whole affair. How Mr. Grogan felt cheated, but didn't mean any harm."

Jess paused, making certain Buddy was all ears. He seemed serious so she went on. "When that's done, over the weekend, you can visit your neighbors. Let 'em read the flyer first. Then see if they want any of their odds and ends returned. It's the least you can do for the guy who saved your hide. Agreed?"

The big boy shrugged but didn't say anything. Instead, his size twelves kept a soft, steady beat on a stool rung. There was no doubt who was in charge of this informal meeting.

"The sheriff owes my uncle a huge favor. When Uncle Bob was a game warden he once kept the man from being roughed up by poachers. Bob's gonna explain the situation. He'll ask that deputies stay away from Mr. Grogan. Then later today, soon as my stepmom arrives, we'll all ride over to the trailer."

Jess let her gaze drop. It pained her just to glimpse Buddy's gargantuan bruise. "Mr. Grogan isn't certain he wants to be there, but he said he'll have the paintings ready. But in case he stays, you guys are to remain with the van. If my stepmom thinks the artwork is saleable, I'll run back and get the two of you. It'll take a few trips to carry it all out."

She looked at Travis, then at Buddy. "Are we all on the same page?"

Buddy put on a sheepish grin. "Yes, fair lady, we all agree. It was my own darn fault that I clipped a tree."

Jess locked eyes with Travis. As if on cue, both groaned.

E P I L O G U E

# Epilogue

Jessie's stepmom didn't just like the paintings, she fell in love with them. She said they were as realistic as any they'd ever displayed.

But what really got her attention was the trailer's interior. She told Mr. Grogan that if he was willing, she'd like to bring the gallery owner up so he could see for himself.

In the meantime, she took dozens of photos. Her thoughts were that the Airstream could be the center-piece of a wildlife art show. They'd happily replace the old camper with a new model—one with more space, better heating and insulation—one that could be occupied in the winter.

Max was so flabbergasted he had to fight to keep back tears. Jess put Travis and Buddy to work lugging can-vases to the Dodge Caravan. While they were occupied, she had an idea, one she shared with her stepmom.

Yes. Her stepmom knew just the person who could do it. The woman was an artist specializing in free-form plastic and fiberglass. It'd be child's play for the lady to make a flesh-toned half-mask Max could use to cover his scarring. The request would be made as soon as her stepmom returned to the city.

That evening, Buddy composed the flyer explaining how he'd come to possess dozens of odds and ends. At first angry that their lake homes had been invaded, most of the neighbors quickly shrugged it off. As one fellow said, "I guess if I didn't miss my old saw, I really didn't need it in the first place. The good news is, this Grogan guy you wrote about saved your skin. We're all happy about that."

Buddy's dad had located a diver willing to go down deep; *Johnny* would be plucked from the depths over the weekend.

On a sun-filled Friday afternoon, two days before he had to head home, Travis took the controls of the two-seater. Pete never said a word. Travis did it all—takeoff, turns and landings. The Cessna only bounced once.

Bob, Betty and Jess looked on from the shade of the huge hangar door. The shrewd old man rested a hand on his niece's shoulder. "Let's hope Travis keeps flying airplanes with wheels. At least until we get the water-birds back in the air. And when we do, what d'ya say we make a flight north, visit a special friend up near the Boundary Waters?"

Jess reached around and gave her uncle a squeeze. "I'd like that, Uncle Bob. I'd like that a lot."

# about the author

Minnesota native Ron Gamer has held a passion
for woods and waters since early childhood days.
Now retired after thirty-four years of teaching in the
Robbinsdale School District, he continues to be active
in the outdoors. When not out fishing, bow hunting,
or piloting small aircraft around the state, Ron can be
found at his computer—creating realistic adventures
he hopes will be enjoyed by readers of all ages. To
read more about the Chance series and Ron's school
presentations, visit www.RonGamer.com.